E. J. Bousfield

THE JEWEL KEEPERS

Book One
Albion

Published in 2009 by Kings Hart Books,
an imprint of Publishers UK Ltd
6 Langdale Court, Witney, Oxfordshire, OX28 6FG
01243 576016
www.kingshart.co.uk

Edited by Eileen O'Conor

Cover design by Helen Waller © 2009
Cover artwork by Kevin Dyer © 2009

A catalogue record for this book is available from the British Library.

The paper used in this book is from sustainable sources, certified by the
Forest Stewardship Council.

ISBN 978-1-906154-14-1

Dedication

For my Mum and Dad who have always believed in my stories and for my
sister who shares many of the gifts described within.
For Clíona, Alex and Isla, the three brightest stars in the sky and
for Steve Donohoe, my beloved and best friend.

Acknowledgements

This novel grew from my love of nature and my need to make sense of the past and how it impacts on us. I have always had an interest in religion and the power that belief systems have on shaping our perceptions of the world, of life and of death.

I have been blessed in many ways. I would like to thank my family; my youngest daughter Isla has read many versions of this novel and her feedback has been invaluable to me. Thanks also is due to Steve Donohoe, my husband, who not only built the website but read the entire manuscript and made some very good suggestions, most of which I took on board. Thanks to Creina Mansfield who teaches the Writers Workshop at the University of Manchester—I found her classes to be both stimulating and inspiring. I would also like to thank Eileen O'Conor, my editor, an intelligent, feisty woman who has taught me many new writing skills. Thank you Eileen.

Thanks also to three of my closest friends, Nicky Jachim who read the very first draft, and to Sue Chapman and Sarah Morgan for allowing me to share Abersoch with them.

Thank you also to Tighnabruaich for just being the most beautiful, restful place on Earth. It was the place where this novel began.

The Arvon Foundation employed two very gifted teachers for a Work in Progress course at Lumb Bank in August 2007. Thank you to Martyn Bedford and Louise Tondeur who helped me think about structure and scene development. The week I spent at Arvon allowed me to shape this novel and to realise that it was a trilogy I was writing and not a single book.

Lastly thank you to Kings Hart Books. It is becoming almost impossible for new writers to find anyone brave enough to publish them. Kings Hart are both courageous and in love with storytelling and the gift it brings to our world.

Author Biography

E.J.Bousfield was trained as a counsellor and still works with young people. Her company runs an online counselling service across parts of the UK called Kooth.com.

She has always enjoyed writing and was inspired to write *The Jewel Keepers* after she attended a short course on Archaeology at the University of Manchester. Two more books will follow and she already has ideas for other novels.

The author invites you to give your opinions of the book on her website:

www.thejewelkeepers.com

I

Yorkshire, England, 1784 A.D.

'Keep still, Stanley, for the love of God!'

The horse quietened immediately, aware of the uncharacteristic note of alarm in his master's voice. With his heart beating furiously, Robert Duke, hand on bridle, glanced around at the silent courtyard. The sun lay dormant in the east and the moon was now a faint sliver in the early morning sky. Soon the birds would begin to sing. It was imperative that he got away quietly and unseen. He looked anxiously up towards his wife's room tucked in the west wing of the house and noted with relief that her lamp remained unlit. The other windows too, were still shadowed with sleep and only the kitchen, deep in the basement, betrayed signs of movement and light.

Deftly, Duke swung himself onto Stanley's back, took up the reins and coaxed the horse forward. The horse turned and made his way slowly and quietly towards the tall gates at the end of the drive. These gave onto the road that led to the City of York, but Duke, instead of taking this road, nudged Stanley towards the open fields.

The horse broke into a gallop. He knew where he was going. Before his master had married Esther, with the fair hair and a mouth that rarely smiled, they had travelled this way many times to see another lady, one with dark hair and warmer eyes. Her name was Hannah. Yet the last time they had seen Hannah something in her had changed. Her eyes had become clouded, sad, her expression mournful. This had troubled Stanley for he had liked the smell of Hannah; her gentle voice soothed him, and his master too seemed to have a sense of peace about him whenever he was beside her.

Stanley breathed in the sweetness of grass and cornflower and felt the wind tear through his mane as he galloped across the wide fields on the way to Hannah's home. As they neared Hannah's cottage, Stanley began to sense something was wrong. His master sensed it too for he suddenly jerked on the reins. A hot bolt of pain shot through Stanley's mouth, causing him to rear up and neigh shrilly in protest.

Hannah's small house was deserted.

The door had been torn from its frame. It hung precariously on one hinge. Overturned baskets of herbs, pots of potions and healing balms were scattered across the grass. Through the lopsided door, the horse could see broken shapes; the furniture had been hacked to pieces and the small table where Hannah had sat many times, smiling and peeling beans for their supper, was split in two. Stanley raised his head and snickered loudly.

This was bad.

He felt fear run through him. There was fear, too, in the house; he knew the cold smell of it. And of something else, sickly sweet, once warm, but now grown cold and hard.

'Steady boy,' Duke commanded him and Stanley felt the firm grip of his master's legs around him.

Duke threw himself off his horse. He ran to the door. He scanned the darkened room; saw the crumpled bed, the upturned chairs, and the blood on the walls. So the rumours were true. They had taken her.

For one long moment Duke stood there, frozen, imagining Hannah, small and dark, being dragged away, begging them to leave her be, crying, perhaps crying out for him? He should have come sooner. He should have known the last time he was here—how many months ago? six, eight—that the madness had come upon her again. He could have helped her then, but no, he had chosen not to, returning instead to his comfortable life, his business affairs, and a marriage that was as cold as the Arctic seas. He had failed her.

'They have taken her and I am lost,' he said, even though there was no one to hear.

Stanley tossed his head in agitation. *What to do?*

But Duke, unlike Hannah, did not have the gift of horse speak and Stanley's thoughts drifted away on the wind.

The horse pawed the ground impatiently. Duke glanced up at Stanley; the answer came to him suddenly. He must find Hannah, rebuild her house, and never leave again. 'Stanley, we're going to York,' he said quietly. But the horse had already turned and was heading swiftly back to the road that would lead them into the city.

II

The sun had risen fully by the time they passed through to the west of the city of York.

The Asylum rose out of the hills, a bleak monolith of grey stone set against the moss of the Yorkshire moors. Duke approached the building from the rear, making his way to the front entrance with caution. He had not fully prepared for this and would have to call upon his position as land owner and merchant to gain entry. Such calls upon his status repulsed him greatly; today, for the sake of Hannah, he would lay such principles aside.

Above the heavy oak door the portal bore the Coat of Arms of the City of York. Duke lifted the great iron knocker and let it fall heavily.

He turned to Stanley, 'Steady boy. I won't be long.'

I need to come with you. I know where she is.

Duke tied Stanley to a tethering post and waited.

I fear the worst.

The door swung open. The man who stood there was gaunt, bent like a thorn twig, his skin grey and bloodless.

He gave Duke a yellow-toothed smile.

'What's wanting?' he croaked.

Duke spoke authoritatively. 'I am here to order the release of a woman by the name of Hannah Joyce.'

The man at the door frowned.

'And who might you be then?'

Duke swallowed his anger.

'My name is Duke, Robert Duke, and I am a close friend of Miss Joyce. I am here to return her to the care of a family that loves her.'

The man smirked, suppressing a laugh behind his hand.

'Well then Mr. Dukes, Sir, p'raps you don't know that it was her very own family as had her committed 'ere. Her being, as you might say, a very sick woman.'

He tapped a grey finger against the side of his head and made as if to close the door, but Duke read his intentions and slammed his leg against the jamb.

'I demand to see Miss Joyce!'

Before the man could answer, another voice spoke from the darkness of the hall.

'Let Mr. Duke in, Jones.'

Jones stood aside with some reluctance and allowed Duke to enter. From out of the shadows a man came forward. He was a large man, not as tall as Duke but his stature was broader and fuller. Dressed in a red jacket and breeches and holding a rider's whip, he outstretched a large hand and clasped Duke by his.

'I saw your arrival from my study window. That's a fine-looking horse you have there Mr Duke.'

He turned to Jones and snapped, 'Take Mr Duke's horse and stable him man. And ensure he has water to drink.'

Jones ducked his head several times, avoiding both men's eyes.

'Yes sir,' he muttered sullenly.

Duke studied the man. He looked to be around the age of forty; thick-set, heavy jawed. From beneath beetling brows stared two eyes of ice blue.

'Forgive me, I have not introduced myself. My name is Edgerton. My uncle, Lord Edgerton, has put me in charge here. He is the owner and benefactor of this asylum.'

Duke knew Lord Edgerton. He sat in Parliament, owning much of the land in Yorkshire and parts of Lancashire. The man was vain, a persecutor of the poor and a religious bigot. It was also true that he held the ear of King George.

Duke regarded the nephew coldly.

'Does your uncle make a habit of arresting young women and holding them here against their will Mr. Edgerton?'

Edgerton's eyes seemed to flicker for a moment.

'Everyone here is held against his or her will, Mr. Duke. It is in the nature of the place.' He hesitated and looked away briefly before meeting Duke's eyes again.

'My uncle has kindly taken it upon himself to establish this Asylum for the mentally afflicted. The insane are not capable of exercising their will. We have to decide what is best for them.'

Duke took a step towards Edgerton. 'And who, pray, determines who is insane and who is not?'

'I am no doctor Mr. Duke, but even I recognise the ranting and delusions of a deranged soul.'

'You declare by your own admission that you are not a doctor. Yet you claim the right to incarcerate people here against their will!'

Edgerton stared at Duke. Duke saw Edgerton's hand clench suddenly and begin to draw back.

'I warn you my good sir,' he said evenly, 'not to take it upon yourself to strike me. I may not embrace violence but I have good connections both here in York and elsewhere. I can guarantee you that I will use them wisely if you lay as much as a single finger upon me.'

Edgerton held his gaze, baring his teeth in an icy smile.

'Sir, I have no intention of striking you. I merely wonder by what right you come here demanding Hannah Joyce's release. You are neither her husband or her brother, or indeed any relation that I am aware of.'

Duke felt the anger rise in his throat. He glared at the impertinent Edgerton, yet knew if he was to progress with this encounter, he had to offer him some part of the truth.

'Miss Joyce, like me, is a member of the Society of Friends. We are Quakers Mr. Edgerton. Quakers refer to each other as Friends. Now take me to where you are holding her so that I may return her to her home where she will be taken good care of.'

Edgerton hesitated. He knew all about Quakers. He knew his uncle hated them. They were a strange order, with heretical ideas about God. They refused to recognise the authority of the established church and they refused to fight for King and Country, claiming all war was inherently against the word of God. They prayed together in damp halls without the guidance either of priest or bishop. Their justification for such heresy was that God was available equally to every man and woman. They postulated via badly written scrolls in towns and villages that the clergy were not a direct channel to God, but mere men like themselves. They were stubborn and unmoveable in their beliefs. Edgerton would have to think carefully. Duke would not be easily appeased.

'Mr. Duke, I fear we have become enemies when really there are no grounds. Miss Joyce, your friend, was brought to these premises Tuesday last with a delusional mind and we are keeping her for her own protection.'

'Then you will not object to me seeing her for I have no wish to harm her.'

'Nevertheless, visitors do make inmates worse. It fuels their delusions. It would be kinder to leave Miss Joyce alone, Mr. Duke.'

'Don't talk to me about kindness Edgerton,' Duke said slowly trying to contain his rage. 'I saw the results of your men's kindness in the damage they inflicted upon Miss Joyce's home. It is there for any one who cares to look; in the broken door, the smashed furniture, her possessions trod into the ground like discarded rubbish.' He stepped closer remembering the blood he had seen spattered on her walls. 'Doubtless I shall see more evidence of it when I meet her face to face.'

Edgerton opened his mouth in reply but Duke would not be delayed further. There was a door at the back of the hall. Ignoring Edgerton's protests, he strode towards it and swiftly turned the handle.

He immediately found himself in a study, opulently painted in yellow and cream. By the window stood a desk carved from the finest mahogany and upon it, a fashionable statuette imported from the east. A fire blazed in a marble hearth and a rug of the finest wool covered the oak floor. Duke scanned the room looking for another door.

There had to be an entrance to the Asylum from this room.

He found it in the furthest corner. It was locked. He shook it hard, tried using his shoulder to break it open. It would not move. In desperation he looked for something in the room he could use; a poker, the statuette, anything that was heavy enough to crash his way through. There was nothing. Sweat broke out on his forehead. Time was against him. At any moment Edgerton would come through the door with half a dozen men in tow. Then he would be dragged away, possibly imprisoned, and Hannah would be lost to him.

Outside in the hallway he could hear scuffling and the suppressed murmurings of voices, and he knew in his heart that Edgerton had already gathered reinforcements. He tried to force the door open again with his foot, but it would not yield. It was then that he heard the sound of galloping and Jones's voice call, "I can't hold him sir; he's just too strong!"

Duke looked up as the study door crashed off its frame and Stanley cantered into the room. Horse and master faced each other.

'Stanley!' Duke cried. Stanley watched his master with wide eyes, neighing loudly and shaking his head from side to side. He trotted over to where his master stood and nuzzled his ear and then, with no warning, he swung his body around knocking Duke sharply off his feet. Duke glanced up just as Stanley reared and smashed his front legs against the locked door with all of his weight. The door splintered and fell with a crash. Stanley galloped through the opening leaving Duke to follow.

Outside Duke heard Edgerton scream at Jones, 'Get the guards man! Hurry, before they get through!'

III

The corridor was dark and damp, sharing none of the opulence of the neighbouring room. Duke kept sight of Stanley, who appeared to know where he was going, his white body a semblance of light in the dimness of the asylum. Duke felt his way through the passage, holding on to the wall, taking care not to slip on the wet stone floor. The place stunk not only of damp, but urine. The sharpness of it clung to the back of his throat and he fought the urge to retch. He had to find Hannah immediately; Duke knew it would only be a few moments before Edgerton came after him. He would be thrown in prison for trespass. Although even a prison cell would not come close to the hellishness of this place.

Suddenly the passage opened into a wider chamber. Duke gasped in horror at what he saw.

Lined against the walls were rows of cells. Inside, women were shackled in irons. There were eight, ten, maybe twelve women huddled together, some lying down as if they were trying to find warmth in the wet hay that covered the floor. Others stood staring out through the bars, their eyes wide and vacant. The walls were dank with mould and the air sang with the stench of human faeces. Duke searched frantically for Hannah, knowing she was here, kept like an animal chained to the floor and lying in the filth and cold.

He called her name, his voice shaking.

'Hannah, can you hear me? Hannah it is I, Robert. I have come for you.'

Someone laughed. He spun around. A woman dressed in brown rags leaned into the bars of a cell, grinning foolishly at him, her teeth black and broken,

'Who do you want my love?'

'Hannah, Hannah Joyce. Do you know her?'

The woman closed her eyes and then opened one to peer at Duke.

'What do you want?' she screamed at him, 'I told you not to do it!'

Duke leapt back in shock. The woman was raging at him, shaking her fist and rattling the bars. Others began to whimper and soon the air was rent with desolate shrieking and weeping. Duke turned on his heel to quickly move away. Another voice spoke evenly yet firmly above the din.

'Hannah is on the next floor sir. I think your horse may have already found her.'

Duke turned around. In the corner of a cell crouched a young woman who could have been no more than sixteen years of age.

'Be quick sir. She is dying.'

Duke turned and ran. He saw the flight of wooden stairs leading to the next level of the asylum and raced up them taking two at a time. Yelling Hannah's name over and over he tore through the cramped corridor of penned and chained women until he found her. The horse was standing next to the cell watching Hannah with careful eyes, his warm breath pluming in the damp air of the asylum. Hannah was lying scrunched up in a corner of a small cell, her legs drawn up to her chest, her hands clenched into fists, her dark hair wet with perspiration. A sharp pain shot through Duke's chest and his eyes filled with tears. He could barely speak.

'Hannah can you hear me?'

Nothing. He shook at the bars and kicked them hard. The clatter of vibrating metal echoed around the chamber.

'Hannah, please my love, speak to me?' Duke could see her frame rising and falling. He looked around desperately. There was no sign of Edgerton. He shook at the bars once more.

'Hannah, please, wake up.'

He needed to speak to her, to tell her he would return with a warrant to remove her from this place, to not give up hope. Just then, Stanley raised his head and neighed not once, but three times. His call resonated throughout the corridor and bounced off the walls. Hannah stirred and then sat up. She looked at both Duke and Stanley. Slowly a broken smile spread across her face.

Duke reached out his hand to her and she stood shakily to walk towards him. He was shocked by how thin she had become and by the hollowness of her cheeks. Her eyes, once dark and dancing with life, had dulled and an angry bruise ran along the left side of her jaw. He touched her face.

'What have they done to you?' he whispered.

'I knew you would come,' she said. She reached out her hand to Stanley who came towards her, his head lowered. She whispered something into his nose and the horse promptly turned and cantered towards the stairs, his hooves clattering on the stone floor. Duke looked after him.

'He will slow Edgerton's men,' Hannah whispered.

'I should have come sooner,' Duke said, 'Hannah what have they done to you?'

'It don't matter. Robert…you have to listen to me. There are things you must know…'

'Hannah, I am going to get you out of here. I will return with a letter from the Commissioner and ensure you are released. They have no right to keep you here—'

'Hush,' Hannah interrupted and touched his face.

Duke took her by the hand and caressed her palm running his finger over the narrow silver line that ran from the base of her left thumb to the top of her wrist. Hannah glanced at the birthmark; a surge of strength momentarily restored itself to her, and she dug her fingers into Duke's hand. 'Robert you must search for something. If I do not return from this place, there are two things you have to find. One will be easy, but the other…is more difficult.'

'Hannah, you will be freed,' but he broke off as Hannah winced in pain, her features contorted as she hunched forward in agony.

'Hannah, what is it my love, pray tell me?'

'Robert I do not have long in this world…'

She closed her eyes and focused on steadying her breathing. When the pain had passed, she opened them again and spoke quickly in short sharp rasps.

'Robert, find the Jewel. It is lost. Until it is found we will continue to suffer. Please.' She slumped towards him.

Duke looked at Hannah, tightening his grip on her hand. So the madness was still in her. He spoke softly, 'What Jewel Hannah? I do not understand you.'

'The Stone, the Keepers' Jewel. Robert…the church…don't allow the church to hide it any longer. Find it. Do whatever you have to.'

She cried out as pain raged through her again.

'Hannah I promise,' he cried. 'I promise to continue our work, the Friends and I, we will always be here; we will return God to all.'

'No, that is not what I meant.' She closed her eyes, leant into the bars and became limp. Slowly she slid to the floor.

He put his hand to his mouth in disbelief then reached out to touch her forehead. Her face had grown whiter and was clammy to touch. He yelled out into the darkness, 'We need a doctor, she is sick. Please someone call a doctor!'

He heard a shout and a rattle of many feet running through the corridor and then the thunder of hooves as Stanley reared and sent Edgerton's men piling down the flight of stairs. Duke released his hand from Hannah's, ran to the stairs and pulled Stanley out of the way. He looked at six men lying at the foot of the stairs, recognising them immediately by their red uniforms. Edgerton had called the King's soldiers. Duke yelled at them as they scrambled to their feet and came towards him, their pistols drawn.

'Can you see the conditions these women are kept in? Can you see the inhumanity of this place?'

One of the men, wearing the insignia of captain, raised his pistol at Duke's head.

'In the name of His Majesty the King, you are under arrest.'

IV

Duke ignored the threat. He ran back to Hannah, crouching down by the side of her, shouting over his shoulder, 'For the love of God, put away your guns! Fetch a doctor, this woman is dying!'

He had no care for the men or fear of any bullet tearing through his flesh. He stretched his hands through the bars, trying to stroke her hair. Her eyes were closed now, and her breathing had become shallow.

He called to her, 'Hannah...Hannah...oh my dear, do not leave me...'

Her eyes flickered open for a moment and she smiled at him. He felt her slowly slip away from him.

'Hannah, stay with me, for a while longer, I beg you.'

But she was no longer breathing and he knew, his heart breaking, that she was dead.

He felt rough hands on him. He was jerked to his feet. With his arms pinned behind his back, Robert Duke was marched away, down the wooden stairs. Two soldiers took hold of Stanley, now subdued and compliant. They passed the cells. Several of the soldiers held their mouths to prevent retching from the stench. The young girl saw them approach. She crawled forward to the front of the cell.

'Sir, the baby...did she tell you about the baby?'

Duke bucked against the men escorting him.

'Wait!' he cried, 'In the name of God, wait!'

Grudgingly the men drew to a halt.

'Baby? What baby, what are you talking about?'

'Hannah's baby, sir. The little girl. They took her.'

Hannah had a child!

'For God's sakes, is it alive? What have they done with it, where have they taken it?'

The captain motioned the men to pull Duke away. The girl spoke frantically, desperate to get the words out.

'It's a little girl...she's with Hannah's sister, in York...she was born gifted...like Hannah, sir...just like Hannah—'

'Move on.' The captain shoved at Duke's back and the soldiers obeyed, pulling Duke away from the cell towards the stone passageway. Duke struggled.

'Let me be!' he hissed. He turned his head towards the girl, his eyes wide with grief, urging her to continue.

'She had the mark on her hand, sir, the little girl did...she had the same mark...'

She was holding up her left hand, pointing to the region just below the thumb.

Duke felt a thread of hope, a mixture of joy and anguish. Hannah was lost to him but there was a child, his child. Through their child, he could reclaim part of her.

As he was marched towards the door, he shouted out to the girl, 'I will return. I promise you. I will come back with a warrant to have this damnable place closed down. Tell everybody...tell them!'

V

Katie 2008 A.D.

'Animals can't talk Katie. Please stop pretending they can.'
The voice was hard and dismissive and Katie felt her blood rush to her cheeks. Red-faced, she returned Samson the hamster to his cage and shut his door. She glanced quickly at Laura, her mother, frowning over a crossword puzzle and cursed herself for getting it wrong again. Animal Talking was the most certain way of earning her mothers' disapproval.

'You do worry me Katie,' Laura said without looking up. 'You just never seem to change.'

'I mean,' Laura continued, her head bent low over the newspaper, 'you bring all this social isolation on yourself. No one will want to be friends with a girl who thinks she can talk to animals. It's hardly cool is it?' She glanced up at Katie then looked away again, shaking her head.

Katie kept her eyes on the hamster. She was a thin, wiry girl, tall for her thirteen years. She had short dirty blonde hair and fingernails bitten so low that the pink nubs of her finger tips were left exposed. As soon as a nail dared to protrude above the parapet, Katie's teeth would move in and mercilessly chew it off. This was another habit that drove Laura mad.

'For God's sake Katie, you're supposed to be a girl,' she would say and hand her a bottle of nail polish. Katie would put it with the others; her wardrobe shelf was an aviary of colours, tiny bottles of blues, greens, golds and reds, glossy and unopened, were stacked, hidden from view under a pile of winter jumpers.

Now she stood on tiptoes and pushed the hamster's cage back onto the top of the sideboard. Turning, she went running up to her room. Once inside the sanctuary of her bedroom, she kicked her chest of drawers hard, several times, finding satisfaction in pretending it was Laura she was kicking. Then she sat down on the edge of her bed. For how long had her mother been telling her that animals could not talk? It felt like a lifetime. It probably was.

'It's not my fault', Katie thought, 'I don't ask for these things to happen'.

In the beginning, Katie remembered, when she was small, three or four perhaps, her mother had found her amusing.

'Lots of children have vibrant fantasy lives and Katie is no exception,' Laura had said to Dad once. That was long before Dad had run off to live with Knickers, a woman who made her living by selling lingerie on the Internet.

It was at nursery school, as she was approaching her fifth birthday, that she first discovered that she was a 'problem child'. She had been minding her own business one morning, chatting to Henry the guinea pig, a small brown and white creature trapped in a chrome and glass cage, perched on the top table in the Reading and Writing Corner, when her mother had walked through the nursery door. Katie had gone to greet her but her mother had looked right through her and disappeared into the storeroom-come-office with Mrs Griffin and Mrs Davidson. Katie had run to the door and was about to tap on it when Sarah Miles had stepped in.

'I bet they are talking about you,' she'd said slyly

Sarah Miles was a plump little girl with wild black curls, a lisp and the hugest blue eyes Katie had ever seen. Katie was mesmerised by those eyes and stood gaping at her, mouth open, wishing she had eyes as blue and huge as Sarah Miles.

'Don't stare,' said Sarah Miles crossly. 'My mummy says it's rude to stare.'

Katie shut her mouth quickly.

'Sorry' she had said, then added, 'You have very nice eyes. Are they real?'

It was Sarah's turn to stare.

'Of course my eyes are real,' she said hotly. She moved in towards the door and turned to Katie.

'Shall we listen?' she'd said, her mood changing dramatically from one of foe to friend. Katie looked behind her to see where the other members of staff were. Mrs Walters was in the Construction Corner sorting out a dispute over stickle bricks and Mrs Crook was outside in the yard administering a sticking plaster to Isaac's knee. Isaac was howling, hot fat tears were rolling down his shiny cheeks and beside him lay the cause of his distress; a red scooter with a bent front wheel. Mrs Crook was clearly busy. Katie turned to her new found partner in crime and nodded.

'Ok,' she'd said and Sarah Miles had giggled and taking Katie by the hand she'd pulled her towards the door. Both girls pressed their ears to it. They could hear the soft murmurings of Mrs Griffin, interspersed with the high pitched voice of Mrs Davidson. Katie listened intently. Sarah Miles was right. They were talking about her.

'It's lovely that Katie has this imaginary world around her, lots of children do at this age,' she'd heard Mrs Griffin say. 'Our concern is that Katie does not isolate herself from other children.'

'You mean other children think she's weird?' Laura replied curtly.

There was a silence in which Katie imagined Mrs. Griffin looking to her colleague Mrs. Davidson for guidance.

'It is true the other children find Katie strange and some do refuse to play with her,' Mrs Griffin said eventually.

'Why is that?' said Laura.

There was another short silence. Katie pressed her ear harder against the door wanting to catch every word.

'It's just that sometimes Katie mutters to herself under her breath. Some of the other children find it a little bit...frightening,' said Mrs Davidson. Katie had heard her mother sigh and then the rustle of her tights as she crossed her legs.

'Animal talking,' she said.

'Animal talking?' asked Mrs Davidson, surprise in her voice.

'Katie believes she can hear animals talk,' Laura sighed.

'Oh,' said both teachers at once.

Katie had turned then to look at Sarah, mortified that her new friend should find out her secret, but the listening space formerly occupied by her was now empty. She had obviously become bored and decided to find better things to do.

Katie felt relieved and turned back to the door. Her ear was hurting now with all the pressure she'd put on it, her palms were clammy and she could feel a hot sting in her bladder; she needed to go to the loo badly but she also wanted to know what Laura was saying.

'Would you like me to remove Katie from nursery?' asked Laura.

'I mean, I don't want my daughter frightening the other children.'

Mrs. Davidson stepped into the breach;

'No, not at all Mrs. McIntyre! Katie is a bright little girl with some lovely qualities—she just gets carried away sometimes with her imaginary friends. We only want her to focus more on making real friendships with the other children.'

Katie could imagine her teachers' doughy faces and well-intentioned expressions. She heard Laura sigh again,

'You don't know what to do and, of course, no one does. I suppose I should take her to a child psychologist but I have little faith in them. Maybe I have indulged her too much.' Katie's mother sounded sad when she said this. Her voice was flat and tinged with regret.

'It's probably best that we all ignore Katie when she behaves in this way. Give her no attention at all. Make her realise that such behaviour is unacceptable.'

Katie felt her insides shrink. Laura was already beginning to ignore her at home and now she was asking the teachers to do the same.

Suddenly, a hand fell onto her shoulder and a sharp voice said, 'Katie McIntyre what are you doing?' She spun around to face Mrs Crook and a triumphant Sarah Miles, standing with her arms folded and an 'I told you so' look upon her face.

'What are you doing?' repeated Mrs Crook, 'You can't go listening into private conversations. It's rude!'

Katie looked down at her shoes.

'She is rude Mrs Crook,' piped up Sarah.

'She stared at me and told me my eyes are not real.'

Sarah adopted a hurt look and the eyes in question suddenly seemed as if they were about to fill with tears. Katie blinked in surprise, 'I did not say that,' she said.

Mrs Crook turned to Sarah, 'We'll deal with that later Sarah. Let me talk to Katie now.'

Katie reverted to studying her shoes, black leather with a single purple butterfly arching across the tops of the toes. She liked Mrs Crook best of all. She didn't want to be ignored by her. She felt heat creep up into her cheeks.

'They were talking about me,' she said meekly.

Mrs Crook sighed and took Katie's hand.

'Never mind,' she said kindly, 'I am sure your mummy will tell you all about it when you get home. It'll be OK.'

'No it won't,' Katie thought. 'It won't ever be OK.'

'I wasn't being mean about Sarah,' Katie said to Mrs Crook.

Mrs Crook smiled. 'I know.'

Katie looked over at Sarah Miles who had dispatched herself to the Painting Table. She was holding a huge paintbrush resplendent with thick green paint, dripping glossy splodges onto oatmeal coloured paper. Yet it was not this that absorbed Katie. It was the red light hovering above Sarah's head and the thin wispy fingers of light cascading down from there, outlining her body in soft pink hues.

Sarah Miles seemed oblivious to the light show going on around her and was chattering noisily to her friend Lisa, her voice rising above the orchestra of the nursery like a violin solo. Katie stared.

'What is it pet?' asked Mrs Crook, worry in her voice.

'Nothing,' Katie had replied quickly, remembering that staring was rude, 'it's nothing.'

VI

*A*nimal Talking. Laura still called it that and she always said it with a sneer, narrowing her mouth and eyes in pure contempt. Katie had often thought that if she could bottle that look it would be sufficient to bring down entire armies; the ferocity of her mother's glare could pickle the skin and turn insides to syrup.

Shaking off this thought, Katie went over to her wardrobe, slid the door open and reached up to the top shelf. Groping beneath a pile of blankets, she found the key she had hidden there. She crossed to the yellow pine chest of drawers and unlocking the top drawer went rummaging through a mass of loose pens, blunt pencils and scraps of old drawings looking for her diary. Finally she felt it, wedged tightly to the back of the drawer. She eased it out, taking care not to litter the carpet with pencil shavings and scraps of torn paper then clutched it with both hands. It was a plain black A4 diary, the kind Dad used to keep in his office; nothing fancy, just a silver ribbon to mark the page and this year emblazoned on the front in gold. It had wide open spaces for each day with plenty of room for writing or doodling. Katie opened it.

On January 5th there was an entry about Animal Talking, made just after Dad had left them.

I saw the blackbird again. He's always alone. The other birds come in twos or threes arguing with each other and fighting over the bird seed. The Blackbird, though, is so aloof. He ignores the other birds; it's like he doesn't even notice they are there. They see him though. As soon as he swoops into the garden and lands on the lawn the smaller birds, the tits and sparrows, fly off squawking. It's almost as if they are scared of him but they won't tell me why. Maybe it is because he is bigger than them, and stronger. I watched him from my bedroom window. I wonder if he is lonely. He has shiny black eyes and a sharp yellow beak, and when he can't get to the best seeds in the feeder he shakes his head crossly and uses his feet to balance on the wooden perch. He swings his head back and pecks furiously through the wire holes trying to pull out the fattest seeds.

Katie paused and chewed on her pen. Dad had never minded her connection with animals, not like Laura. Laura had asked him only last year if he thought Katie should see a doctor about her 'habit.' Dad had said no, she would grow out of it.

'Besides,' he had added, 'your mother has seen more doctors than I've had hot dinners and look where it got her—a big fat nowhere. You don't want Katie pumped full of drugs do you?'

Katie sighed at the memory and returned to her diary.

'The blackbird looked up then right up at my window. He looked me straight in the eyes and that's when I got the fizzy feeling in my stomach. I knew then it was going to happen because it always starts like this. The warm fizzy feeling is a bit like Christmas - you feel excited and happy and scared all rolled into one because you don't exactly know what you are going to get. Well it's the same with animal talking. You never know what you are going to hear. Sometimes it's very clear but other times you don't hear anything; you just sense what the animal is feeling. The blackbird was looking at me and the warm fizzy feeling began to spread from my stomach into my arms and legs, running into my hands and toes like warm water. I concentrated on the warmth, feeling it cover me and then, when I was completely covered, that's when I could sense what the blackbird was feeling. He was frustrated. He was impatient with the bird feeder. If he could have stamped his feet and thrown things he would have done so. He chirped then, a cry that quite clearly said, 'These seeds are stale.'

Katie stopped reading for a moment and lay on her back, staring at the ceiling which was white and spotless with not a cobweb in sight. A costume chandelier hung above her head. Laura's obsession with keeping the house impeccably tidy, trendy and clean, was there even in her choice of light fittings.

On that blackbird morning back in January Laura had been out. Katie had gone downstairs and emptied the feeder onto the grass. Damp pumpkin, sesame and sunflower seeds had skittered into the neatly shaved lawn. She had replenished the feeder from a new freshly opened packet of wild bird food, leaving the lid open so that the blackbird could easily get to the contents. When he had finished filling himself, he flew off without even acknowledging Katie. She replaced the lid on the feeder. When Laura returned home from work, tired and hungry, she had complained about the seed all over the grass saying it would bring the rats. Katie had blamed the squirrels.

'Bloody squirrels,' Laura had said, 'They need shooting.'

Katie felt upset then; it was hardly fair on the squirrels and she didn't like to hear her mother curse them like that. If Dad had been here he would have just laughed, but he wasn't. Dad was miles away, living with Knickers in Exeter.

Feeling miserable, Katie turned over, moving her left hand, which had been tucked tightly against her stomach. She shook it to dislodge the pins and needles, catching sight of the birthmark that ran like a single silver railway line from the base of her thumb to the top of her wrist. She changed into a more comfortable position on her bed, flicking through the pages of her diary with her birth-marked hand until she came to Saturday April 19th. She re-read the entry for the tenth time in two weeks.

Today Laura announced that we are moving to Manchester.

That Saturday, April 19th, Laura had called Katie downstairs to the kitchen. It was a dark stormy day and huge grey clouds pregnant with rain hung low in the sky. Katie had sat at the kitchen table and fiddled with a coaster made by Laura at one of her ceramics night classes. Laura sat opposite her daughter and announced, 'I have something to tell you Katie.'

Katie's stomach had lurched. Those were the precise words Laura had used when she told Katie that she and Katie's father were separating.

Katie had tried to sound unconcerned.

'What news?'

'We are moving to Manchester,' Laura had replied matter-of-factly.

Katie had stared at Laura, not knowing what to say. Manchester? They had lived in their house in East Dulwich ever since she was born. She could still smell Dad in the house—traces of his aftershave lingered in the bathroom. The window seat in her room, where he would sit and talk to her, had been left as it was on the day he departed; the cushions had not been moved. She remembered him sitting there when she was small, reading her *Fantastic Mr Fox*; she remembered the times he smuggled bubble gum to her when Laura wasn't looking; competitions to see who could blow the biggest bubble and laugh the loudest when the gum collapsed onto their cheeks. They couldn't leave London!

'Manchester?' she had asked, her voice tight with tears.

'Yes, Manchester,' replied Laura impatiently. 'Houses are cheaper in Manchester, Katie, and since your father left we have only the one wage. I need to reduce our expenditure accordingly. I have been offered a new job as a consultant for a firm of interior designers. It is a wonderful career opportunity for me.'

She had paused then and scowled at Katie, 'You're not going to make a fuss are you? You know I can't bear tears. They are such a waste of time. They don't get you anywhere you know!'

That was it. Discussion over. Kaput. They were moving.

Katie fiddled with the corner of the diary page until it became mushy from the sweat on her fingers. She had written, *I just wish we could take the house with us. Not that Laura cares. I hate her! Where is Manchester anyway?*

Katie had Googled it.

It looked pretty grim; all red buildings, tiny streets and cobbled alleyways cluttered with rubbish. Katie had tentatively shared these findings with Laura in the hope that she would change her mind.

'For God's sake Katie, what do you mean its all cobbled streets and poky little houses? The trouble with you is that you watch too much *Coronation Street!*'

How would she know what I watch, Katie had retaliated in her diary, *she's never in!*

She turned the page, ready to make her next entry, her stomach suddenly full of butterflies. Her diary was the only place where she could truly express herself and share deep thoughts, like admitting she hated her mother and missed Dad. She picked up her pen, thought for one moment and then wrote:

I have made Laura cross, again! She is in a foul mood. And tomorrow we have to go to see Nana. Laura doesn't want to go and I must admit that I'm not too keen either. Nana has been ill, scarily ill, hearing voices again. I just wish everything was normal. I spoke to Nana on the phone and she said that she has something important to tell me; something that will change my life. And, apparently, on no condition must I tell Laura.

VII

L aura was standing at the foot of the stairs. 'Come on Katie,' she called, 'we are going to be late unless you get a move on.'

Katie bounded down the stairs two at a time although inside she didn't really feel like bounding at all. It was all for show. Laura had been a bit off with her all morning. Perhaps she had heard her 'animal talking' to Lottie, the terrier from next door, even though she had tried to do it discreetly.

The dog had been distressed because Mrs. Green, her owner, had gone out and left her alone in the house.

'She's only gone shopping,' Katie had whispered through the wall.

Gone gone! panted Lottie.

Katie sighed deeply, 'Nonsense. Don't you remember last Saturday? She left you at home then. She does it every Saturday Lottie. She's gone shopping!'

Lottie howled. *Gone gone. I go too!*

'Lottie,' Katie had become quite exasperated by now, 'They don't let dogs into shops. She had to leave you at home. She will be back in an hour.'

The dog had lifted its head and wailed pitifully, a long high wail that made Katie's ears burn. 'Lottie, please calm down,' she had begged. 'How about if I come round and talk to you through the letter box. Will that help?'

Katie had gone round to Mrs. Green's and prised open the letter box, squatted down and chatted on to Lottie through the door about football, the dreaded move to Manchester and going to see Dad in Exeter. She was about to tell the disinterested dog all about her new high school when she heard Mrs. Green's car pull up behind her in the road. Katie stood up quickly, straightening her skirt and clearing her throat as a puzzled Mrs. Green walked up the garden path.

'I was just checking on Lottie for you Mrs. Green. She was getting rather upset.'

'Oh, all right dear,' Mrs Green replied quietly. 'Well I'm back so you can go now. Aren't you moving to Manchester *soon*?' she added.

'No, not yet, in another week or so. But we are visiting my Nana today, so I had better get going.'

Katie gave a nervous smile, hopped over the low fence separating the two houses and went back indoors, feeling Mrs Green watching her all the way.

Laura was arguing on the telephone with Dad as Katie walked through the front door.

'No Jim, we said two weeks! You know I'll need that time to get the new house straight.'

She glanced at Katie, motioning with an impatient hand for her to go away. Katie went slowly up the stairs. She guessed her parents were arguing about her again. She could hear Laura's voice rising higher and higher and she began to feel sick. All the poisonous hatred her parents felt for each other flowed from them into her. She tiptoed across the landing and pressed her ear between the gaps of the banisters.

'No you are being unreasonable. As usual, Jim, it's all about you and what you need. Well, I have needs too! I'm moving to Manchester for Christ's sake, and I will need the time to get things sorted out. I have a career too you know! You promised Katie could stay for two weeks.'

There was a pause. Then Katie heard Laura say, 'Well that's just typical isn't it? I'll tell you what, how about if I put Katie on the phone? Maybe you can explain to her that your girlfriend doesn't want a kid around while she's entertaining her clients!'

Another moment's silence followed, and then a sigh of relief in her mother's voice.

'Thank you. For goodness' sake, Jim, I don't ask you for much.'

The conversation became quieter then and, predictably, tightly polite questions followed about each others' health and their respective careers. Katie left the landing and went to her room to get ready.

She focused on the journey to take her mind off her parents' row. So, Knickers didn't want her in Exeter and neither did Dad by the sound of it. Well, that was fine by her. She would go to Exeter and not say a single word; she'd ignore Dad completely, be as obnoxious as she could; that would teach him a lesson. She stamped about her room looking for her iPod and her PS3 game console, thinking through her instructions from Nana.

'Bring a large envelope,' Nana had said on the telephone, 'I have a letter for you.'

Katie had wondered why she needed to bring an envelope; surely if Nana had paper to write a letter on, she could find an envelope. Then she remembered Nana's last episode of ill health.

Laura had found Nana at home sat on the floor of her living room. In the centre of the room she had built a tower of paper. Tiny pieces of torn paper methodically placed one on top of the other, piled high, supported by a base of newspaper sheets. It had been a fire hazard, Laura said and proof that Nana needed to be in hospital again. Nana's social worker had agreed. Laura had driven Nana to the local psychiatric hospital only to find that six days later not only had Nana made more towers, this time from scraps of food she had commandeered from the hospital bins, but also that she had been left unwashed and unfed too. Laura found Nana in a pool of urine.

'That's it!' she had said to Katie's Dad.

'I don't care what it costs I am moving my mother. That bloody hospital is just making her worse.' Nana was in a posh hospital this time, all marble stair cases and gold taps according to Dad. Laura had paid for it, another source of moans and complaints, but perhaps, thought Katie, that's why Nana has not got envelopes. They don't want her making towers again.

Katie went into the spare room that Dad used to have as his office and found an old brown envelope in the desk drawer. It had a water mark on it, a picture of a crown. She returned to sit down on her bed. She ran the telephone conversation she'd had with Nana through her mind.

'On no account must you tell your mother what I am about to tell you,' Nana had said.

'Why not?' Katie had asked, thinking that she didn't tell Laura anything anyway.

'All will be explained Katie,' Nana had said, 'but if you tell her that I want to talk to you, she won't let you be alone with me. What I have to tell you Katie, well it's important. Can I trust you girl?'

Katie had sighed.

'Ok.'

'Good. Oh and Katie don't tell Dr Bennett either.'

She did not sound very ill Katie had concluded. In fact she sounded better than she had done for a long time. Then of course Katie remembered the delusions.

'Nana's delusions are the worst part of her illness Katie,' Laura used to say.

'I can cope with her stupid voices and mad obsessive behaviour, but I can't bear the bloody delusions.

'Why?' Katie had asked, not really understanding what delusions were.

'Because she can sound so damned convincing, that's why!' said Laura. 'Once when I was small she convinced the local police that a bloody spaceship had landed on top of the chip shop. Before we knew it the entire police force had arrived with sirens wailing, guns, grenades, and the lot. And Nana still managed to sound calm and self-assured. They wouldn't believe she was ill until Mr Parrot from number six called Nana's psychiatrist.'

So the delusions were stories.

'Stories can't hurt you though,' Katie had said.

'Oh yes they can Katie,' Laura had replied firmly.

'Stories that have no basis in fact can leave a person hurt and confused. If Nana ever starts telling you stories, and it's clear that she doesn't know it's a story but thinks it's the truth, change the subject. No messing. Do you understand?' Katie had nodded.

Later Dad had told her that when Laura was a little girl Nana often used to get unwell.

When Laura was only three, neighbours had found her sat inside the coal bunker; thin, cold and wet in a yellow frock with black spittle around the corners of her mouth. She had been eating coal because there was no food in the house. The neighbours had found Nana sitting in the living room staring into space, endlessly muttering nursery rhymes in a deadened monotonous voice. Nana had been taken into hospital and Laura went to stay with the first in a long line of foster carers. Dad also told her how once Laura had been woken up in the middle of the night by Nana banging saucepans and shouting at the top of her voice, convinced that she was on the Titanic, and that it was her job to wake up the sleeping passengers before they all drowned in the freezing sea. Dad said there were lots of stories about Nana that he could share with Katie but Laura didn't like him talking about it because it upset her too much. Katie guessed this was why Laura did not seem to like Nana at times, and referred to her as 'the mad old bat' and other things, like 'the bane of my life.' Katie wondered whether she was also a bane, whatever that was.

'Katie! What are you doing up there? Get a move on!' Katie's thoughts were interrupted by Laura calling again from the bottom of the stairs.

She picked up her denim jacket from the floor and stuffed her feet into her trainers. Folding the brown envelope neatly into four she placed it in the inside pocket of her jacket and went downstairs.

'Thank heavens you are ready,' said Laura.

'Now for goodness' sake get into the car, we have a long drive in front of us.'

VIII

The Sanctuary was a Victorian hospital, built from pale yellow Yorkshire stone on the banks of a blue lake. Ducks swam on the water and Katie spotted Canadian geese and swans too, serenely enjoying the late afternoon sunshine. The gardens were sloped and well kept, the neat lawn interspersed with beds of summer plants and flowering shrubs of purple and pink Rhododendron. Wooden benches were dotted throughout the gardens, on the paths and around the lake. Katie could see patients sitting, talking and looking out across the still waters.

They crossed the sloping lawn and entered the building through the front entrance. Warm oak panelled walls and polished floors greeted them in a cavernous hallway, and a huge crystal chandelier hung proudly from the ceiling, brightly lit up like a choir of electric angels. There was a smell of lemon disinfectant, mixed with roses, mingled with freshly polished mahogany. A marble statue stood to the right of the front desk. Katie went over to inspect it. She ran her fingers over the inscription that was etched into the base.

Robert Duke, Patron and Founder of the York Sanctuary

Katie spoke the words out loud, and the woman at the desk raised her head.

'Ah you've found our Robert' she smiled. She leaned over the desk. 'He founded this hospital in 1822. He was disgusted by the conditions of the asylums. A Quaker Friend of his, Hannah Joyce, died in the old asylum here in York so he built this hospital to prove to the world that mentally unwell people had the right to decent treatment and dignity.'

'Yes if you can afford it,' Laura muttered under her breath.

The woman frowned. 'Can I be of any help?' she asked coldly.

Laura gave her a taut smile, 'We've come to visit my mother, Dolly Stephens.'

The receptionist gave a short smile, 'Oh yes, Dolly, a very interesting lady. She has not been with us long has she?'

She swivelled round on her chair and addressed herself to her computer, rapidly tapping a number of keys.

'Ah yes here she is. Dolly is one of Dr Bennett's patients. If you can just give me two minutes, I will call him and tell him you are here. He has just finished giving your mother her medication.'

Picking up the telephone she dialled a number.

'Dr Bennett, Dolly Stephens' daughter and granddaughter are here in reception. Shall I send them down to you or will you come up to meet them?'

She replaced the receiver. 'Dr Bennett will be with you in one moment.'

Dr Bennett was a skimpy man who did not fit his clothes properly. His shabby jacket hung off his slim shoulders and the seat of his trousers was baggy and crumpled. He had dark hair and brown eyes and was not much taller than Laura. He nervously insisted on shaking Katie's hand as well as Laura's. His own hands were clammy and rather limp. He then led them down a long well lit corridor to Nana's room. Katie could feel her hand still wet from his touch and she surreptitiously wiped her it dry on the back of her jeans. The remembered feel of his hand on her skin made her shudder.

The hospital walls were painted a subtle shade of yellow and paintings of mountains and rivers adorned them, separated by mirrors and monochrome photographs of the staff. They passed through a part of the corridor which widened to reveal a coffee area.

'The patients can meet here to chat and have a drink,' explained Dr Bennett. Discarded cups and spoons lay across the long coffee table and someone had left a half eaten sandwich in a pool of spilt tea.

'Tsk,' said Dr Bennett, clearly embarrassed, 'I do apologise for the mess. I will ask one of the staff to clear this away.'

Laura made polite conversation.

'How is my mother?' she said in her professional voice, the voice she used when trying to be socially impressive.

'A little better, but she still has a way to go before she is well enough to leave. I think you will find she is very comfortable in her new room,' Dr Bennett replied. 'She has her own television now and an en-suite bathroom and we have just decorated.' He sounded proud of this. They reached

Nana's bedroom. On the door a china plaque read *The home of the living dead*.

'She seems to have a macabre sense of humour, does Dolly,' Dr Bennett joked. He opened the door and poked his head into the room, retracting it quickly as a plate whizzed past his head and smashed on the door jamb.

Katie heard Nana yell out, 'You dirty little goblin. You can't keep me in here any longer. I know you are trying to kill me.' Katie glanced at Laura, who was raising her eyes to the ceiling

'Not again,' Laura said under her breath.

'Hmmm,' Dr Bennett said, 'I think your mother may be experiencing another paranoid delusion. She has been having a lot of them lately. Yesterday she was convinced that I was one of God's spies. We may have to increase her medication.' He turned to Laura, locking Nana's door behind him, 'Would you mind coming along to my office Mrs. McIntyre? I could do with you signing the consent form and, of course, there was that little chat you wished to have with me.' He glanced at Katie as he said this and Laura nodded. She turned to Katie.

'Katie you stay here. But don't go in, you understand? Nana could be dangerous.'

Katie swallowed and gave a small nod. Dr Bennett smiled broadly at Katie, 'You can always go and help yourself to a cup of tea from the visitors' kitchen,' he said. 'You could sit outside in the garden whilst I talk to your mother. It's just that we may be a little while.'

Katie shook her head, 'No, it's all right, I'll wait here.'

She watched Dr Bennett and Laura disappear along the corridor, then sat down leaning against Nana's door. Dangerous! Nana might be barmy, scary, but she was never dangerous.

'Katie, have they gone?' Nana's voice came through the door.

Katie stood and peered through the key hole.

'Nana?'

'Well who else do you think it is you fool?!' Nana said, 'Now, open the door. We don't have all day you know.'

Katie hesitated.

'I haven't got the key. Dr Bennett took it with him,' Katie said, 'I think he's locked your door.'

Nana let out a short delighted laugh.

'Oh he has, has he? Well that don't matter see, because I have another one.' There was the sound of rustling. A key was pushed under the door.

'Now open it,' Nana commanded.

Katie thought for a moment.

'Nana you are not going to try and run away are you?' She suddenly had visions of Nana escaping down the corridor and across the exquisite lawn with Laura and Dr Bennett taking chase.

'No, of course I'm not! My god girl, have you seen the state of my legs?! I wouldn't get far on these I can tell you. No, I just need to talk to you before your mother gets back. Now are you going to open that door or not?'

Katie hesitated.

'I don't know how long they are going to be Nana,' she said pressing her mouth up close against the wood of the door, 'They could be back here any second, and she'll kill me if she catches me in there with you.'

Nana snapped, 'Don't be such a wet lettuce! Where's your back bone girl?'

'Laura is in a terrible mood,' whispered Katie, 'I don't want to make it any worse.'

'Ah,' said Nana, 'well you can't make it any worse Katie. That one was born with a scowl across her face. Now open the door. I can't do it from the inside.'

Katie thought for a bit. 'Ok,' she said eventually, 'I'll come in for ten minutes, but no more.'

'There's my girl,' said Nana.

Katie picked up the key, opened the door and stepped inside the room.

IX

It was just as Dr Bennett had described; it had been decorated recently. Katie could smell fresh paint and unlike the faint yellow of the corridor, Nana's walls were a refreshing pale green. Nana was not so fresh looking however. Katie could see she had aged since her last visit; the skin on her face had grown thinner and more papery and her brown eyes had sunk deeper into their sockets. They were watering furiously. Nana wiped them with her hand.

'You don't look too well Nana,' Katie said truthfully, giving her a large hug. Nana felt brittle and small and Katie felt sure that if she squeezed too hard she would crush her grandmother to dust.

'Of course I don't look well!' said Nana crossly, disentangling herself from her granddaughter's arms.

'Neither would you if you were drugged up to the eyeballs like I am. That's all they do here you know, give you nasty drugs and try and stick needles in your bottom! I mean take a look at this!'

Before Katie could protest Nana had lifted her skirt and bared a part of her bottom cheek. Her saggy flesh was mottled blue and green. Katie stared.

'They did it two days ago,' Nana continued. 'They call them Depot injections. They came in here at six o'clock in the morning and stuck a great big whopping needle into my bottom and then wondered why I yelled so loud.'

Katie was shocked.

'Why did they do that?' she asked.

Nana moved closer to Katie, looked suspiciously around the room as if to make sure no one was listening, and whispered, 'To keep me quiet. They don't want the truth to come out do they?' She gnashed her teeth and shouted suddenly, 'Goblins, the lot of them!'

Katie felt her heart jump in her chest. Perhaps she had made a mistake coming into the room. She swallowed hard and looked at the door. Nana touched her on her arm.

'There's no need to be scared of your old Nana. I promise to behave.'

'So what have you been up to Nana?' Katie attempted to change tack, get Nana chatting about normal stuff, avoid the delusions. Nana snorted, 'Why I've been waiting for your visit Katie. I have something I want to show you. Did you bring the envelope?'

Katie nodded and dug into her jacket to retrieve the envelope.

'Good,' said Nana, taking it from Katie.

'Now come and sit with me.'

Lighting up a cigarette, she sat herself down in one of the chairs by the window. Seating herself in the other, Katie said, 'You're not supposed to smoke in here, Nana. This is a hospital.'

Nana waved her hand dismissively and then with her other hand she opened the window and blew the smoke out into the courtyard.

'Let me tell you something girl. In this life, never do everything they tell you to do.'

She blew more smoke out of the window and then whipped out a small bottle of gin from under her chair and swigged hard on it.

'That's better,' she sighed with a small burp.

'Now, sit closer to me because I want to talk to you.'

Katie shifted her armchair so it was almost touching Nana's. Nana leaned in so close to Katie that she could see the bristles on the old lady's chin and smell her warm ginny breath.

'Katie, I want you to open my bedside cabinet. There is a packet wrapped in a plastic bag. Pass it to me will you dear?'

Katie found the bag and handed it to her. She watched as her grandmother fussed with it, finally pulling out a wedge of black and white photographs.

'Here, take a look at these Katie dear. These are your ancestors. The ones your mother likes to forget,' Nana said. She handed the photographs to Katie,

'Careful, they are very old and very precious.'

Katie leafed through the faded yellowing photographs. They were street scenes, mainly of children playing hopscotch in bare feet. One photograph in particular caught Katie's attention. It was of a young girl, about the same age as Katie, standing in the back yard of a terraced house. In her hand she held a broom. She was dressed in a long dark dress with a white apron tied around the middle. Katie saw she was beautiful. Her face was finely boned and her eyes were big and open, seeming to stare straight at Katie. The girl's face, unsmiling, strangely knowing, seemed familiar to Katie, though she couldn't think why. A slight chill crept down her spine.

'That's Millie,' said Nana.

'She's so pretty,' murmured Katie. 'Somehow, she looks alive.'

Nana smiled proudly.

'Well in some ways she is Katie. Perhaps she's not that unlike you.'

Katie looked up at Nana.

'What do you mean?'

Nana shifted in her chair.

'Millie was my grandmother, Katie. She was my mother's mother, which makes her your great-great grandmother. She was a very special lady.'

'Why special?' Katie was still gazing at the photograph.

Nana moved in yet closer to Katie.

'Well, for one, she could hear animals talk just like you.'

Katie's face flooded with colour. How did Nana know about her speaking with animals?

'No need to be ashamed Katie. It's a gift, and Millie had many more gifts which I believe she has passed on to you. She saw the lights that people carry with them. That was not her greatest gift of course; even I can do that,' Nana said complacently.

'No, her greatest gift was that she could talk with those who had passed on into death and because of this she learned the secret.'

'What secret?' Katie said.

Nana leaned in even closer.

'The secret of the Jewel,' she whispered. Her watering eyes lit up like bright stones.

Katie swallowed.

The Jewel; what was Nana talking about now? She remembered Laura's words of warning, 'If Nana begins to say strange things that make no sense Katie, change the subject. We must not encourage her in her delusions. The Doctors have told me that to pay her attention when she talks rubbish will only make her more ill.'

'So have you been following the cricket Nana?' said Katie weakly. She felt unsure of how to derail Nana from *the delusions* but knew that Nana did have a liking for cricket. It might just work.

Nana bought her hand down hard upon her knee.

'Cricket?' she said, sounding insulted, 'I don't want to talk about cricket. I need to tell you about the Jewel!'

Katie quickly looked at her watch. She had been in the room ten minutes.

'Don't you be worrying about Laura returning just yet,' Nana said. 'They will be an hour at least. Dr Bennett is an old gas bag once he gets talking.'

Katie sighed; she may as well listen to Nana's story. Part of her felt it could do very little harm. No one would know that she had listened. As long as she was out of here in another twenty minutes, she would be all right.

'I will have to tell you the brief version Katie,' said Nana, 'but don't worry because the rest will be explained by others. It's the Travellers you see. They will torment me for telling you but for now they have left the room.'

Nana hesitated before adding sadly, 'I wish I could remember the spell for warding off bad voices but they stole it from me...'

Before Katie could interrupt to ask her what a Traveller was, Nana had cleared her throat and continued with her story.

'A long, long time ago, long before the Bible was written, an ancient stone, a Jewel, was placed at the top of a tall tower. The tower was so tall it disappeared through the clouds and you couldn't see the top no matter how hard you looked. It was called the Tower of Babel. Do you know the story of the Tower of Babel, Katie?'

Katie shook her head. Nana looked at her resignedly.

'What do they teach you in school these days?' She took another swig of gin, puffed at her diminishing cigarette and continued.

'Well, the Tower of Babel was built by Nimrod the Babylonian King, after a great flood had washed over the earth. There had been weeks and weeks of the heaviest rain people had ever seen. It fell like some raging torrent out of the sky, Katie. And it just kept on raining and raining as if it was never going to stop. So that when it finally did stop, the people were so happy, they decided to build a tower all the way to the heavens, to get closer to the Gods. At the top of the tower they placed a Jewel that was red as blood yet clear as running water. No one knew where the Jewel came from, although I have my suspicions!' Nana tapped her nose knowingly.

'Some say it was given to Nimrod as a gift by a travelling merchant. Some say he stole it! Some claimed that Nimrod took the Jewel from the line of Adam, then buried it deep beneath the temple where the floods could not reach it! But that was a lie!'

Katie sat forward, her chin cupped in her hands, hanging on to every word. She loved Nana's stories.

'Now Katie,' Nana continued, 'The Jewel was a gift from the Gods to all of humankind. A very special gift. We were instructed to protect it at all costs for it was a channel to the Gods themselves. The Jewel gave humanity knowledge and wisdom, the sort of knowledge that only comes to those who are tuned in to the world around us, the sort of knowledge that you get if you use your mind and your soul. Through the Jewel people were able to communicate with the spirits that live in the plants, the trees, the rivers, the lakes, the animals and importantly, to those ancestral souls that have departed this life and gone on to another plane.'

Nana stopped.

'Are you listening Katie?'

Katie nodded.

Nana wiped her mouth on her sleeve and sat forward, her eyes dancing with excitement.

'Now, the other gift the Jewel bestowed on humanity was the gift of language,' she said.

'Language? You mean people could not speak before they had the Jewel?'

'No, of course people could speak child!' Nana said. 'The Jewel bestowed the gift of one language on all of life. The whole of the Earth spoke in one tongue and communication between the peoples of the world and the world of nature was commonplace. It was a happy time and a peaceful time.'

That's beautiful Nana,' Katie said gently.

'It was Katie. The Jewel was like nothing you or I have ever seen. It gave out a glorious light that flooded the entire land and through its power the past and the future could live side by side. Are you with me Katie? Do you understand everything I have told you?'

Katie nodded.

'Good,' said Nana. 'We haven't got a lot of time. Now comes the dangerous bit, the part of the story that explains where we are now.'

Nana sighed deeply. When she began the story again, her voice had a different quality; it was distant, as if it was not really her speaking at all, but someone else speaking through her from a time long ago.

'In that part of the world, there was one particular God, a tribal God of war, a God who was very jealous. He was also powerful. He disapproved of the people having the Jewel. He felt that if the human race could be like the Gods and communicate with each other in life and in death, then they would grow stronger and more knowledgeable. They would become like him and he didn't like that one tiny bit. So, he declared war on the other Gods, saying that he was the only one fit to be a God and that all life came from him and all life should worship him and only him!'

Nana hesitated. She shifted in her chair.

'This God decided to wreck the tower and strike the people with a terrible disease so that they could no longer understand each other. He attacked the Tower with a mighty storm and the builders scattered in confusion and fear. Then he tried to destroy the Jewel with a bolt of lightning.'

Katie's eyes widened. 'Did he destroy the Jewel Nana?'

'Almost,' said Nana, 'But one of the builders, a poor man from the local village, saw what this God was doing and climbed the tower right to the very top. He unclasped the Jewel from its place at the top of the tower and hid it in his clothes. All this time the jealous God was firing lightning bolts at him, one after the other and each one more fierce than the one before. The builder felt sure he would burn to death.' Nana took another slurp of gin and leaned in towards Katie.

'But apart from one small bolt that caught the man on his left hand, the God kept on missing! The other Gods saw what he was doing and they protected the man in the best way they could. Down, down the man climbed fighting to overcome his terror. The pain in his hand grew fiercer by the second; so much so he was sure he would lose his grip and fall from the tower to his death. But he didn't. He reached the bottom, picked himself up and ran and ran into the mountains with the Jewel. The story says that he hid in the mountains for seven years.'

'What happened after seven years?' asked Katie.

Nana was quiet for one moment, lost in thought. Then, she spoke again, 'The man returned to his village, hoping that after seven years of hiding away the God would have forgotten him and forgotten the Jewel.

Yet what he found on his return made him very sad. The jealous God had destroyed everything. He had achieved his goal. The people now only believed in him and called him the one and only true God. They had become slaves and had lost all connection to the world of the Gods. They had lost their knowledge, their inner light had dimmed; the jealous God forbade them to remember the Jewel and the gift it had given them to talk with spirits. They could no longer understand each other or the world of nature. They had no doorway to their ancestors. When the builder tried to remind people of how things once were, they called him mad, evil, and a blasphemer and they threatened to stone him to death. The builder fled the village.'

A sound outside in the corridor made both Nana and Katie sit up suddenly. Frozen in their chairs, they waited for Dr Bennett and Laura to burst in and find them talking. Both Nana and Katie let out sighs of relief when the buzz of a vacuum cleaner vibrated through the walls from the corridor outside. Katie quickly looked at her watch. She had been inside the room for almost thirty minutes.

'I'll have to go soon Nana.'

Nana nodded, 'I know you do, but before you go let me tell you one more thing about the Jewel. It concerns you Katie.'

Nana sat forward, resting her hands on her knees. She looked tired, Katie thought, but there was also something else about her; a sense of urgency to finish what she had to say. Katie knew she had to stay and hear the rest, despite Laura's warnings, despite her anxiety.

'Ok,' she said, 'but do hurry. I really don't want Laura to find me in here.'

Nana continued, 'The builder kept the Jewel safe for many years more. Yet all the while, in his heart he knew that the God would never stop searching for it. He would never rest until the Jewel had been destroyed. But the builder knew that as long as he could keep the Jewel safe it was possible that one day the people might be free again; they may learn once more the secret of the Jewel. He knew that he would not live forever, that one day he would die. It was vital for him to appoint another Keeper before he died—another Keeper who, like him, would safeguard the Jewel for the human race. So he began the long hard search for someone worthy enough to carry such a burden. But it was to prove to be a difficult quest. Over time the man grew very old and increasingly afraid that he would not be able to find anyone at all. The jealous God had spies everywhere, watching, listening out for signs of the Jewel, looking for the Keeper, determined to find both and destroy them for good. Everywhere the man went, people were increasingly frightened of him and his story. They were afraid of the memory of the Jewel.'

'Did he find someone Nana?'

Nana nodded, 'Oh yes he did,' she replied, but it was not someone from his own land. To find a Keeper he had to travel across many seas.'

'Where did he find him, Nana?' She could barely stand the suspense.

'Here,' Nana said.

Katie looked about her, puzzled. 'Here?'

'In England, Katie,' said Nana.

Nana smiled then, and said softly, 'In this land of such dear souls. This dear, dear land…'

Katie stared at her.

'That's Shakespeare,' Nana said, 'don't they teach you anything at school?'

Outside the vacuum cleaner ceased its low hum and Katie looked at her watch for the third time. 'I really must go.'

'Yes you must,' said Nana, 'but first let me give you something.'

She took the brown envelope and inside it she placed the photograph of Millie.

'Now Katie, I have something else for you.'

Nana fished inside the carrier bag and pulled out a letter, neatly tied with a white silk ribbon. She slipped it into the envelope, licked it shut and handed it to Katie.

'The letter will explain what the Jewel really means. Read it when you are alone, you understand? Do not let your mother know that I have given you this letter. Read the letter and look at the photograph of Millie. Do you promise me you will do that?'

Nana gazed at Katie, gripping her hands tightly. 'Now go!' said Nana, 'And look after yourself Katie. Strange things will start to happen for you, but be brave. You are going to need all of your strength.'

Katie bent over to kiss Nana on the cheek.

'Thanks Nana,' she said. 'Thanks for the story.'

Nana smiled.

'It is no story Katie,' she heard Nana call as she walked out of the room, 'it is your destiny.'

X

Albion 23 A.D.

Albion was the land of the White Stallions. Huge and bold, they reared up and out of the steep chalk cliffs, a pure symbol of defiance and battle; any fool daring to invade these shores would be met with both in plenty. Much blood had washed the shores of Albion, invaders from the far North but more recently the threat came from Rome. Julius Caesar had failed, twice, to capture Albion and bring her into the domain of the Roman Empire but the lure of her remained.

On a warm day, when the sky wrapped the island in a cloak of blue and the sea was at peace with itself, Albion looked like a plum waiting to be picked; a land of tin, copper and silver, with fields and forests that were rich and fertile. The Romans saw Albion in this way. However, on a cold day when the sea raged and lashed the cliffs, and the fog sat heavy as a wet blanket on the shoulders of the island, they became less buoyant and boastful about taking Albion. They grew afraid thinking about it. In Rome, legionnaires whispered darkly to each other about the mysterious and magical shores of Albion. They claimed that the Celts that inhabited the island could harness the sea and control it; with a whisper their Seronydd elders could magic the waves into tumultuous water giants with the power to smash ships and men's bones into dust.

Other claims were made about Albion being a cold and barbarous place, where the language spoken was from the belly, guttural and savage. It was said to be a land where the skies rarely cleared and the sun hardly shone; where crops turned rotten in the ground due to the poor weather. Some said the Celts were often so starved they resorted to eating each other.

These were just some of the stories that circulated about Albion. Those who visited Albion frequently saw that the stories were only partly true.

The merchants that traded with the southern tribes of the island knew them to be wily and shrewd, friendly and hospitable yet quick to turn on you if they sensed you were trying to cheat them. They saw a land that was warm in spirit and plentiful and a people well accustomed to the moodiness of their Gods. The Celts had learned to plan well for the wild fluctuations in weather; they had had to in order to survive. No merchant had ever witnessed the Celts eating another human being, but it was true that in battle with neighbouring tribes, Celtic warriors delighted in removing the heads of their opponents and bringing them back to the homestead as trophies of war.

The land belonging to the Brigante tribe, the kingdom known as Brigantia, lay in the north west of Albion. Its furthest border was mountainous and rugged, purple rock and shrub land dominated the landscape, and the farmers barely scraped a living from the earth. Further south the land grew more generous; the hills were softer and greener though still high enough for the Brigantian tradition of building hill forts in times of battle.

Huge looming fortresses protruded from these hills, protected by escarpments carved from rock and mud, dug deeply into the flesh of the hill.

It was cold on the hill fort and, in this time of war, Mortunda would often look longingly out across the valley to the lower lands where the wind could not bite your cheeks and lift you off your feet. The Brigante *oppida,* their main settlement, was sheltered at the bottom of the valley. From the top of the fort, if Mortunda stood on her tip-toes, she could make out the lines of the streets, the oppida walls and the outlines of the districts; the rounded roof of the meditation house where the Seronydd elder lived; the granary houses stacked in peacetime with heaps of grain and barley, the yard where chariots were assembled, then tested, their wheels forming deep ridges in the dust, and lastly the Royal residence, where they would live again when the war with the Parisi had been settled.

Princess Mortunda, small and dark-haired, the daughter of Brennus, King of Brigantia, traced the path to her father's dwelling as it wound its way around the back of the temple, past the cook houses that remained smokeless and abandoned today. There she stood, gazing upon the roofs of the Royal Houses rising above the stone wall that surrounded her father's domain.

She could visualise the pigsties and the stables in the royal enclosure, and she wondered again how long they would have to wait before they could return. Her father had said it would not be long; the Parisi were ready to make peace, and the Briganti would emerge as victors. Yet the war had lasted all winter, and she and the rest of the tribe were weak and tired from the fighting, the long waiting and living on the wind swept hill.

Mortunda flopped down into the grass, her mind busy and hot with thinking. She had often been told that she had been born with the qualities of a leader, a queen, the one to follow in her father's footsteps. It was not something she wanted. She sat on the grass with the chickens, the only reminder of Roman influence that her father allowed in his Kingdom, chewing on a stalk and pondering deeply upon the collection of river stones she had gathered in her lap.

'What are you doing Mortunda?' a voice said, 'Why are you here on your own?'

Mortunda looked up and saw that her father was watching her.

He stood, hands on hips, feet parted slightly, a concerned frown wrinkled across his brow. Mortunda could not lie, not just to her father, but to anyone. It was a trait that had caused her much grief in her eleven years of life, for there had been many times when a small lie amongst peers or her teachers would have saved her from severe embarrassment or humiliation, even the occasional beating. However, it couldn't be helped; lies would merely stick in her throat whilst her tongue spoke the truth.

So she said, 'I am thinking of Belisama,' knowing that Brennus would disapprove.

Brennus bent and touched his daughter's head, parting her dark hair away from her eyes.

'You are too young to be communing with the spirits, Mortunda,' he said. 'You should play with the other children while you can.'

'Maybe,' replied Mortunda thoughtfully, running her fingers over the smooth surface of the stones. She wondered how much of Belisama's spirit resided there; was it all of her, or just some? She could feel the warmth radiating from them, but Mortunda was unsure whether this was Lugh, God of the Sun, kissing the stones, or was due solely to the presence of the River Goddess herself.

'What are you thinking now?' said Brennus, touching Mortunda's nose, a gesture he always used when teasing his daughter. Mortunda looked up at her father, took in his broad shoulders, muscled arms and the deep green of his eyes.

'I can feel Belisama's power in the river stones and I would like some for myself.'

Brennus frowned in disapproval, then sighed heavily,

'One day, Mortunda, you will lead our people, and that is power enough. You are a child of the land. Now go and play, it is wise to do so while you can.'

Mortunda looked at him, a serious frown creasing her forehead. 'I think I will make a poor leader, Father, but a good Seronydd. I would rather talk to the spirits and let someone else be leader. I am not as strong as you.'

Her father hesitated. Mortunda knew she was his favourite child and that scolding her hurt him deeply. She also knew that she alarmed him with the things she said; filled him with anxiety for the future. She had heard him telling her mother so enough times, in the dark when he believed Mortunda was sleeping,

'Why does she have to be this way?' he would whisper.

Mortunda's mother, Leticia, would smile; Mortunda could see the whites of her teeth through her own partially opened eyes, gleaming in the darkness.

'Mortunda is who she is Brennus. The Gods have given her gifts and it is not our business to meddle with them.'

Brennus was not convinced, 'Well the Gods had better make her Queen, that's all I have to say. The tribe is going to need an intelligent leader once I am too old. There will always be wars to fight and trade to make.'

Leticia would fall silent for a while.

'Mortunda will lead us, of that I am sure,' she said once, 'But it may not be in the way that you hope for Brennus.'

'Mortunda.' Brennus's voice broke her reverie. 'Why do you have to say such things?'

Mortunda looked up at him, the memory of her mother fading in the weak sunlight. She shrugged. 'I don't know,' she said. 'I just think I will make a better healer and seer than I would leader.'

Seronydd seers were highly valued by the tribe, as much as warriors were, perhaps more so, especially in times of trouble. Seers were the eyes of the Gods, and could see into the future. More importantly they could interpret the present and guide the tribe on matters of war, birth, sickness;

they were the source of clarity in times of indecision. They gained insight from the spirits who resided on the Middle Plane alongside the human world and they were also the interpreters of dreams. Every man, woman and child had access to the Gods through their dreams though some were more open than others to hearing what the Gods had to say. Those with the widest channel to the Gods became seers, but the training was hard, and took many years. Mortunda wanted to be a Seronydd seer, an elder one day. She felt the calling in her blood but her Father was adamant that she was mistaken. Brennus glanced quickly over his shoulder, making sure no-one else could hear his words. He took his daughters hand in his.

'Mortunda, I have worked hard to lead us and as my daughter you are in a good position to carry on my work. Of my children, it is you I name. I command that you take the throne. You were not born to be Seronydd. There is a special calling for such work and they have not chosen you. You know what Sego has said on this matter. Now I will hear no more of this nonsense!'

XI

Sego had said she was not chosen.

Sego was a Seronydd elder and had lived with the Brigante for two summers. He had left them the summer before to return to Mona, the heartland of the Seronydd, to further his training and deepen his understanding of the knowledge. It was he who had advised Brennus on the timing of the war with the Parisi and should he return this evening, he would be instrumental in helping Brennus draw the peace terms with the Parisi, once the battles were over.

'Mortunda is not gifted enough to be a student of the Seronydd,' she had heard Sego say to her father in his deep velvet tones.

'The Gods advise that Mortunda marry a warrior and breed strong sons to enrich the tribe.'

Mortunda had felt her stomach turn over; she knew in her blood that Sego was wrong but she did not know how she could convince her father of this. Brennus had pressed the issue of Mortunda's destiny further with Sego, but not in the direction Mortunda wanted.

'Sego, tell me, do the Gods say that Mortunda will be Queen one day?' he had asked. Sego had hesitated and gone off to meditate upon the question. When he returned, Mortunda made sure that she could hear his reply; she had hidden inside an empty oak barrel inside her Father's house and sat as still as a mouse, her ear pressed against the grain listening to every word the elder spoke, her heart beating thickly.

'The Gods see that Mortunda will be Queen and she will give birth to sons who will lead this tribe into great prosperity and long life. One of them will be a great King.'

Brennus had laughed aloud and clapped his hands in glad approval, whilst inside the damp barrel Mortunda tried not to weep. Later that evening in the sleeping quarters she shared with her parents, Mortunda had overheard her mother's response to Sego's words.

'He said what?!' Leticia had said incredulously.

'Forgive me Brennus, but sometimes I think that man's channel to the Gods is filled with mud and fallen leaves. Any one with half a brain can see that our daughter is highly gifted. And the way that man goes on about sons all the time makes me think he has more Roman blood in him than Albion. Has he not recognised that the female line of the Brigante fosters as many great queens as it does kings? Does he not recognise the wisdom of the female line or see the contribution women make to our tribe? We do not hold such lowly opinion of women, we leave that to Rome!'

Leticia, Mortunda's mother, had been incensed and Brennus had taken a while to calm her down.

'Leticia, you can not go around accusing the elder assigned to the Brigante of being a Roman,' he hissed at her as they lay in the dark. 'You will get him killed!'

Mortunda smiled; part of her, even though it was wrong to think it, would have been glad to see the back of Sego. Mortunda suspected that she was probably already a better seer than the burly humourless elder with his muddy channel to the Gods.

Mortunda stood and brushed the grass from her clothes. She would not argue with her father today. She put her stones in her pocket, gave her father an enigmatic smile and walked towards the small gate that led out of the chicken enclosure.

XII

She felt her father watch her walk away. Small for her age, slender and yet agile, she knew many saw her as a determined child. Other children and some adults too, would visibly shrink in her presence, as if she were already Queen of the Brigantes. It was a personal trait that did not please her. It meant she often felt cut off from other people, as if she were apart from them. Behind her, she heard her father sigh. He had other matters on his mind apart from the worry of Mortunda; tonight the leader of all the Seronyddion was coming to speak with the Brigante concerning impending uprising in Gaul. The talks would go on into the deep of night and through into the next day. Brennus needed to keep his strength for that.

The evening air was thick with the sound of drums. The meeting with the Seronydd was an important one and Brennus and his elders were preparing themselves in their houses, dressing their hair in braids and ensuring the maps and plans for war were ready for discussion. There was an atmosphere of heightened tension and, whilst the warriors banged upon drums, others lit torches around the inside perimeter of the fort and out into the enclosures. The hill fort would stand alive and alight tonight, a shining fiery beacon in the darkness of the surrounding countryside. The pathway to the King's dwellings was soon lit up with orange flame and smoke rose from the opening in the roof of the meeting house. Inside the King's meeting house, the place where Brennus would discuss matters of war and politics, the hearth had been lit in preparation for the visitors. Soon they would be partaking in roast pig and lamb and supping on ale. Outside the meeting house in the open circle, food was being prepared for the banquet. The air buzzed with the shouts of cooks, and smells of sizzling succulent meats and warm oatcakes wafted across the enclosure.

Mortunda had heard two important pieces of news that evening. A messenger had ridden into the fort in early dusk amid great cheers and jubilation. The Parisi had petitioned for peace.

'They have surrendered some of their land in the south to the Brigante,' the messenger had explained breathlessly to Brennus.

Brennus had nodded.

'Also they have promised cattle, wool and wine to be sent across the new border at first light.'

Brennus frowned, 'Tell them we do not want their wine.'

Seeing the messenger's puzzled look, Brennus exploded, 'Are you stupid man? I do not want wine. It is a filthy lousy Roman drink poisoned with the breath of their Empire. I want grain instead; food for my people and enough left over to make ale. Go now messenger, deliver my word and tell Greta the Warrior Leader I will join her again tomorrow. Tell her that great rewards await her here.'

Loud cheers had thundered around the fort and music and singing started up; there would be plenty of dancing tonight and the feasting would be rich and go on long into the early morning.

The other news to have reached the fort had concerned Gaul. The Romans had long ago defeated the lands of Gaul, a country much larger than Albion on the other side of the ocean, but still, years later, small important victories continued to be won by scattered members of the tribes that had once dominated the continent. The Romans had recently been defeated in small skirmishes along the Western coast and continued to be surprised and outsmarted by bands of Celts that appeared from out of nowhere, and then disappeared into the interior without trace. With this news however came a warning that caused Mortunda's father much concern. Rome knew that the Gauls gained inspiration from the Albion tribes and Albion had long been the refuge of fallen Kings and Queens of Gaul. Now there were stories that had begun in the South of Albion where the coastal tribes were situated, of an impending attack upon the southern shores of the island. There was a possibility that the Romans would invade Albion. This very night the Seronydd elders were bringing a visitor with them—someone who knew the Romans and what they were capable of only too well. He was the former King of Veneti, one of the largest tribes of Gaul and had fought the Romans on many occasions. His tribe had been defeated and his lands taken, but he had escaped to Albion. This prime enemy of Rome was riding in tonight with the Seronydd elders to discuss business although Mortunda did not understand precisely what that business was.

Mortunda watched the orange flames of the torches dancing in the black night and tried to shut out her fears of Rome. She closed her eyes to feel the combined pleasure of heat and cold upon her cheeks. Her joy was interrupted when Aed her brother came up behind her and grabbed her by the waist, making her squeal with indignation.

'Caught you out dear sister,' he teased, 'No time to weave your magic on me that time.'

Mortunda punched him in the ribs and he fell to the floor in mock agony.

'Oh do not kill me dear Mortunda,' he cried, 'Do spare my life for I am nothing but a fly on your horse's turd.'

'And those are your words!' said Mortunda, stretching out her hand to pull her brother to his feet.

Aed grabbed her hand, pulled her over and then pinned her to the ground with his knees. He put his hand gently around her throat, 'Surrender?'

Mortunda nodded. Aed grinned in pleasure. His superior strength restored, he stood up and yanked Mortunda to her feet. 'How are you this night?'

Mortunda shrugged, 'I am well enough,' she replied.

'Have you spoken to them yet?' Aed pointed to a small group of girls sitting around one of the fires talking. Mortunda shook her head. Aed glanced quickly at her. 'You could try talking to them Mortunda,' he said. 'I think our Father worries about you not mixing with the other girls in the tribe.'

'I know he does,' Mortunda shrugged. 'I just find it hard to know what to talk about.'

'Why that bit is easy,' he said. 'You just talk about the things that we talk about.'

'I don't think those girls are very interested in my dreams,' she sighed. 'They are not like you Aed. They only seem to care about dancing and beading their hair.'

Aed laughed, 'What's wrong with dancing and looking beautiful Mortunda!' He nudged her gently in the ribs and looked over at one of the girls sat around the fire, 'Well if you get stuck for words you can tell Sirona that I love her.'

Mortunda pulled a face. 'That's disgusting!' she declared, 'I will say no such thing.'

She looked towards the campfire at the large group of girls huddled around it. Sirona sat towards her left, her legs crossed and her hands moving excitedly as she retold a story to her laughing companions. She was a round girl with large rosy cheeks and fair hair that was left loose and long, to do as it pleased. The flames of the fire danced in her laughing eyes and the light flickering on her young skin heightened the animation of her expressive face. Sirona caught Mortunda's gaze and raised a hand in awkward greeting. She flashed a broad smile at Aed and then, aware of her newly acquired audience, she continued her story, embellishing it with further flamboyance and receiving louder shrieks of laughter from her friends.

'Father says you are never too young to find your future wife,' murmured Aed. 'Come Mortunda.'

He grabbed his sister's hand and pulled her with him to the edge of the group.

'Any room for us?' he asked and immediately the girls shuffled round to make room for the two to sit down. Aed sat down next to Sirona and extended his hand in greeting.

'Hello sister,' he said, 'what were you and your friends laughing about?'

Sirona tilted her head in the small courtesy bow observed by the Brigante.

'I was telling them about the day Cedric fell into the swine pit and became so covered in pig poo that his own mother did not recognise him and chased him off with a broom,' she said.

Aed grinned, 'Ah yes poor Cedric. He is not known for his navigational skills—I heard he went head first over the fence and straight into the steaming pig droppings. He shall not make a warrior; the sow chased him off with her snout if I recall and he ran screaming to his mother.'

Everyone laughed. Mortunda watched her brother laughing and talking with the girls and she wished that she could do the same. She wished she had Aed's effortless way of being with other people and his easy social grace. He would make a far better leader than she ever would. She thought hard on what she could add to the conversation and as usual came up with a huge blank space. The conversation turned around to the impending feast.

'I wonder what time we shall eat this evening?' Sirona was saying. 'I am so hungry I can barely think.'

There was a murmuring of agreement.

'We won't get to eat until all the boring talks are well and truly underway,' added another of the girls.

Mortunda looked up at her sharply. 'They are not boring talks.' She knew she sounded sharp, disapproving. 'I heard my Father say they expect a King from Gaul. How can these talks be boring if they concern our future?'

'I thought all the Kings from Gaul were dead,' replied the girl flippantly.

Mortunda stood up, her heart banging angrily in her chest. 'You should not say such things! The Gauls are our friends, and if they lose everything to Rome, it will be us that Rome turns to next.'

It was true. Rumours had reached the North that some of the Southern tribes along the coast of Albion had befriended Rome and that some would welcome Albion falling under its rule. Years of prosperous trade between Roman merchants and the tribes of Southern Albion had softened the latter's mistrust of the great Empire, and Mortunda was aware that her father feared an invasion; the friend turning to foe, the southern tribes duped into passivity, allowing the Romans an easy capture of the shoreline of Albion. The Romans would march north, then, and attempt to take the Brigante. Mortunda imagined her own tribe caught in a bloody battle and her father captured and imprisoned by Rome. The thought made the blood freeze in her veins. She had heard the stories of what Rome did to those they captured. The Romans gave Celtic royalty a choice; either bow to Rome and hand ownership of the land to them or die. She knew her own father would never agree to hand his lands over to the Latin pigs. She could not bear to think of him tortured and killed, or captured and sold in Rome as a slave.

'Sorry, I did not mean to offend you,' the girl replied sulkily.

'No, we did not mean anything by it at all,' added another girl. 'We know they are important talks really.'

The mood had changed now from one of light frivolity to acute embarrassment. The children sat around shuffling their feet not knowing where to look. Even Sirona was lost for words.

Mortunda got slowly to her feet. 'I am sorry for spoiling your fun,' she said, 'I will go now and find out when we can expect the visitors.'

'I'll come too,' said Aed quickly.

Mortunda could read the mixed emotions playing out on his face; irritation for her quickness to take offence, and concern for her lack of social grace. Her own brother was embarrassed by her. She shook her head. 'No, you stay Aed.'

She forced a smile.

'I'll come and find you when they arrive, I promise.'

XIII

Mortunda made her way toward the open circle where, later, the tribe's leading families would sit together and eat. The circle was situated just outside Brennus' quarters, and periodically, throughout the evening, Brennus would leave his place inside the house to join them to share in eating and drinking.

Mortunda feeling mournful and lost after the encounter with the girls hoped that she would find some warmth and emotional sustenance here. Around the large open fire the cooks sat on stools carved from oak. Mortunda admired the beauty of the wood. The woodcutters would have performed the necessary rites before they took the wood from the tree. Trees were sacred to the Brigantes. Spirits resided in the oaks, some were ancient spirits that had been present since the beginning of time and they carried much wisdom. The Seronydd would seek their guidance on matters of fertility, whether the land was to be rich with food in summer or barren; whether the tribe was to receive an abundance of boy births or girls, or whether the numbers would be balanced. The Brigantes often left small gifts beneath oak trees in thanks for their shelter and beauty. Permission would have to be sought from the spirits themselves before an oak tree was ever cut down for the benefit of the tribe. Helen, the craftswoman, had carved the cut wood into elegant loops, creating stools that were light enough to lift and move back from the fire should the heat become too intense. The light from the fire danced and flickered on the surface of the wood and Mortunda could see the faces of wood elves move in and out of focus. Away from the fire there sat a large round wooden bench and, near to that, a heavy oak table. Here the chefs prepared the cooked meat ready to be taken into the food house. Other tribal members would eat around their own smaller camps and join up by the large fire to hear stories and sing songs later in the evening.

The cooks were under a great deal of pressure to get the meat prepared in time for the visitors. Some of them, celebrating the fact that the fighting with the Parisi was over, had drunk a little too much ale. Tempers were getting short. Fighting would often break out on occasions such as these, and so to avoid the scuffle of grown men made giddy with drink, rolling around punching and kicking each other, Mortunda decided instead to head for the eating and meeting house, where her father, the guest and the Seronydd elders would sit later to eat and discuss events in Gaul and the likelihood of war with neighbouring tribes.

Pushing the door open she entered a large room thick with wood smoke. Shielding her eyes from the choking heat and fug, she picked her way across the room to the sitting rug at the far end and sat down. Giles, the chief organiser was ranting at a scrawny looking boy, 'For the love of the Gods, deaden that fire! We want to warm Brennus, not burn him alive!'

The boy began hurriedly to splash water onto the leaping flames. Giles watched for a moment, then, turning away, caught sight of the small, rather forlorn figure of Mortunda at the back of the house. His heart warmed and he crossed the room to join her.

'Mortunda, what makes you look so sad?'

Mortunda smiled. Giles, large and dependable, was a permanent feature in her life. It was he who had helped carry her mother's body to the burial chamber two summers past. The fever had claimed many Brigante lives and Leticia had been taken swiftly. Her face had grown wet with sweat and her complexion, usually soft and dewy, had over night turned green and lined, until she was no longer recognisable. Mortunda too had almost been lost to the fever. Giles had ridden out for two days searching for the right plants in order that the healers could save Mortunda's life and had sat with them, nursing her and coaxing her spirit back to the Middle Plane. Mortunda had responded well and lived. Ever since then, Giles had held a special place in her heart.

'It's nothing,' Mortunda shrugged in answer to Giles' question. Giles raised his eyebrows and folded his arms. He could always tell when Mortunda was holding something back.

'I upset Sirona and her friends,' she admitted grudgingly.

'Oh,' said Giles, 'And how did you manage that?'

Mortunda told him what Sirona and her friends had said.

Giles nodded, 'And you became angry?'

'I did!' retorted Mortunda.

'That is no bad thing Mortunda. You were right. They are crucial talks.'

He sat down beside her, leaning in towards her, 'I wouldn't worry too much about Sirona,' he whispered conspiratorially, 'I hear she is frightened of the dark and throws the most massive tantrums when she can't get her own way.'

Mortunda giggled, then added seriously, 'Aed likes her.'

Giles pulled a face of mock horror, 'Never! And I thought the boy had impeccable taste.'

Mortunda snuggled into Giles' large arm and sighed, 'Yes he does Giles. For all I know one day Sirona and I might be related by blood. Aed said he might be handfasted to her if Father will permit it.'

'Well I am sure you can handle Sirona! Those eyes of yours, they are magical. You could knock her to the ground with a single glance if you so chose. Now tell me what else possesses your mind so.'

Mortunda bit her lip. She did not know where to begin or how to untangle the many things she felt.

'I just feel different,' she said eventually, 'and I do not know what to do about it.'

'Why do you need to do anything at all?' he asked, 'Maybe you are different. Your Father feels sure that one day you could lead the tribe.'

'Exactly!' Mortunda exclaimed. 'I do not want to lead the tribe Giles, yet I cannot let my Father down.'

There, she had said it. She watched for Giles' reaction. He was thinking carefully. Unknown to Mortunda, Giles had always questioned Brennus' declaration that Mortunda was his favoured heir to lead the tribe. It was, in his opinion, a foolish thing to say. Brennus was a popular leader in this time of war and had been the right person to lead the Brigante into battle with the neighbouring tribe the Parisi, but Brennus knew, as they all did, that leaders did not last forever and that new ones could emerge from any family within the tribe if they won the confidence of the leading families. It was true that Royal bloodlines had become more stable in recent years, with more tribes handing the leadership down to sons and daughters of the incumbent monarch, but to assume they could never be challenged was folly. Mortunda was a child, and she would only lead if the tribe decided she was right and the circumstances fitted. Giles felt Brennus had placed a heavy and unnecessary burden on very small shoulders, but to say so out loud would be to undermine Brennus' reputation as a man of wisdom and foresight. In dangerous times such as these, that would be equally foolish.

He had to be careful with his choice of words and yet offer some comfort to the child.

'Being leader is a big responsibility; your father is young and there are many summers before him Mortunda. I would not spend too long thinking about it.'

Mortunda looked at him, her eyes weary with tiredness.

'But I do think about it all the time.' She struggled for a moment, wondering whether to tell Giles what was in her heart.

'I keep dreaming of Sequana,' she said eventually. She waited for his response, afraid that Giles would shout at her or speak sternly the way her father had.

'Sequana the Goddess?' asked Giles incredulously.

Mortunda instantly regretted having said anything. 'I know of no other,' she said defensively.

'What have you dreamed?' Giles asked. His skin prickled. Mortunda had been visited by a Goddess! Giles feared such closeness to the deities. He was happier fighting in battle than hearing spirits speak, and he hoped he would never be visited by the Gods. He cleared his throat, 'Will you seek the advice of Sego?'

Mortunda shook her head, 'My father has spoken with him before, but I have not.' She hesitated. 'Sego does not like children,' she said simply.

Giles nodded, 'Ah Mortunda, I think Sego likes only himself.'

The pair laughed then. It felt delicious to break taboos with Giles. Seronydd elders of all levels, whether they were seers or healers, were fiercely respected by the tribe, and yet sometimes it felt good to poke fun at them, but only with people you could trust with your life. Since Leticia had died, Mortunda had had no one else to speak frankly with. Giles filled the gap beautifully.

'Go on then little sister, and tell me what you have dreamed. I can't pretend that I will understand, but I am a good listener,' Giles said. Mortunda nodded.

'In my dream Sequana came to me as a pretty lady. She had long flowing hair, dark as river mud and eyes the colour of cornflowers. She said I must go down to the oppida and meet her by the river. She said there is something bad about to happen and we must make talks with people in the south to stop it. She said all our lives depend on it.'

Giles grunted, 'Mortunda your father will not permit you to leave the fort to meet anyone, even the Goddess Sequana. We have only just finished battle with the Parisi. Greta and the warriors have guarded the oppida well, and the war is over, but the oppida may still be unsafe.'

'I know,' said Mortunda mournfully. 'Are you pleased the battle is done with Giles?' she asked.

Battle with the Parisi tribe had been bloody and victory had come to the Brigante at a price. Giles had lost his son to their sword and Mortunda knew the pain was still raw. He grunted and ran his fingers through his hair.

'Of course I am pleased!' he said. 'The extra land will be good for us. It is fertile and has many established crops. I have heard the wheat is the best for miles around. It will mean more food in winter for us, that is for sure.'

There was a silence. Mortunda could see Giles search around the room, as if he were looking for someone or something.

'You still miss him,' she said quietly.

Giles sighed deeply and placed his huge hand on Mortunda's knee. His eyes filled with tears.

'Sometimes, I can still smell that rosemary he used to put in his hair,' he said. 'I can hear him too, telling his daft jokes and stupid stories. He liked a laugh our boy. He made his mother laugh all the time. The poor woman hasn't smiled since he left us. Still, what can you do? The Gods took him and there's nothing I can do about that.'

The Parisi sword had cleaved the boy's spine in two. Giles had held the broken body against his own; held the boy in his arms, watching the light slowly fade from the wide, staring eyes; watching as his son's spirit gradually and with extraordinary gentleness, withdrew itself from the poor broken body until it was gone, gone to Arawn, the God of the Dead. According to the Brigante warriors in battle that day, Giles had wailed in grief and several Parisi tribesmen lost their heads to his anger. Now, in mentioning the Parisi, Mortunda watched Giles shake off the memory of his son lest it engulf him, drown him again in his loss.

'It will be good to return to the oppida,' she said with a note of hope in her voice.

Giles nodded. The pair thought of the warm settlement nestled in the valley below. Everyone hated living on the fort; it was crowded, windy and cold, but it was safe in times of fighting, much safer than the spread of a wide open settlement where the land, animals and the people were harder to protect.

'I know it is dangerous to return,' said Mortunda, 'I would explain my wishes to my father if only he would listen, but he gets cross with me when I speak about such things. He does not believe that I should become a Seronydd.'

Giles ran his hand through his hair.

'The Seronydd, are a difficult breed Mortunda. They choose their future elders in closed whispers. Their ways are a mystery to me.'

He shuddered as if a spider had suddenly found its way under his clothes and was tracing patterns into his skin.

'I am sure that if I could speak with the leader of the elders today, I could persuade him to take me to Mona and train me to be a Seronydd,' replied Mortunda. Her eyes were wide and plaintive. Giles clasped his hand over Mortunda's, 'Mona is far away from here and we know little about it,' he said gently. 'Your father would miss you too much and so would I.'

Mortunda looked glum.

'What do you know about Mona, Giles?' she asked.

Giles thought for a moment. 'Well, I don't know a great deal,' he confessed, 'but what I have heard is enough to convince me that I never want to go there.'

'What have you heard?' Mortunda asked excitedly. 'Please tell me!'

Giles smiled. 'Ok,' he said, 'I have heard it is a dark place, full of forests and tall mountains that loom above the heads of men and glower down at them. The Seronydd have a temple there, a huge temple made of rock carved from the side of the mountain, and inside their temple they practise their rituals to the Gods and study the stars.'

Mortunda listened, her eyes wide. She could feel the skin tingle on the back of her neck as she imagined the temple in the mountain and the dark gloomy forests.

'It sounds wonderful,' she said.

Giles clicked his teeth, 'I wouldn't call it wonderful. I have heard that the forests are full of goblins that snare Seronydd children and take them prisoner to the Lower Plane, where they feast off their souls and steal their bodies. Goblins are ugly creatures with gnarled skin and huge bony hands. They work with the Travellers; cruel spirits who delight in journeying to the parents of the dead Seronydd children to torment them with their children's voices.'

Mortunda stared in horror.

'That is despicable! I thought Travellers were good. I thought Travellers carry messages from the Gods to the ears of humans,' she said.

Giles nodded, 'Most are good, but just like humans, you get some that are good and kind and some that are nasty and harmful. Some Travellers cannot be trusted. Leave me with the human world any day, Mortunda. At least you can drive a sword through a bad man. Malevolent spirits are far trickier to deal with!'

Mortunda swallowed.

'I suppose a Seronydd has to learn how to tell the good Traveller from the bad, doesn't she?'

Giles smiled, 'Yes she does.'

'There are lots of good things about being a Seronydd though,' said Mortunda.

'Like what?' asked Giles.

'Like being able to travel wherever you want,' said Mortunda.

Giles nodded thoughtfully, 'I suppose that's true,' he said. 'A Seronydd is respected and feared by all tribes. He or she can cross as many tribal borders as they wish to without being kidnapped and held to ransom.'

Mortunda was quiet for a while,

'I would have to make sure I was well disguised if I were to go to Mona,' she said, 'otherwise I could get killed.'

Giles laughed, 'Yes that's for sure. If anyone recognised you as the daughter of Brennus you would be swiped straight away and your father's land ransomed in return for his daughter. But Mortunda, you would not leave us to go to Mona would you?'

His tone had turned to one of great seriousness now and he laid his heavy hand on Mortunda's head. She was about to answer him when a roll of the drums, together with various loud cries of delight rippled through the enclosure interrupting any further conversation. Scrambling to her feet, Mortunda ran to the door. Standing on her tiptoes she looked towards the outer rim of the fort. Coming up the hill was a procession of men on horse back led by Brigante warriors, painted in blue woad, their decorated skin glistening in the torch light, long dread locks held stiff by the herbs and dye they had woven in to keep the hair firm and unyielding. Behind the painted men, also on horse back, came a figure, tall and stern, wearing a cloak of fur, the fallen King from Gaul.

But Mortunda's eyes were on the three silent, black-clad figures who rode with the King. Austere, unsmiling, their faces stark and bloodless in the moonlight, they looked neither to left nor right, yet such was the power of their presence that everyone present felt himself observed, his secrets discovered, his soul lay bare.

The Seronydd elders.

Mortunda, her heart suddenly beating loud in her ears, felt her legs grow weak.

XIV

Mortunda watched as the men dismounted. One of the Seronydd, Mortunda noted with great surprise, was in reality no more than a boy, possibly younger than Aed, a freckle-faced lad with yellow flopping hair and dark shy eyes. The other was Sego. So, he had returned to Brigante.

He was a huge man who towered above her father. His arms bulged with muscle and his chest was as wide as a boar. His hair was dark and his eyes a deep brown. His colouring was unfamiliar in these parts and some whispered that Sego came from overseas. The rumour was not true. Sego was a descendant of one of the southern tribes, and this was all Mortunda knew about him. She had often sensed that Sego felt apart from the rest of them. It was almost as if he believed that fellow humans were beneath him. He certainly felt no regard for her or Aed. On occasion she and Aed had wandered into their father's house whilst Brennus was seeking Sego's interpretation of his dreams, and whereas Brennus had waved the children out with a half-hearted dismissal of his hand, Mortunda had felt Sego glare at them as if he despised them. Today he did not even acknowledge her but looked straight through her; she could feel the chill of him. He was a man she mistrusted and feared in equal measure.

The newly arrived company had travelled a long way and signs of tiredness were etched into their faces, black rings circled their eyes and their jaws were slack from lack of sleep. The eldest of the three Seronydd elders, the leader of all Seronyddion stumbled slightly and was immediately assisted by one of the painted Brigante warriors who had ridden with them. Leaning on the younger stronger man, the elder righted himself and nodded in thanks to the tribesman. It was then that he caught the glance of Mortunda's eye. He raised his head and looked deeply into the child's face. Mortunda felt her cheeks redden and her throat grow dry but somehow she found that she could not pull her eyes away from the vivid blue of his stare. She stood rooted to the spot, her arms and legs heavy and immobile. She wanted to look away but was unable to; her senses felt flooded by his looking, as if he could see right inside her soul. It felt to Mortunda as if her head no longer belonged to her but was being operated by an outside force. She could feel his thoughts imprinting themselves into her body and her mind as if they were physical things; she sought them out and read them instantly, as quickly as birds from the forest read the signs of oncoming winter. He was saying, 'Who are you child?'

Mortunda answered quickly with her mind. 'Mortunda, daughter of Brennus.'

Then suddenly Brennus her father came forward, his hands held wide in greeting, blocking the view between Mortunda and the elder.

The connection was broken.

'Lovernicus, Gwr Doeth, leader of all Seronyddion, we are honoured. Come inside and receive food and warmth.'

Lovernicus embraced Brennus and then turned to face the King from Gaul. Brennus bowed his head and held out his hand. The other man took it and the two embraced warmly, hugging each other tightly as if they were kin. The Gaul released Brennus from the embrace.

'Ah Brennus, it is good to see you again. My brother, I bring bad news but I bring it with a hopeful heart,' he said.

Brennus smiled widely, 'Torrance, my brother, we will listen to you with gladness and we will do all we can to help you and the people of Veneti. Let us go inside and warm ourselves by the fire.'

Torrance slapped Brennus on the back and the two men, followed by the boy Seronydd, Sego and Lovernicus, walked towards the house that Giles had prepared earlier. The horses were led away to be fed and watered. As they made their way across the slippery mud towards the food house, Mortunda looked across at the one they called Lovernicus, the one who had almost burned her with his eyes, but he did not return the look. He kept his gaze straight ahead.

The feasting and talking went on into the deep of night. Song had broken out around the smaller campfires and the oldest members of the tribe had begun the storytelling that would continue until dawn broke through the night sky. Most of the stories were well known but on occasion new chapters would be created and interwoven into the fabric of the old, embellishing the richness of the original story and bringing new meaning to the ears of the times. Mortunda loved the stories of the ancestors and if she had not felt so anxious she would have sat and listened, her grey eyes glowing with love and anticipation in the dark, her heart beating faster with a kind of fearful excitement, as she imagined the sounds of warriors' swords clashing against their enemy, feeling the wind rush under her feet as she was transported to lands where battles were fought and won. Tonight however, Mortunda stayed hidden in the shadows, away from the stories, the triumphant celebrations of defeating the Parisi, the laughing and drinking. She ran Lovernicus' words over in her head, *Who are you child?*

She looked towards the house where her father was locked in talks with Torrance the King from Gaul and the Seronydd elders. The key to her concerns lay in there. Before the night was over she had to share her dream with her father and the elders, but getting into the house and finding a valid excuse for her interruption was not going to be easy.

She looked longingly across to the settlement and pondered briefly upon leaving the fort and making her way across to the river as she had been instructed to do in her dream, but each time she considered it, a bolt of fear shot through her heart and she knew she would never do such a thing without her father's blessing. She wondered, not for the first time, why she had been born with gifts if it was known that her father would not allow her to follow her destiny.

A strong breeze was blowing in from the north; she could feel it spinning its cold fingers around her arms and legs and, unable to sit any longer amidst the merriment of the fort, she made her way towards a clump of trees on the edge of the hill fort enclosure to seek shelter. The trees were swaying heavily in the gathering wind and Mortunda sat beneath a large oak, leaning against the heavy, gnarled trunk. She could feel the hard ridges of the bark bite into her skin and she felt thankful for something solid; the oak was a symbol of confidence and durability, something Mortunda needed badly. She filled her nostrils with its scent and exhaled deeply. Immediately, she felt the calm of the tree's spirit enter her bloodstream and wash over her anxiety. Breathing in again, she began the visualisation. She saw the roots of the tree lying deep beneath the earth, spreading out across the land and in her mind she travelled along them. She felt the roots, firm and thick, holding the trunk on the surface of the earth and feeding it with nutrients from the soil. With deep breaths she drew upon the tree pulling the wisdom and knowledge it carried within the roots, up from the ground, into the trunk and through her body. She allowed the spirit of the tree to circulate around her and felt it tingling in her fingers and toes. As Mortunda sat with her eyes closed she asked the tree the question, 'What does Sequana want?'

The answer was immediate and came in a loud rush.

Go and speak with Lovernicus.

Mortunda tried another question, 'What is my destiny?'

The answer rode in upon a whisper but was as clear as early spring waters, 'Lovernicus can tell you. Swith him.'

Mortunda sat still and focused again. 'What will happen if I cannot speak with Lovernicus?' peak

The answer flowed into her veins, *The Brigante will be lost.*

Mortunda gently eased the spirit of the tree back into the trunk and then, by breathing out, she blew it gently back down to the roots. She praised the tree for its knowledge and thanked the spirit for helping her, but inside she felt irritated, frustrated and dissatisfied. She had wanted a different answer, one which would cause her less grief. She knew that she had no choice but to make her way to her father's house. Despite the contempt of Sego and the wrath she would endure from her father, she had to speak to Lovernicus.

She walked back towards the interior of the settlement searching for some inspiration, some plausible method of gaining entry to her father's quarters. The question of how she was going to gain an audience with Lovernicus churned in her head.

'I have to find a reason,' she said under her breath, 'I have to find a way of making him take me seriously.'

She found it suddenly in the bobbing flames of the campfires.

She could call upon the Request of the Flame!

Her father and Lovernicus would have to grant her a hearing if she called upon the Request—every man, woman and child had the right to do so, though few chose to; it was a dangerous journey. She took a deep breath and resolutely made her way toward the food house. As she crossed the mud she saw Aed leaning against a disused war chariot. She hurried towards him, anxious to tell him of her plans, hoping that in doing so her heart would become lighter. She called out to him but to her surprise he did not turn in her direction.

'Aed,' she tried again and waved at him furiously in the dark.

'Aed over here!' Her brother turned, not to her, but to another figure on his left. Mortunda stopped dead in her tracks. The figure was in darkness, but she could see from the subtle hints of hair and clothing, a certain grace of movement, that it was a girl Aed was holding gently by the shoulders. She heard soft laughter and watched as her brother leaned forwards to remove the girl's hair from her eyes. The girl reached up and touched Aed's face and the pair moved in closer until the girl's head was resting on his shoulder. Mortunda turned on her heel and walked away. Her stomach was churning and hot tears burned in her throat. Sirona! It had to be her of course. She thought of her brother's soft dark hair and open face. She recalled how he would tease her and then comfort her when she felt forgotten by others. He was her Aed. How dare Sirona try to steal him from her! She walked toward the house, head bent low, thinking angry thoughts, and before realising it she had reached the door of the house. She leaned for a moment against the frame, easing the thought of Aed and Sirona from her mind, controlling her jealousy and steadying her breathing. With a deep breath Mortunda forced herself to focus on the task in hand. It was a skill she had learned from her mother.

'Look inwards Mortunda,' she could hear her mother say. 'Find the core, the heart of the matter and do what needs to be done.'

She knew that she had to be strong to face Lovernicus; she could not afford to look foolish. It was important that she appeared to be in full control of her emotions. If Lovernicus saw her as a silly child he may accuse her of wasting his time and of disrespecting the sacredness of the Request. That would make her father look foolish too. She straightened her hair and pushed her shoulders back and, quelling the uneasiness that rose in her stomach, she pushed open the door and walked into the room.

XV

Katie 2008 A.D.

The night she returned from the hospital, Katie could not sleep. Nana's words burned in her ears, 'It is no story Katie; it is your destiny.'

What did Nana mean? She was imagining things of course, she had to be. People did not have destinies, not really. Laura had always said that people had to make their own lives because no one else would do it for you. Katie turned onto her back and sighed. Sleep was not going to come. She may as well read the letter. She flicked on her bedside light and padded to the wardrobe door, slid it open and reached for the key. She unlocked the chest of drawers. Her hand hesitated over the handle of the drawer. Suddenly she felt frightened of what the letter might contain. She chewed nervously on her bottom lip, then took a deep breath and pulled the drawer open.

Sitting on her bed she untied Nana's silk ribbon and let it fall to the floor. Unfolding the pages, she began to read. Nana's handwriting was surprisingly neat but the letters were packed tightly together and the writing was thin and scratchy. Katie had to hold the pages close to her eyes in order to decipher each word.

My dear Katie by the time you read this letter, I will have already told you the story of the Jewel. The Jewel has played a big part in the history of our family for many years. Katie, it is going to play an enormous part in yours too.

Do you remember me telling you about the builder being attacked by bolts of lightning? If you recall I told you how the jealous God kept on missing him. Oh he tried all right! Bolt after bolt of pure white light flashed from those dark thundery skies, but all to no avail what so ever! He reduced that tower to a pile of rubble, but he could not hit the builder. Except for that one time, when a fragment of light hit the builder's hand. Remember I told you that Katie? The bolt of lightning seared the builders hand and left a mark. If you look at your hand you'll that same mark on you, a thin silver line that begins at the base of your thumb and runs to your wrist. This is the mark of a Keeper.

Katie stopped reading for a moment. Nana was saying that she was a Keeper of the mysterious Jewel? She looked at her birthmark. She had never paid it much attention before. She ran her finger down its silvery track. Numb. It had always been numb. Laura had said it was more like a scar than a birthmark because it had never had any feeling in it. Yet she had been born with it; even on her baby photographs it was there, standing out clearly on her hand, a flash of silver surrounded by warm pink baby skin. She shrugged and carried on reading. Nana's delusions were interesting, even if they were off the wall.

Before he died, the builder found a new keeper and the Jewel was passed on to several keepers for many generations more. However, somewhere along the way the Jewel has gone missing.

'Missing?' Katie said aloud.

We don't know how, but we fear for its safety. We know that the God still pursues the Jewel and we fear that he is close to finding it. We think it is with a Keeper who is struggling to pass it on. In fact we know this is the case. It has to be. The Jewel has not been seen by any of us for many years, although our family has always known it and felt its presence, weakened though it has been. Katie, you will need to take out the photograph of Millie. I want you to look closely at Millie, examine the picture and remember what you see. If you look properly, you will find the evidence that shows I am not just a crazy old woman telling my grand daughter fancy stories. Look now Katie before you read on.

Katie placed her hand inside the envelope. She noticed that she was shaking. She slid her fingers round the back of the photograph and, remembering it was old and fragile, pulled it out gently. Millie looked up at her and that same chill she had felt in Nana's hospital room came over her once again. If she hadn't already been sitting down her knees would have given way. Gazing at Millie's face she could see traces of herself in the dark eyes, in the way her chin came to a triangular point. The sloping of Millie's cheekbones resembled Katie's own. Millie was small, shorter than Katie, but then this photograph was at least a hundred and twenty years old; people were shorter in the 1880s. She glanced at Millie's hand grasping the handle of the broom and it was then that her heart almost stopped beating. Along Millie's left hand Katie could see a mark. At first she had assumed it was a mark on the photograph, a piece of grit on the camera lens, but when she held it up close, she could see it was a squiggly line running from the base of her thumb to the top of the wrist. It was the same birthmark. Katie stared. It was coincidence of course, a strange genetic twist in the story of evolution, nothing more. She returned to the letter to see what Nana made of it all.

The mark on Millie's hand is the mark of a Keeper; the scar left by the lightning bolt. Millie should have been a Keeper of the Jewel and so should you be. But where is the Jewel Katie?

Katie shook her head.

'I don't know,' she replied as if Nana was in the room with her.

She returned to the letter.

This question has plagued our family for generations. You can have no idea of the harm its loss has caused us. Your own mother was deprived of a loving childhood. The Travellers, agents of the God, have besieged me for years, filled my head with hurtful words and bullied me with their voices, tore me from my own daughter, made me too ill and confused in my head to care for her. I do not bear the mark myself, but because I am from the line of Keepers they have tormented me. They did the same to Millie and her mother before her. We have been a motherless family Katie; our daughters have been stranded and abandoned. We need to find the Jewel. The line of Keepers has to be restored, not just to our family, but to the whole world. This is your destiny. Find the Jewel Katie. Track it down. Bring it home. Return it to the world. Watch for the signs; your journey is about to begin. Remember to trust what others would fear and take care. My love is with you always, Nana xxx.

Three kisses. Nana had signed the letter with three kisses. She ran her fingers over the crosses and realised that her own mother had not kissed her for many years. Frowning thoughtfully, Katie walked over to her window. The garden below was in darkness. She stared out into the dark. All about her lay a deep, almost unnatural silence. It was very late; around two o'clock in the morning, yet she felt wide awake. The words 'motherless family' rang in her head. She knew what Nana meant. Katie too was motherless. Although Laura was next door, sleeping, sharing a house with her, eating with her sometimes, she did not share in Katie's life. No one did. Was this her fault, Katie asked herself. Did she unwittingly invite Laura's disdain? Was she wrong to hide things from Laura or to avoid the friendship of others her own age? Katie sighed and looked into the dark. A feeling of someone watching her crawled up her arms and down her back and she shuddered. Turning away from the window she reached over and placed the letter back in the drawer, switched off her lamp and lay down.

Her head was dizzy with fragments of images—birthmarks, hospital gardens, Nana's watery eyes, the blackbird, the photograph of Millie. She lay there for what seemed like an age, turning to her right side, then onto her left, and waiting for sleep to come. She had just begun to succumb to its embrace when the telephone rang. She opened her eyes and listened to Laura stirring from her sleep.

'Hello,' she heard Laura say sleepily. 'Who is it?'

She sensed her mother shift from sleep into wakefulness, heard her voice become sharper and more anxious.

'Dr Bennett. What's wrong? Is my mother ok?'

She heard the mattress creak as Laura eased herself into a sitting position.

Silence.

Then she heard Laura sigh deeply and say, 'Thank you for letting me know.'

The telephone clicked back into its stand. Katie sat up, her senses now on full alert, waiting. There was the snapping of Laura's bedroom light being switched on and scuffling as Laura searched the bedroom for her slippers; there was the sound of Laura easing herself into her dressing gown, the shuffle of her feet walking across the landing and the turning of Katie's door handle. Laura appeared in the doorway, the landing light silhouetting her like an angel. Her face was wet with tears. 'Nana died tonight,' she said simply.

XVI

They buried Nana the following Saturday.

'There's no point in hanging around,' Laura had said gruffly.

Dr Bennett had explained to Laura on the telephone that Nana collapsed with a heart attack several hours after Laura and Katie had left the hospital. He hadn't rung straight away because during the doctor's attempts to revive her, her heart had started beating again. Sadly she had had another heart attack soon after and the second time all attempts to resuscitate her had failed. Dr Bennett said he was sorry.

Katie sat through the funeral in a daze.

Nana was dead.

She'd gone without any warning at all. The vicar's words, reaching her from the pulpit, seemed meaningless. He hadn't known Nana at all. His voice hung dreary and emotionless in the musty church. At one point he mispronounced Nana's name calling her 'Dilly' instead of 'Dolly.' There was very little to be said, except some talk about Dolly being returned to Jesus and eternal life. She wondered what Nana would have made of such a humourless parting. Katie imagined Nana sat in the back pew with her bottle of gin, a dry smile on her face. She would, no doubt, have said something to upset Laura, something funny, something off the wall, something mad. A world without Nana suddenly felt dry and dull, all the fun squeezed out of it, leaving behind nothing but dust. Katie felt more alone than she had ever felt.

The funeral was held in York at a small church not far from the Sanctuary. They lowered Nana's coffin into a small plot close to a sycamore tree. Katie watched the men shovel the brown earth back into the ground, each thud of soil burying her Nana's body deeper and deeper until at last it was done. Nana was gone.

Katie turned and followed her mother back to the hospital. She could hear the sound of her footsteps as she crossed the tarmac of the car park but her feet felt as if they were not attached to her legs; every part of her felt as if she were made of cotton wool, airy, light and not real.

Dr Bennett had arranged a small tea for Katie, Laura and the staff that had cared for Nana. Dad had not been invited. Over sandwiches, coffee and a glass of orange juice for Katie, the staff shared their memories of Nana. The receptionist who had welcomed them in just a week before was telling the group about Nana's sense of humour,

'She was such a dear,' she said fondly, 'always up for the crack. We shall miss her.'

Dr Bennett nodded gravely, 'Yes she was. She certainly had a spirit about her.'

The receptionist, who was called Jackie, said suddenly, 'Oh and she was so intelligent too. She loved the library. She was always down there reading about all sorts. She showed an enormous interest in the story of Duke.'

'The chap who built this hospital?' Laura asked.

Jackie nodded, 'That's right. The library is in the basement, built on the grounds of the old asylum where Hannah Joyce died. It's a bit creepy down there.' She shuddered.

'I wonder why Nana would be interested in Duke?' said Katie.

Dr Bennett cleared his throat.

'Maybe your Nana identified with Hannah Joyce, the lady who inspired the building of the Sanctuary,' he suggested. 'After all she lived in a time when the world was very cruel to the mentally ill. Hannah died a horrible death in the old asylum. Your Nana probably felt sorry for her, understood her in a way that maybe we cannot.'

Katie nodded and took a bite of her sandwich. The bread was dry in her mouth, her throat too tight to swallow. She took a sip of juice to wash it down.

'What happened to Hannah?' said Laura.

Dr Bennett put his coffee cup on the table.

'The library has the full record. I am afraid I do not know the entire story, but the bare bones are that Hannah died in the old asylum, not from her mental condition, but from childbirth. She was pregnant when she was admitted to the York Asylum and gave birth there. She was not properly cared for and died, I assume of a haemorrhage; she lost a lot of blood.'

Katie felt sick.

'That's terrible,' she said, 'what happened to the baby?'

'Died alongside the mother I should imagine,' Laura said quickly. 'The graveyards are full of dead babies from the 18th century.'

'Actually no,' Jackie said. 'The baby didn't die. According to what Dolly found out, the child was taken away to be placed with Hannah's sister. Duke never found her. He died without ever knowing his own daughter.'

'Was Hannah his wife then?' Laura asked.

Jackie smiled and her eyes glittered briefly with conspiratorial delight.

'No!' she said, 'It would have been a major scandal if the truth had been revealed back then in the 18th century. I mean, a man like Duke; married, respectable, rich, having an illicit relationship with a poor uneducated woman like Hannah. It was only when the family handed his diaries over to the Sanctuary that the truth was known. Hannah Joyce and Robert Duke were more than just friends.'

Katie thought about Nana. Duke's story was tragic, romantic in a way she supposed, but she wondered why Nana would have been so interested in an 18th century love affair. Somehow it did not seem like Nana.

'Was there anything else unusual about the story?' she asked.

Jackie looked at her. She shrugged, 'I don't think so.'

'What happened then, did Nana ever get to the bottom of it?'

'Well,' said Jackie, 'it seems that Duke became a bit of a King Herod in reverse.'

Katie frowned, 'How do you mean?'

'Duke didn't just search York for his daughter,' explained Jackie, 'he searched the whole of England and America. He sent messengers to track down the child through the network of Quakers, and put up a substantial reward for anybody who could find her. He was determined to seek her out, not to kill the child of course, as King Herod wished to do to the baby Jesus, but to claim her as his own. He searched for all of his life, but the child was never found.' Jackie looked sad.

Laura sipped her coffee then said, 'How would he have known the child. I mean it does surprise me that no one came forward to claim they had the girl, especially if a large reward was on offer. I would have thought plenty of poor families would have been willing to sacrifice one of their children for the right price.'

Jackie nodded, 'Yes, I thought that too, but Dolly seemed to think he would have known her.'

Dr Bennett swallowed a mouthful of food, 'The mark,' he said, his voice muffled with bread. 'According to Duke the little girl had a birthmark just below her thumb on her left hand exactly the same as Hannah's. Duke looked for a child with a white birthmark.'

Katie's heart leapt. Instinctively she closed her fingers over her thumb and put her hand behind her back. She glanced quickly at Laura, who seemed not to have registered the doctor's remark, and was clearly bored with the story. Her mother was looking at her watch, probably calculating how long it would take them to drive home. Katie thought for a moment. She had an idea. She picked up another sandwich and put on her brightest smile.

'Would it be all right if I took a look at the library? I'd love to see the diary and—well I love books anyway, so I'd really like to have a look around down there…and see what it was that fascinated my Nana.'

Jackie looked at Dr Bennett who nodded his approval. She smiled. 'I'll take you down there,' she said. 'We'll need a torch because the light has gone at the top of the stairs. Come on.'

Before Laura could protest about time and traffic, Jackie had grabbed a torch and was leading Katie down the hallway and across to the basement stairs. Katie was about to see the ground floor of the old Asylum and be led to the diary of Robert Duke.

XVII

The air was musty in the basement. Katie had thought she would have to stoop to avoid hitting her head, but the ceiling was almost as high as the ones in the upstairs rooms. There the similarity ended. Unlike the splendour of the entrance hall, in the basement cobwebs hung in thick grey clumps and the shelves, where files were stored, were coated with a film of dust and muck. The smell of damp punctured the air, and a chill hung around the back of Katie's neck.

'The library is this way,' Jackie called from ahead. Katie looked around her. Built against the far left wall she could see cells with iron bars, just large enough to contain human beings; in some there were chains still attached to the floor.

'What are these cells for?' she called out.

Jackie turned to face her. She grimaced.

'Those are from the old asylum,' she said. 'The patients were kept there. They were chained to the floor, six or seven of them to one cell. They were treated no better than wild dogs.'

Katie felt a wave of shock. She reached out and touched one of the bars, felt the cold metal and tried to imagine Hannah Joyce, damp to her bones, frightened and pregnant, captured in a cage with no prospect of escape.

Jackie led her through the basement until they came to another room. This room had a door and efforts had been made to ward off the damp. Inside the walls had been plastered and painted and a carpet lay down. A ventilator hummed, circulating air around the room. It was wider, cleaner, brighter here, and from floor to ceiling there were shelves packed with pamphlets and leather bound tomes, some behind glass cases, others just waiting to be lifted up and read. Katie looked around her. Reds, greens and browns, the favoured colours of Georgian literature, looked out at her and there was something else she could not quite place; a feeling, a sense of something else being present with them in the room.

'Do you mind?' she asked Jackie as she picked a book off the shelf, titled *On the nature of God*.

Jackie shook her head. 'Not at all, please be my guest.'

Katie opened the book and felt the thick yellowed pages between her fingers. The paper felt soft but not smooth and a smell of musty abandonment lifted off the opened book. It had lain unloved and forgotten for many years. 'Like Hannah,' she thought, and then a strange connection formed in her mind, 'Or like Millie.' She placed the book back on the shelf and ran her eyes across the titles; many were about Quakers, most were about God and the Church and written in language she did not understand. She wondered how Nana had read these and understood them.

'They are all a bit boring really,' apologised Jackie, 'A bit above my head I am afraid. Not for your Nana though. She used to explain them to me a little. The diary is over here if you want to see.'

Jackie was unlocking one of the glass cabinets. 'Here it is,' she said, taking out a brown leather bound book. It was small but heavy. She brought it over to Katie.

'See if you can understand it. I am afraid the language is too tricky for me, but you seem to be a clever girl.'

'Thanks,' said Katie.

Jackie checked her watch, 'I am going to pop upstairs to see if Dr Bennett needs me back on reception. Will you be all right if I leave you down here for a while? I'll come and fetch you in half an hour?'

Katie nodded, although she was a little nervous at being left in the cellar with so many ghosts. Seating herself on one of the high-backed leather chairs, she opened the diary to the first page.

I, Robert Duke of Oak Stone house, in the District of York swear by the Lord My God and Father to record all I have learned on the whereabouts of the child of Hannah Joyce.

Katie read on, but the rest of the passage was written in cryptic language on the nature of the Quaker faith, and did not mention Hannah again. Katie was more confused by the end of the passage than she had been at the beginning. She flicked through the pages looking for something interesting, but most of the diary was not about Hannah at all. It contained long passages about Duke's business dealings, detailed descriptions of hunts he had led, tedious meticulous lists of foods consumed at dinner parties and records of Quaker Meetings and the folk who attended them.

Katie was about to put the diary back, disappointed and bored, when she felt something bulky in the centre of the book. It felt out of place, an alien object that should not be there; something that had been folded and attached by a clip to the inside of the diary. Katie unfolded it carefully because the page was worn thin, almost transparent, and had frayed around the edges. It was a letter written on a long sheet of paper that unwound itself until it touched the dusty floor of the library. Katie caught her breath. It was from Robert and was addressed to Hannah. She began to read, acutely aware from the prickling of her skin that what she was viewing was deeply personal, almost sacred. She felt like an intruder, that she had no right to be here in this room unravelling a mystery that began over two hundred years ago and yet she felt compelled to read as Nana must have done before her;

October 20th 1814

My dearest Hannah,

I write to you in the knowledge that you will never read my words. It has been thirty years since I witnessed your passing from this world and still to this day the pain of losing you is too great for me to bear. True, no man would see evidence of my pain nor guess that I am anything more than a business man going about his daily affairs of commerce, fishing, riding and fulfilling his duties as a husband and father. And yet the truth is, my love, I am dead inside. Not a day goes past Hannah when I don't long to be with you, to hold you, to see your face, to, God forgive me, embrace you once more. My arms ache from the lack of you, my heart beats a hollow sound, and my bed is a grave. My life is empty without you. The day you left me stays with me forever; the stink of that dreadful place, the agony in your eyes and your gentleness. Even at the point of your departure you could only think of me.

He must have meant the day he found her in the asylum, Katie thought. She could imagine him now standing by the cell, banging on the bars, begging Hannah not to die. It could easily have been the cell she had seen earlier in the basement. She imagined Nana behind the bars of one of them, and her stomach knotted in anger. She was glad places like that didn't exist any more. She read on.

Hannah I am writing this letter to tell you that I have failed you in death as I failed you in life. In life I did not come to you soon enough; instead I allowed Edgerton's men to take you from me; I placed my social station and all that it demanded of me above my love for you. Not a day goes by when I do not berate myself for not being a stronger man. I should have put you before any other consideration. We should have married and escaped to the New World. But no instead I chose to hide you away and commit you to sin whilst I played the lie of being Robert Duke, respectable tea merchant and married man. In truth, I am no more than a liar and a fraud. Yet the pain of knowing this is nothing to the pain I feel at not having you with me. The devil himself could not punish me more.

The New World; Katie thought, what did he mean by the New World, and then she realised Duke meant America. She returned to the letter.

My darling Hannah, let me tell you how I have failed you in death as well. Your last wish was for me to find a lost Jewel – the Keeper's Jewel. You told me, do not let the Church hide it any longer.

Katie started in her chair. The Jewel! She read on fervently.

My darling, I have been unable to find any such object. At first I thought the Jewel was one of your imaginings, a moment of delusion, a fragment of the madness that often claimed you, but then I began to question such prejudices. Perhaps, I thought to myself, Hannah is right and such a stone exists. I have studied the history of the Church, made an inventory as far as it was possible, of all the idolatry' stored by the established Church, and I have sought out this Jewel in as much of this world as I know to exist and no one has heard of such an object. I am left thinking you must have meant something else.

On leaving you that terrible day, a young girl told me of the existence of our daughter. In my grief I assumed that our daughter and the Jewel were two different things. However with the passing of time I have come to realise that she is the Jewel; my darling Hannah, a child of yours would be the most beautiful creature on Earth and it would only be right to refer to her as a Jewel, a precious thing that could and would save my soul, mend my broken heart if only I could reclaim her.

Hannah, I have spent the last thirty years in search of our daughter, looking for the child with the silver mark on her hand, the mark that you claimed gave you your gifts of healing and of communing with nature. I have searched high and low throughout England and the New World but alas I have not found her. I will spend the rest of my life looking for her Hannah but today I wanted to write to you to let you know that so far, I have failed miserably. I do not pretend to understand what you meant when you said return the Jewel to the people but I do know that I, wretched creature though I am, would feel happy once more if our daughter, our Jewel could be restored to me. I will continue in my search for the rest of my life, of that I promise you
With all my love,

Robert.

Katie sat very still, yet all her senses were alive and fully awake. She realised she was crying softly. Nana. Her poor Nana. So this is where she first heard of the Keeper's Jewel from the words of Robert Duke, not from a biblical myth. The Jewel itself did not exist. Duke's lost daughter was the Jewel. She had been all along; nothing to do with a sacred stone that once sat on a tower. Katie folded the letter away, attaching it with its clip to the diary page, placed it back in the glass cabinet. So, Hannah's daughter had disappeared and like Millie, and like Katie, she had a birthmark on her hand. Katie looked at her hand, turned it over in the dim light of the basement library. Well so what? It was just a birthmark, nothing more. Many people had birthmarks; they did not go around saying they were Keepers of magical Jewels. Laura was right. Nana's mind wandered and made up made things that were just not real. And she had been convincing too. Katie had almost believed Nana's story, almost believed that she was special and different in some way. She wasn't special, at least not in a good way. For the first time, sitting in the dingy, damp grounds of the old York Asylum, Katie seriously pondered her future. If she was not careful she too would end up here like Hannah, or Nana, tormented and ill, unable to function at times, making up stories about things that did not exist. Somehow she had to change. Somehow she had to become normal.

XVIII

Albion 23 A.D.

Mortunda stood in shadow by the door, watching her father's guests. She did not want to be seen, not just yet, so she kept very still. She saw Lovernicus, the Gwr Doeth, shift his position on the hard ground as if his bones had grown too old for sitting still. The meeting had a long time to run before all things needing discussing had been dealt with; Mortunda could see the maps spread open on the ground. Torrance, the King of Veneti, sat poring over them, his huge rugged face lost in thought. Lovernicus wiped his hand across his mouth to dislodge a fragment of mutton and stood up shakily.

'Excuse me my companions,' he smiled, 'I need to stretch these old legs of mine.'

Deseus, the boy with the blonde floppy hair and dark eyes, stood to lend Lovernicus his arm.

'Thank you Deseus. You see my friends,' said Lovernicus, 'the first lesson we teach our young Seronydd pupils is how to assist the elderly and infirm.'

Laughter broke out around the fire.

'Do not let his fragility deceive you,' said one of the elders sat with his back to Mortunda, 'Lovernicus is as strong as he is wise.'

Lovernicus glanced at the speaker. It was Sego, the elder. Mortunda wondered whether Sego would accompany Lovernicus back to Mona or if he would remain with the Brigante to draw up the terms of the Peace Treaty with the Parisi. Her feelings were torn on the matter; if she was to be successful this evening in her quest to go to Mona as a trainee Seronydd, part of her would want Sego to remain with the tribe. She feared travelling with the man and did not trust him. On the other hand she would prefer a rather more human elder to help her father with the drawing of the new boundaries. Perhaps the younger one. But looking more closely she could see he was no older than fourteen summers. It would be some years yet before he could take on such a responsibility.

If Sego did remain, his task would an important one, one of the most important of all the tasks performed by the Seronydd. He would be called upon to consult with the spirits of the Earth for guidance, ensure the peace terms were fair and that the Brigante, victors of this recent battle, would only take a small proportion of Parisi land. The Parisi would need enough cattle and crops to survive and prosper; Brennus could take some of the land he had conquered, but the Seronydd Code forbade the victorious to take all. The new boundaries between Parisi and Brigante would be drawn up by the Seronydd elders according to Seronydd law, signed in the blood of the Kings. Yet Mortunda knew that new wars would soon follow, resulting in yet newer boundaries, sometimes within a few short moon months of the last battle. It had always been this way with the Brigante.

Mortunda looked at Sego again. She wondered what Lovernicus thought of him. Sego was clearly not a learned man like Lovernicus. With his huge arms and wide torso he appeared more like a warrior than a man of the spirit.

Lovernicus spoke, his voice full, melodious and strong, 'Sego, share with us your thoughts on the situation facing the peoples of Albion? What do you make of these latest developments in the south? Is Albion in danger of capitulating to Rome? These matters are of far more interest to us than any debate about the state of my old age.'

Mortunda guessed that prior to her slipping into the room the party had been discussing the plight of Torrance's people across the sea in Gaul, and the pervasive Roman incursions into the Albion coastline. Sego's reply came as no surprise to her.

'Our elders from the south tell us that the tribes are mixed in their responses to Rome. The Trinovante in the south east have, as we know, a long relationship with Rome, although Comminus their King has recently changed his mind about them.'

'I hope that is the case!' said Brennus angrily. 'The man is a traitor. It is he who has let Rome into Albion with his bleating to Caesar about the Catuvellauni. The man should have fought his wars like the rest of us do, not gone running to Rome like a frightened baby!'

Lovernicus frowned. 'That may be the case Brennus, but the Catuvellauni broke the terms of the peace treaty on several occasions. They were warned by the Gods not to take too much land, but they chose to ignore them and now dominate much of the south east of Albion. The Trinovante were concerned for their future and that is why they ran to Rome. However, the good news for us is that after all these years of trying to convince the tribes of Albion to buy into Rome's plans; it now appears that Comminus has changed his mind. He is willing to see that Rome has darker intentions on Albion and I think we should nurture this new understanding of his and try to forget old grievances.'

Brennus shook his head. The bitterness he felt for the Trinovante betrayal ran deep. Yet, much as he hated to accept it, he knew Lovernicus was speaking some sense. 'Continue Sego,' he said begrudgingly.

Sego cleared his throat.

'I was saying that the Atrebate and the Cantiaci have also been trading with Rome for some years and this trade has brought increased prosperity to these coastal tribes—many of them have survived cold winters only because of the goods Roman trade has brought them. They do not see Rome as a threat, but as a commercial necessity. Some say that talk of Rome being an enemy is driven by envy and not threat.'

Brennus was shaking his head.

'Yes, yes, we are all aware that this is what some say, but what do you think of these conflicting opinions Sego?' Lovernicus was impatient.

Sego was aware that all eyes were upon him, that both Torrance and Brennus would hang on his every word. Without Seronydd guidance the tribes would be lost, driven only by their base desires to fight and kill and appropriate each others lands. Without the elders, the rivers of Albion would run permanently red.

He smiled humbly, 'My thoughts on the matter are that it is complicated. My sense is that the tribes of the south do not trust nor care for the opinions of the northern tribes. They see the north as being a bigger enemy than Rome. I give as an example the Atrebate, who have just recently declared Rome a friend and potential ally against their foe and closest neighbour, the Catuvellauni. Once again the Catuvellauni have grown to be over-ambitious in the eyes of the Atrebate, taking much land that once belonged to them. As Lovernicus has already explained, the Catuvellauni do this despite advice from the Gods that such actions are unwise.'

'The king of Catuvellauni is a powerful man,' Lovernicus said. 'He hates the Romans as much as he loves vanquishing other tribes. He was once your king, Sego. It must be difficult for you to hear of your father's people going against the Gods.'

Lovernicus was looking intently at Sego, watching for his reaction.

Sego reddened. 'I do not think of my father very often Lovernicus. My duty is to follow the Seronydd Code, not to concern myself with matters of home. That is no longer my domain.'

All eyes were on Sego, and Torrance shifted uncomfortably on his seat.

Sego, his face still flushed, continued, 'I must add that our Seronydd brethren serving the tribes in the south struggle to persuade some of their leadership of the danger that Rome poses. Again, the Atrebate is a good example of this. The Atrebate elders have spoken with the King about the threat from Rome and warned that the Gods have declared Rome an enemy, but he has ignored their advice. He has insisted on courting favour from Caesar. The elders have concluded that, in order to keep any influence within the tribe, they must honour his decision and accept that it flies in the face of guidance from the Gods. As long as their hearts remain true to the Gods, they have done no wrong. I am increasingly afraid that in the south of Albion, it is only the Catuvellauni that continue to view Rome as a threat. The Seronydd seek to persuade the others of this but their success in doing so remains unseen.'

'Except for the Trinovante,' said Brennus, 'Don't forget that Comminus is changing his mind about Rome. He may come on side with us.'

Sego sighed, 'Yes, for the moment,' he said, 'but Comminus is old and will no doubt die soon. He has three sons, all of whom want the Trinovante throne. They are divided in their loyalty to Rome. I have word that the youngest of the sons is well disposed to Rome and the riches she brings.'

Torrance the Gaul had been listening to Sego speak, the look of rage on his face growing with every word. He burst out suddenly, his voice thick with fury, 'Then these tribes from the south are fools! The Romans, they ingratiate the people with gifts and trade and promise protection to the weaker tribes. They say they will look after you and keep your enemies at bay and bring wealth to your lands. Then they come, not as friends, but as invaders!'

Torrance smacked his huge hands together, 'And then they have you, all of you. They take your cattle, your women; they steal your sons for their armies and leave you with nothing, nothing more than a mere token of power.'

Torrance spat angrily and slammed his sword into the dirt. Lovernicus placed a hand on his shoulder.

'Torrance, we know this. We know what the Romans do. We will consult with the spirits, with the Gods; we will seek a way to ensure that this does not happen here. You shall have a place to stay with the Brigante and if we can help restore your people we shall do so. The Seronydd are more than aware of the Romans' lack of respect for women, children or anything other than power, silver and fur.'

He glanced at Sego as he said this, but Sego appeared lost in his own thoughts.

Brennus sighed wearily, 'We still have much to discuss,' he said. 'I think it would help us and our esteemed brother Torrance if we looked at a map of the tribal boundaries of Albion and made plans to thwart Rome. There is much the Seronydd can do still in working with these southern tribes, in persuading them to cool off trade with Rome. However we cannot make the mistake of ignoring the possibility of a military solution. The future of Albion may lie with the northern tribes. The map will show us where the weaknesses are along the coastline and where the Romans are likely to attack.'

Sego broke in, 'We must not alarm ourselves unduly Brennus. There are no plans for an impending Roman invasion. Rome is busy in Gaul,' he glanced briefly at Torrance as he said this, 'and their last attack on this island failed. They will not lightly try again. There will be months of planning, plenty of time to allow the Seronydd to do their work in the South. The latest news we have from Rome is that Albion is safe.'

Brennus shook his head, 'I disagree with you Sego. Rome is a capricious snake. She will not allow her military plans to be known. They could be planning an attack as we speak. We need to be prepared.'

He turned to pull out a map of the tribal boundary. As he did so, Mortunda stepped out of the shadows. Everyone looked towards the doorway, Brennus with a large scowl on his face and his sword ready. Mortunda clutched her arms about her waist and took a deep breath.

'Father,' she said, 'I have something to say.'

XIX

'Mortunda, is that you?' Brennus asked more in surprise than annoyance.

For one brief moment as he watched her standing in the doorway, Brennus was reminded of her sleepwalking as a younger child and wondered whether she had newly woken from a dream and wandered in not realising that talks were going on.

'Are you asleep Mortunda?' he asked.

Mortunda stepped further forward into the light of the fire and nervously cleared her throat.

'No Father, I am very much awake. I have come to ask for some guidance.' She glanced nervously at Lovernicus.

Brennus' voice rose in shocked disbelief at her words, 'Child, this is neither the time nor place! You know not to enter my house at such a time and when we have such important guests!'

Mortunda stepped forward. 'Father,' she said, her voice cracking with fear, 'I only came because I had to. I am so afraid. I cannot sleep. I have a burning terror in my heart for our people and it worries me greatly. I only wish to request a few moments of your time and that of the elder.'

She glanced briefly at Lovernicus, too afraid to meet his eyes.

'I promise I will leave you as soon as I can. I understand the importance of your discussions.'

An awkward silence fell about the room. Everyone was waiting for Brennus to speak again. Lovernicus placed a hand on Brennus' shoulder, 'Maybe it is best if we allow the child to speak.'

She could feel Lovernicus studying her face, taking in the grey of her eyes, the determined line of her mouth, trying to work out what she wanted.

'Is this your daughter Brennus?' he asked, sounding surprised. 'I noticed her on the way into the fort.'

Turning to Sego he said, 'I think our esteemed elder forgot to mention you had a daughter. Is this child your only daughter Brennus?'

He kept his eyes fixed on Sego, who visibly reddened and looked at the floor.

Brennus nodded, 'Yes, she is my one and only daughter and I apologise for she is as stubborn as a goat and rude as a pig,' he said. 'Mortunda, I must ask you to leave.'

Lovernicus held up his hand.

'Wait,' he said, 'maybe we should ask the child why she came here, find out what ails her so. It could be important. I have to confess to feeling some admiration for the child's courage.'

He glanced at Sego again, 'No mere child destined to be a minor queen or wife of a warrior would have the courage to enter her father's house during talks with kings and elders. That takes a special child, a gifted child, perhaps; someone with something important to say?'

Sego, looking embarrassed, was staring at the ground. So, Mortunda thought, Sego had also told the Seronydd leader that she was nothing special, just the child of a King, destined for nothing great. She thought of the open camps where the Seronydd elders and tribes came together to discuss which children had been sighted as gifted in communing with the Gods. Any son or daughter of the tribe could train as a Seronydd. They had to be nominated by other adults in the tribe; a mother, father, brother or uncle, whether it be a foster relative or blood—any of these could name a child and give witness to why they had chosen them. The Seronydd elder serving the tribe would journey to the Upper Plane to talk with the Gods and the spirits to seek their guidance on each nomination. If the answer was affirmative, the Seronydd would agree to take the child to Mona. Mortunda knew her mother had, despite Brennus' objections, nominated Mortunda but Mortunda had been refused by Sego. Mortunda had been right all along; Sego really did not like her.

Brennus stood up. Ignoring Lovernicus he walked over to Mortunda and took her roughly by the shoulder.

'You must leave,' he said gruffly.

Mortunda felt a lump rise in her throat. She looked at Lovernicus. *Help me*, she pleaded with her mind.

Lovernicus spoke up, his voice cheerful and yet appeasing, 'I think we should hear what she has to say Brennus, and then she will be unburdened. Young hearts sleep better when they are not burdened wouldn't you say?'

He smiled hopefully at Brennus and cocked his head slightly to one side. Brennus remained indignant but hesitated,

'We have no time to listen to her Lovernicus. There is still a lot to discuss and the night wears on. I could more easily grant her an audience with you in the morning, if you would be so kind then as to indulge my daughter's impertinence. For now, I think it best that Mortunda returns to her quarters and shows her father the respect he deserves.'

Brennus glared at Mortunda, who shifted onto one leg. She felt she would cry at any moment.

Lovernicus intervened gently again, 'Maybe just grant her a few moments Brennus?' he suggested again, 'and if your daughter's request needs a considerable length of time, we can proceed in the morning.'

Brennus looked down at the floor and Mortunda watched him trace her mother's face in the dust.

She felt a stab of pity for her father. He had loved her mother so much. When Mortunda closed her eyes, she could still see Leticia's eyes, blue like the spring sky and her jaw line, smooth and defined; her determined mouth smiled back at her from the dirt. She missed her terribly, missed her guidance in situations such as these and if she were here this evening Leticia would advise her father to listen to Lovernicus. She had always had the greatest faith in Mortunda and the deepest respect for Lovernicus. She would have trusted Lovernicus to make the right decision. The question was, would her father do the same?

Brennus looked up at Mortunda.

'You have a few moments only Mortunda. Whilst our guests refresh themselves with ale, you may speak with the elder and then you will leave the house and you and I will speak tomorrow.'

Mortunda nodded and bowed her head,

'Thank you Father. I will be speedy with my request and then as you ask I will leave and not bother you again.'

Brennus turned to leave but Mortunda touched his arm,

'Father I would like you to stay. I want you to hear what I have to ask the elder. I think it concerns everyone here. I wish to call upon the Request of the Flame.'

'No!'

Brennus had turned white.

A gasp ran around the room. Even Lovernicus looked startled. For a while nobody spoke and then Brennus said, his voice shaky,

'The Request is an extremely dangerous journey Mortunda, you know that! It is only undertaken by those with highly developed souls. It could kill you.'

He slammed his sword into the hard floor sending a sharp clang echoing around the room. Her father's eyes were now blazing with anger.

'Mortunda, you have to retract your words now and apologise to our guests for your lack of respect and impertinence. You will leave now and go to your chamber.'

Mortunda raised her head and met Lovernicus' eyes.

Help me, she pleaded again.

Lovernicus held her gaze as if he was looking for traces of foolishness and facetiousness, but he found neither. He turned to Brennus, choosing his words carefully. 'Brennus, the Request is as you say, a highly dangerous journey and I am surprised that a child of so few summers has requested it. However I have a sense that your daughter is being neither bold nor stupid.'

He looked softly at Mortunda before turning back to face the outraged Brennus.

'You have long been seen by those far and wide to hold great wisdom and power. Your victories on the battlefield have left your enemies in fear of you and your people. We elders, who talk with the spirits and channel their powers, merely do so in order to serve. I would be greatly indebted to you, Brennus, if you would allow me the opportunity to hear what your child has to say. The Request of the Flame is held in the highest regard by our order. Your child has displayed some of the courage of her father in coming here tonight. I feel I can grant your daughter the Request and can do so in a way that would keep her safe. You understand we are living in difficult times and maybe the Gods have chosen Mortunda as their conduit to us. They may have an important message they wish to convey to us through her.'

Brennus looked gravely at Lovernicus.

'Lovernicus,' he said hoarsely, 'I lost my wife only two summers ago and I do not wish to lose my daughter. She is too young to undertake such a journey. I have never witnessed the Request but I have heard tales of it leaving grown men used to battle weak for days, unable to leave their beds, unable to walk. Mortunda is quite a small girl Lovernicus. Such a thing would be foolish for her. I ask you to decline the Request. Put it down to a misunderstanding from a silly girl who really should be asleep in her bed.'

'I hear what you say,' said Lovernicus, 'and I sympathise with you. However I have other ways, not known to most, of keeping Mortunda safe. If I give you my word that she will be all right, will you allow me to proceed? I do feel, Brennus, that your daughter possesses a gift which is rare and precious. I also feel that this has come at a moment of great change in Albion. I think we should grant the Gods their wish. After all, it is really they who are making the Request. They have merely chosen Mortunda to be their channel.'

Brennus coloured, his pupils dilating dangerously. He was clearly struggling to keep his emotions under control.

'Lovernicus, she is a mere child! We do not send children to the higher plane to consult directly with the Gods. It is unheard of! Even a child of advanced knowledge would perish under such conditions. No! I cannot allow it.'

Brennus glared at Mortunda, angry that she should place him in a situation where he was in direct conflict with the Gwr Doeth of the Seronydd seers. Mortunda felt her skin shrink under the ferocity of her father's eyes. Lovernicus stepped forward to face the angry and frightened King.

'I will do what you wish Brennus. But hear this for it affects us all deeply.'

Lovernicus spread his arms wide and turned to face the group.

'I too was sent on the Request when I was merely ten summers old as was my mother before me. It is my mother's experience that I want to share with you all now. It was the time of the first invasion attempt by Rome. The Gods met my mother in the Flame and told her that Rome was coming, and they were right. Within thirty days Caesar's ships appeared on the horizon. The Seronydd elder passed the wisdom to Cassivellaunus, the ruler of the Catuvellauni, who were able to thwart Caesar in his attempt to invade the southern shores of Albion. The Romans came to shore but were met by Cassivellaunus and his warriors on the beaches. The Catuvellauni hid in the dunes and attacked Caesar's men in chariots. The Romans had never seen such skill in charioteers and many of Caesar's men were felled and beheaded.'

Lovernicus sighed.

'As you all know, Caesar's men did win some ground that day; the sheer numbers of men were too great for the Catuvellauni to hold off. Yet the wisdom of the Gods had been passed to my mother and she was able to aid the tribe in a far more powerful way than the sword.'

Lovernicus chuckled softly, 'The Romans were never sure whether it was the mighty warrior Cassivellaunus who defeated Caesar's men in that final battle or the spell cast by my mother on the seas. The spirits listened to my mother's wishes and created a great storm that destroyed Caesar's boats. Many of his men perished in the sea. He was defeated. Rome was sent home.'

Lovernicus glanced at Brennus. The stories of Caesar's failed attack on Albion were known to all.

'Of course,' Lovernicus added sadly, 'Rome has never reneged on her promise that one day she will have Albion for her Empire and the fact that a few of Caesar's men crossed Albion all the way to the mighty river in the south east has left us with an unpleasant legacy. Rome knows what treasures the lands of Albion hold, they know our ways and they understand our weaknesses. The Romans will be back. It is my belief that they will return soon and our time is running out. We need the Gods to help us to defeat them. Please Brennus, let your daughter enter the Flame.'

Silence fell around the room when Lovernicus finished speaking. Brennus folded his arms, 'Yes I know all this is true,' he said, 'but how can I be certain that sending my daughter to the land of the Gods will help us with our battle plans?'

Lovernicus sighed.

'We are witnessing a request from the Gods,' he said. 'They have asked to speak with Mortunda and it would be folly to ignore them.'

Brennus looked thoughtful for a moment, obviously turning over in his mind the story relayed by Lovernicus. Mortunda watched her father. Suddenly he appeared to be weary, older and tired, worn down by weeks of battle and grief for her mother, beaten by his daughter's stubbornness and determination. She felt sad for him, sad that she caused him so much pain. She wished she could be like her brother, fun, straightforward, able to just obey her father's commands and not be in a constant battle of wills with him. Instead, she had been granted the qualities of her mother; endurance, stubbornness and an uncanny connection with the Gods.

'Such qualities, if harnessed, will give you the power to control an army Mortunda. Men will die for you because they will know that what you command is only true and right,' her mother had once confided to her. 'Your father sees a natural leadership in you. You have qualities that Brennus knows he does not possess. Your father won the right to lead the Brigante through his warrior prowess, but Mortunda, you will lead with your mind.'

Sometimes it felt to Mortunda that such qualities were a curse; if only she had been born an ordinary member of the tribe then she would be valued purely for her Seronydd abilities and life would be simple.

Brennus looked up and turned to Lovernicus.

'Very well,' he said reluctantly, 'you may proceed. But please ensure that you do all you can to secure her safety.'

He turned to the others and raised his hand,

'I would like you all to stay and witness what is about to happen. If my daughter survives the Request of the Flame, surely that is proof to all those who doubt her, that she is destined to one day lead the Brigante as Queen.'

XX

The room had gathered more shadow and was now cloaked in silence. Torrance the Gaul cleared his throat, impatience written all over his face.

'There are matters of war and retribution to discuss Brennus,' he said jumping up from his seat on the ground. 'We do not have time to mess about with matters of magic. There is a time and place for Seronydd wisdom but right now we need to defeat Rome with this!'

He brandished his sword and glared at Mortunda.

Brennus drew himself a little straighter. 'I have given my answer Torrance,' he said gruffly, 'The Gods have ordained this and, as guest in my house, I ask you to honour my decision.'

He turned to Lovernicus. 'Please proceed,' he barked, throwing a second glare at Torrance. Torrance slunk back down to the ground, his face tight with frustration.

'It will not take long my friend,' said Lovernicus soothingly to Torrance, 'once we have finished with the Request, we can return to the discussions we were having with further enlightenment.'

Torrance remained silent, his mind churning over the events in Gaul. Mortunda noticed that Sego caught Torrance's glance, and once again she felt the bite of distrust for the burly Seronydd.

Lovernicus bade the party to form a circle. Using his staff he carefully drew a ring of protection in the dust at the centre of the room and placed four rocks at equal distance to represent Fire, Earth, Water and Air. Mortunda lay inside the circle. Lovernicus knelt beside her. He held his hands above her head where her soul was located and spoke to her in gentle whispers,

'Mortunda, who do you wish to speak with?'

Mortunda answered, 'Sequana, Goddess of the River.'

'Mortunda you have made the Request of the Flame. Those who make the Request claim that the Gods have contacted them; they claim to have been in dialogue with the spirits who inhabit this world with us and as part of us. The Request of the Flame asks a Seronydd to go into the fire with the Requester to talk directly with the Gods of the Upper Plane. You have a question you wish to ask Sequana, Goddess of the River. It is a dangerous journey and I have to ask you one more time; do you speak the truth? Have you truly been called? If you speak a falsehood then one of us will die. The Gods will vanquish any man, woman or child who makes a false claim in their presence.'

Mortunda's voice trembled as she replied, 'I am speaking the truth Lovernicus. Sequana came to me in a dream and asked me to visit her by the old settlement beside the river. She said we were all in danger and we had to talk to the people in the south to prevent war. I meditated this evening by the Tree and was told to come and talk with you.'

Lovernicus listened carefully, his eyes alight with amazement. The child was already consulting with the Tree of Life! He had not encountered such understanding at so young an age since he himself was a boy, and that was a long time ago.

'And you are sure this was Sequana and not a false spirit such as a Traveller disguised as a Goddess?'

Mortunda shook her head vehemently. 'No it was not a Traveller. The Goddess had the smell of the river about her and her eyes were pure cornflower blue.'

He nodded, 'Thank you Mortunda. You have given me your word that your intent is pure and I accept. I will now begin the Request.'

Lovernicus slowly turned to face the circle of people behind him. He went to the stone representing Fire and around it he placed twigs and other rocks. Within a few moments Lovernicus had lit a small fire, and fanned the flames until they danced brightly in the darkness of the house.

'I must ask all present to close your eyes. If you open them you risk being blinded. When it is safe to open them again I will tell you. Close your eyes.'

One by one, the members of the party obeyed the command.

Sego closed his eyes but allowed a tiny fraction of light to seep through his eyelids, just enough to allow the flickers of light to penetrate. He was disturbed. Why had Lovernicus asked them to shut their eyes? It was most unusual. With his partial vision he scanned the others in the circle and saw that they had followed the order. Deseus the boy, Brennus too had clenched his eyelids closed; the other tribal elders who had participated in this rite several times had closed theirs. What was Lovernicus going to do? How could anyone bear witness to the Request if they all had their eyes closed? He listened to Lovernicus talking in a low voice to Mortunda.

'Mortunda, you must too close your eyes and take deep breaths. With each deep breath I ask you to think of your dream and picture Sequana as she came to you. I will accompany you on your journey and ask Sequana to share with me the meaning of her visit.'

Mortunda let her body relax. She breathed in deeply and out again and then took a deep breath inwards. Her eyes flickered behind her closed lids and she very gently began to fall into a trance. With each new breath in and out she moved more deeply into her dream until she was no longer a child laying on a dusty floor in her fathers house but was free, somewhere in a land vastly different, walking across a soft green glade towards a young woman with long flowing hair the colour of mud and eyes as blue as cornflowers.

As Mortunda drew close to the Goddess's outstretched hands, back within the confines of the circle Lovernicus took from his tunic something wrapped in the finest wool. He held it in the palm of his hand for a moment before slowly and reverently drawing away the soft layers to reveal a dark red stone about the size of a pine cone.

Its edges were sharp, jagged; a stone that had been roughly hewn centuries ago from the deepest rock. It lay there dull and lifeless, cradled in Lovernicus' hand. Gradually a light began to emerge from within, and the Jewel slowly came to life. The light inside sparkled, then flashed, igniting, growing brighter and more dazzling until the room was filled with a pure fierce white light. Lovernicus focused intently on the glow of red that lay at the heart of the Jewel buried deep within the silver white rays of light spilling outwards. The Jewel responded to his gaze and began to fizz and spark again. Its centre became a ball of fire. The heart bled into the white light until it had merged with it; the light grew softer then, less harsh, until the entire room and the occupants within it were clothed in a warm soft red glow.

Mortunda was carried in its embrace, deep into the glade towards Sequana, safe from harm.

Through his partially closed eyes Sego saw the scarlet blaze of the light. Very carefully he opened one eye.

Immediately, a sharp pain struck him with the force of a fist and his eyes closed tightly, pinched together in a reflex. He was lifted slightly off his feet by the force, and his face burned. For one moment it felt as if his eyes would melt in their sockets. He spread his hands desperately over his face to make sure his features were still in place, that his eyes were not liquid, not running down his cheeks, and that his mouth had not become a soggy mass of burned flesh. His face felt in one piece—with relief he knew it was just an illusion.

Breathing deeply to keep himself steady on his feet, Sego very gently used his fingers to coax his eyes open again. For a brief moment, before the light pierced him for the second time, he saw a vision of a red Jewel suspended above Lovernicus' open hands. The Seronydd elder, with his head held high, was muttering to the light in a language Sego did not recognise. Lovernicus' voice grew louder, chanting words that sounded like water running over stones and wind running through trees. His voice undulated and rippled in tones and symbols of an unknown language, an ancient language, older than any other in the world. Sego felt his soul drawn towards it; to the power and beauty of the words and to an unseen force, pulling him closer and closer to the centre of the light.

XXI

Katie 2008

The week after Nana's funeral the skies above Britain turned an ominous lead grey. On the first Sunday in July at 1 a.m., they opened. For the following three weeks the country was pounded by heavy rain that fell in torrents. River banks burst and entire village and towns became awash with floods. Starved of sunlight, crops died in the gardens and fields, insects did not break free from their cocoons but withered and died; flowers did not bloom but mournfully bowed their heads in the dark. It was as if the light had been squeezed out of existence. The British public mourned the loss of yet another summer.

In southern Europe, it was a different story. Here the land was plunged into a vicious heat wave that roasted the ground and burned the fields. 'Global Warming' and 'Heat Wave Due To Last All Summer,' dominated the headlines in France and Spain. Across the world the cry of 'Arctic floods—sea levels rising' filled the news, prompting several debates on radio and television on the future of the planet, and the damage caused by the human race to the Earth's ecosystem. Images of polar bears desperately searching for ice floes to rest on, haunted the peoples of Europe. Politicians announced new measures to reduce the use of fossil fuels, and in the glossy halls of the United Nations another new, and probably useless, International Treaty was forged.

Katie lay in her bed, thinking that she should get up but not really wanting to. She felt as if she could not breathe and was unsure whether this was due to the dampness of the summer weather or the heavy stone she had carried in her heart since Nana died.

It had been a heart attack that killed Nana; she had come to believe that. At first she had wondered whether Dr Bennett had killed Nana with one of his depot injections, but then she had reminded herself sharply that Dr Bennett's badness was all part of Nana's delusions. The letter she found in Duke's diary proved that; Nana had been prone to making things up – wild things that had no real basis to them. Nana put things together that did not belong together. No, Dr Bennett was not a murderer -he was just a doctor doing his job. It was as simple as that. There was nothing 'goblin-like' about him.

She lay there thinking about Nana, the move to Manchester and her new resolution that she would give up listening to animals, or watching lights or believing fantastic tales about strange Jewels and Keepers. Instead, she would become an ordinary teenager. Surely it couldn't be that hard to do? After all, millions of other teenagers managed it perfectly well. She had watched them. Moving to Manchester could be a new start for her and Laura.

She swung her legs out of bed, and pulled on her jeans and a tee-shirt. Then she heard the wind crack sharply against the window.

The ferocity of it startled her. Wondering whether the wind had dislodged a branch and cracked the glass, she opened the curtains.
What she saw made her gasp and jump back towards her bed.

There standing against her window, blocking any small semblance of light, stood a fortress wall, stones glistening with rain, part covered with spongy green moss. A dank smell wafted through the bedroom wall, and Katie could hear the dripping of water echoing from inside the fort. With a shaking hand she yanked the curtains closed. She stood still for a moment, and then quickly pulled the curtains open again.

The fortress wall was still there.

A startled yelp came from her throat. She placed her hand over her mouth. Her eyes filled with frightened tears. This was impossible. How could a fortress appear out of nowhere? Of course it could not. This was the beginning she told herself; proof that she was mad like Nana had been. There was really nothing there, just her stupid stupid mind playing tricks on her again. Yet the wall looked real. Maybe it would feel real too? Or maybe, if she went outside to it, she could make it go away. It was all a matter of will power; if she refused to see it, it would have to go away.

She made her way downstairs, creeping through the sitting room where Laura was sat discussing work on the telephone with a friend. So Laura had not noticed anything unusual. Katie slipped quietly out of the back door. Her heart was thumping wildly, her breath stuck in her throat, anxiety raced through her veins, but she knew she had to explore further.

Outside, the wall loomed ominously. It was huge, rearing above Katie's head, a mountain of stone stretching out across the back of the garden and into next door to the boundary of the garden beyond; the fences separating the gardens had gone, splintered like matchwood, Katie assumed, by the weight of the wall. Katie nervously reached out a hand and touched the icy stone. It felt real. It was slimy under her fingers, clammy to the touch. Slowly she began to walk alongside the wall, searching for an entrance. She could not see one on her side of the garden and decided she would follow the structure all the way into the gardens next door and beyond. She nervously made her way around the wall until she was standing in the centre of Mrs Green's garden. At the edge of the lawn on the furthest side, two gardens down, the fortress wall turned and stretched two thirds of the way up where it simply faded away and disappeared. Yet the thing that caught Katie's eye was a tall black iron gateway in the centre of the wall in Mrs Green's garden. Looking at it made her tremble. She could feel herself being pulled towards it; it was as if it was daring her to enter. Then the whispering began; soft insistent voices from some place elsewhere were calling her name over and over. Dreamily, she reached out and touched the cold iron shoulder of the gate. With one push it opened. Katie could see a long stone passage way running into an inner courtyard that then faded away into the green of her neighbour's lawn.

The Greens' neglected barbeque and garden furniture sat rusting incongruously in the centre of the courtyard and even more amazingly, Mrs. Green was sitting in one of the chairs wiping mud off her wellington boots. She looked up at Katie, her surprise causing her glasses to fall off her nose.

'Katie dear, how did you get in?'

'Umm...my tennis ball came over into your garden so I climbed over to look for it,' Katie lied.

Mrs. Green frowned.

'Well knock next time dear. You'll crush the begonias if you climb over the fence.'

Katie looked behind her. So Mrs. Green could not see the wall. Yet it was still there, monstrous and gloomy, its bleak stone staring at her, its cold walls sucking the warmth from her skin. Nana's illness was beginning to take hold of her. She felt herself wobble and grow faint.

'Are you all right dear? You're shivering.'

Mrs. Green immediately leaned forward and felt Katie's forehead. She sat Katie down in one of the chairs.

'You seem to have a bit of a temperature, love- probably catching a cold wandering around here in just a tee-shirt and jeans. Sit here a minute while I fetch your Mum.'

In a trance like state Katie sat down. All around her the wall was fading, the courtyard too was gradually disappearing into the grey mist of the day, until suddenly, all signs of the fortress were gone. Katie's mind was racing. The madness was here. It had come to claim her. Just like it had claimed Nana. And yet Nana always seemed so wise—batty yes, mad yes, but wise too. Was she, Katie, imagining the wall? Or had it been there—a sign of the strange things to come spoken of by Nana in her hospital room? Her head throbbed; she could feel a fever mounting and her fingers tingled. Through the blur she could see Mrs Green returning with a disgruntled Laura in tow, clutching a copy of *Interior Design Today*.

'I think you should put her to bed,' suggested Mrs Green. 'I suspect she is coming down with influenza. Her head feels very hot.'

Mrs Green's words floated in and out of Katie's awareness; her head was spinning, slowly and heavily, like an asteroid in space, and her eyes could not focus properly. She saw two, and then three images of Laura, and Mrs. Green's face was distorted and twisted. Laura took Katie's arm and pulled her out of the chair so that she stood, her legs wobbling perilously beneath her. Together the two women helped Katie back to the house and up to bed. She was fast asleep within seconds of her head hitting the pillow.

Laura thanked Mrs Green who gratefully returned to her garden and the cleaning of her boots. It was only later when she was inspecting her flower beds that she noticed that, despite the long drop from the fence to the ground, not one begonia was squashed in any way.

Katie was ill with a fever for three days. When she finally had the strength to get out of bed, she cautiously approached her bedroom window and drew back the curtains. The fortress wall was not there - everything looked blessedly normal. She breathed a heavy sigh of relief. Maybe, she told herself, the appearance of the wall was a one off event and if she concentrated hard enough, her 'abilities' to see things and feel things others did not, could become manageable once more. Feeling slightly more assured of herself, Katie made her way downstairs to get some breakfast. Laura was out at work. The kitchen floor was covered with assorted boxes, some already crammed with old copies of Laura's magazines, others with books, Katie's clothes and stacks of crockery they no longer used. The move to Manchester was to happen in three days time, and Katie would be visiting Dad in Exeter whilst Laura moved their things into the new house. Katie slotted two slices of bread into the toaster and began loading the dishwasher. She found the small tablets of soap in the cupboard and turned the washer on.

By now the rainfall across the UK had increased substantially. Floods continued to hit the South of England. Today however, the rain had ceased for a while and the sun had momentarily broken through the shield of cloud. A strange heat rose from the ground; the air was oppressive and warm, as if a huge thunderstorm was brewing. Pushing a sweaty strand of hair from her eyes, Katie opened the back door in a vain attempt to circulate some air around the stuffy kitchen. To her surprise, a small breeze floated in and hung around her ankles. Katie got on with her chores, enjoying the welcome relief of the breeze until she noticed that it had grown colder and stronger. The breeze gave a sharp tug on her lower legs. Katie looked down. She gave a start. A wispy white mist had wrapped itself around her calves and was spinning faster and faster, and as it spun, it increased in size until Katie's body was encased in her very own personal whirlwind. It tugged at her waist and pulled her out into the garden, spinning her around until she felt quite sick. It stopped suddenly.

There standing on the lawn in front of her, was the fortress.

This time there was more of it.

Mesmerised, Katie reached out to touch the wall and felt cold slime freeze on her fingers. With a wildly beating heart she again walked around the perimeter to the first gate. A dank smell of rotting fish oozed from the cobbled passage way. Katie cautiously placed one foot on the path and almost lost her balance; she would have to be careful, wherever the fortress had come from, it had been raining there a lot too; the stones were glistening and slippery. Then she heard a voice shout out from the broken guard house at the end of the pathway,

'It's your time Katie, and we're waiting for you. She knows you're coming.'

Peering through the iron gate, Katie looked for the person attached to the voice, but no one was there. She cautiously walked towards the inner courtyard. Looking up at the wall she could see now that it was made not only of stone, but hardened mud and moss; it smelt of damp earth and mildew. Where the stone and mud had eroded away shafts of weak sunlight shone through. Katie shielded her eyes from the sun and it was then that she saw something glitter sharply in the wall.

At first she thought it was the sun bouncing off the stone, but then it glittered again, red gold and bright. Katie placed her hand into the wall and tugged at the edge of the rounded hard object that was causing the glare. It would not budge. Using her fingers she scraped around the edges of the rock and mud that were holding it in place and within minutes she worked it loose and pulled it from its ancient hiding place in the wall. It was a coin. She held it up for a proper inspection. It was thin and worn and was inscribed in a language Katie did not recognise. On one side was an engraving of a beautiful woman, her head held high, her nose proud and straight, and her hair tumbling around her shoulders. Above her head was inscribed the word MORTVNDA.

Beneath the engraving there were some more letters, something she recognised as a Roman date etched into the surface of the red gold metal—DCCXCVII A.U.C

She held the coin in her hand engrossed in the picture of the woman but as she held it, it began to dissolve, melting as if it was made of ice, until it was gone completely and Katie was left staring at the pink flesh of her palm. Gradually the wall began to fade too, until once more the entire fort had disappeared and Katie was standing in her garden listening to the hum of the dishwasher and the smell of toast burning in the toaster. Something strange was going on, stranger than her ability to understand the language of animals, stranger than the lights she saw around people's heads and Katie did not know how to make any sense of it.

XXII

Manchester Central Library was a large circular building that stood on the edge of St Peter's square. The reference room on the third floor sat directly beneath the great glass dome; a round room full of echoes, the rustling of papers being shifted on desks and the hum of computer screens so old that they gave off a dull green light. Katie sighed and stretched her legs.

'Where do I go next with this?' she asked herself.

She had thought it would be easy tracing dead relatives through the Internet but so far, after two hours of searching, she had come up with a huge fat blank. She tapped her foot impatiently against the wood of the desk, prompting a glare from an elderly man wearing a blue bobble-hat who was scribbling down poetry opposite her. Katie glared back at him. She was in far too tetchy a mood to be apologetic. She stood up and wandered over to the towering book shelves of the reference library.

'Maybe I will find something here,' she reasoned under her breath. She ran her hands along the dark green spines of the reference books marked 'Local History' and then remembered that she was now in Manchester. Her heart sank. Katie's family, as far as she was aware, had always lived in London. She would only find history local to Manchester here.

'Damn,' she said aloud.

'Can I help?' a voice behind her said.

Katie turned round to find a young woman wearing a librarian's badge smiling at her. Katie glanced at the name—*Louise Kennedy*.

'You look a bit lost,' the librarian said.

Katie gave a half smile.

'I am,' she confessed. 'I am trying to trace my family tree but seem to be getting nowhere. I thought the Internet would be helpful but it seems you have to pay for any useful information.'

The librarian grimaced, 'Yes, I know. Family trees are big business. Have you tried the local reference section? We have an excellent collection here.'

Katie nodded forlornly.

'I think any information on my family would be in London,' she said sadly. 'I am from East Dulwich and my Nana was born in Elm Park near London, and I think her mother and grandmother were too, or somewhere around there.'

Katie felt her eyes begin to mist. She dug her nails into the palm of her hand to distract herself from crying. Any mention of Nana and the tears threatened. The young librarian pretended not to notice the obvious sadness in the young girl's eyes and smiled.

'Are you doing a project for school?' she asked gently.

Katie shook her head,

'No.' She hesitated for a moment and then added, 'It's really just a personal interest. I want to try to understand some things about my family that are a bit mysterious to me.'

The librarian studied Katie closely for a moment.

'Tell you what,' she said suddenly, 'I have a personal account with a family tree website. It happens to be a hobby of mine. Maybe we can sit down together and you can tell me what you want to find?'

Katie's eyes lit up.

'Thank you,' she said, and for the first time since leaving London she felt a surge of hope.

The pair made their way back to the computer terminal. Luckily the grumpy man in the bobble hat had gone home for the day and the room was now fairly deserted, apart from the odd student dotted here and there.

'Grab a chair,' the librarian said. Then she seated herself and began to type in her user name, *LouiseK23*. Katie tugged a huge black leather armchair over to the table and sat down. She peered over the librarian's shoulder.

'Now, let's see what we can find,' the young woman said.

Katie checked her watch. 'I have to be back at the railway station by 4 p.m. to meet my mother.'

Louise sucked in her cheeks.

'Ok, so we had better try to find what you need pretty quickly. What is the name of the person you want to trace?'

Katie reddened. 'That's one of my problems; I'm not totally sure,' she said.

Louise frowned. 'That does make it a bit difficult,' she said, 'but never mind. Tell me what you do know and we can start from there.'

Katie took a breath. She suddenly felt exposed, as if she was naked and raw and on view for the world to see. She had never shared any of her secrets before; she and Laura never discussed family, and the only place she had ever allowed herself to be open was in her diary. Now she was about to disclose information, personal information, with a complete stranger, even though she was a friendly one. Yet she also knew she had little choice. This search was important to her; finding out who Millie was and if she really was her great grandmother; whether madness did run in her family and if it did, would it strike her too? She needed to understand what had happened to Nana's mother, and her mother before her and, although she would not allow herself to think too much about this, to answer a question that had been growing stronger in her mind since the day of Nana's funeral; was Hannah Joyce part of her ancestry, did the strange birthmark on her hand link her to Hannah Joyce or was it just a strange coincidence? Glancing at Louise, she wondered where to start. She took a deep breath.

'You could try Dolly Stephens. She was my Nana,' Katie said.

Louise typed in Nana's name.

'Wow,' said Katie as a long list of Dolly Stephens appeared on the screen.

Louise grinned. 'That's the easy part,' she said. 'Now we need the finer detail. Do you know the year of your Nana's birth?'

Katie thought for a moment.

'1929,' Katie said, 'and her birthday was 2nd March.'

Louise tapped the keyboard. A shorter list of around twelve names appeared on the screen.

'Now,' said Louise, 'Where do you think she was born?'

Katie peered at the screen.

'I think she was born in London, in the East End. I vaguely remember my Dad saying she was a true cockney.'

'Good,' Louise said 'That means she was born within a mile of the Bow Bells. Bow is in the East End of London and look here!' Louise pointed to the screen.

Five names down Katie read, *Dolly Stephens born 2nd March 1929 in Bow, London.*

Katie felt a bolt of joy run through her. Louise smiled.

'So,' Louise said brightly, 'Let's check your Nana's details and see what we can find.'

She clicked with the mouse and slowly a new page began to emerge. Documents began to unfold onto the screen; large images of official looking forms with blue and green edges appeared on the computer. Both Katie and Louise watched breathlessly as Nana's life materialised before them. Louise exhaled noisily.

'That's amazing,' she said.

'What is?' asked Katie.

'This,' said Louise pointing at the page of documents. 'Usually you have to search for hours to gather this much information. Yet here they are, just sat there waiting for you. It's almost as if someone knew you would need to see these and has arranged for them to be viewable. Do you think your Nana asked for her documents to be made available before she died?' asked Louise.

'I don't know,' said Katie truthfully. 'Maybe she did. She was very keen to tell me about her and Millie and some other things just before she died. To be honest, I, well my mother mainly, thought Nana was mad. Actually she was mad.'

Katie said all this in a rush, part of her wanting Louise to question her about Nana, the other part hoping she wouldn't. Louise however was absorbed with examining the documents.

'Here is your Nana's birth certificate,' she said. 'It says she was born in Bow to a seamstress called Florrie Webster and that her father Augustus Stephens, a Docker, registered her birth on the 10th March 1929.'

Katie felt a wave of sadness. Despite her good intentions her eyes filled with tears. Louise gently touched her hand,

'Hey, it's all right,' she said softly, 'we can stop here if you like. Sometimes all this digging about in the past is just too painful.'

Katie shook her head, 'Oh no,' she said, 'I need to dig. There is so much more I need to know!'

Louise shrugged. 'Ok,' she said, 'just so long as you are sure you want to continue.'

She clicked around the screen again. 'I can try to find out some more about Florrie,' she offered.

Katie nodded. 'I want to know when and how Florrie died and who her mother was,' she said.

Louise followed the links from the various documents until she had pulled up Florrie's birth certificate and below it, her death certificate. Katie held her breath as she read the death certificate.

Pneumonia.

Her great grandmother had died in 1939 of pneumonia at the age of 40. Not madness, but pneumonia. Feeling relieved, Katie scanned the birth certificate, screwing up her eyes trying to read the smudgy writing on the document. It was impossible to decipher.

'I can't read it,' she said helplessly. Louise laughed.

'Let me,' she said. 'I'm used to this. I could read the Dead Sea scrolls if I had to!'

Rapidly she began copying down details from the screen. After a moment she gave a smile.

'Gotcha,' she said. 'Right, this is interesting too. Florrie's mother was called Millie and her surname was Stanton, but there is no mention of a married name and the father's name is blank. It looks as if Florrie was illegitimate. That would have been hard for both of them back then. The world was not a friendly place for unmarried mothers and their babies.'

Katie was silent, her mind racing. So Millie did exist. She forced herself to ask the next question.

'Would you mind if we found out some more about Millie?' she said. Louise checked her watch.

'We haven't got much time,' she warned, 'It is almost 3.15 p.m. and I really should get back to the desk.'

She paused, seeing Katie's look of disappointment. Glancing around she saw the library was relatively quiet. 'Okay, we can go on a bit longer,' she said.

Louise returned her attention to the screen and clicked the various links but this time nothing appeared.

'We need to know which part of England she was from,' said Louise desperately. 'It could be that she was not from London, although her daughter and grand daughter were born there.'

Suddenly Katie remembered Duke's diary.

'Try York! Millie may have been from York.'

Louise typed in Millie Stanton, birth place York, then hesitated over the year of birth.

'We have no way of knowing her precise birth year have we?' she asked Katie.

Katie shook her head. Louise thought for a moment.

'Let's see,' she said eventually. 'If Florrie was born in 1899 that means Millie may have given birth at a fairly young age, seeing as Florrie was illegitimate. Of course, it's no guarantee she was young; women can have illegitimate babies up to their forties, but let's see what we get if we type in the years from 1884 which would make her 15 when she had Florrie to 1874 which would make her 25.'

Louise typed the parameters in and waited while the screen filled with around fifteen names. Two were from York.

'What makes you think it could be York?' she asked.

'Just something my Nana read,' Katie replied. 'It's a wild guess really.'

Louise followed the trail of the two York names and then grinned from ear to ear.

'I think we have found your lady,' she said. 'Millie Stanton, born 1884 in the city of York, died in 1902 in Bow, London.'

Louise sighed and looked at Katie.

'Her little daughter Florrie was only three when she died.'

Katie nodded, 'Nana called us a motherless family,' she said quietly. She recalled Millie's face in the photograph; the dark hair and chiselled bone structure, the intelligence behind the eyes. For a moment Katie seemed to feel some of Millie's anguish across the years. To have a baby at 15, just two years older than Katie, and then to die at the age of 18 seemed to her to be terribly cruel and unfair. To leave poor Florrie without a mother to care for her was terrible too. Katie wondered what kind of life Florrie would have had without a mother to look out for her, to hold her and comfort her. Then she remembered Laura. It suddenly became clear to her that Laura too, in many ways had never had a mother, not a mother you could rely on. Nana had been ill for so long. Laura had been left alone, young and frightened, never knowing which foster carer would be next in line to take her in or when her mother would return from hospital. For the first time she felt a flicker of understanding of her mother's personality and why Laura was so brusque, cold and uncaring at times. She was still hurting.

A wave of sadness swept over her. She realised that she, too, was almost motherless; her ability to speak with animals, her strange visions and hallucinations had created a gulf between her and Laura that neither of them seemed able to cross. Suddenly it was as if she could see things clearly for the first time. She knew she must try to accept the apparent strain of madness in her family and find a way to understand any sign of it in herself, or she too might be lost forever, and the pattern never be broken. First though, she had to be totally sure that there was a pattern that wove and spun its dark threads across the pages of her family's history. If there was, she had to find where it began and from there, how to break it, change it, make it into something more positive. Without speaking she rummaged in her bag and brought out the photograph of Millie that she had kept carefully wrapped in the brown envelope. She showed it to Louise who stared hard at the photograph.

'Is this Millie?'

Katie nodded. Louise looked up at Katie.

'She looks just like you.'

'I know she does. That's why I need to know what killed her. My Nana seemed to think we were linked in some way and although Nana was ill I have a feeling she might have been right.'

Her voice faltered. 'I'm frightened that I will die in the same way Millie did.'

Louise touched Katie's hand.

'Katie, people do not inherit deaths.'

Katie said nothing.

Louise returned to the keyboard but then hesitated. 'In case we don't find out all we need to know today I am going to give you the library telephone number. You can ring and ask to speak to me any time because I can do more of this searching at home. I'd really like to help you all I can.'

'Thank you,' Katie said gratefully.

She watched as Louise typed in Millie's details. The little hour glass at the bottom of the page spun as it searched through the millions of pages stored in the Genealogy website, until eventually the death certificate appeared. It was patchy and yellow in colour but this time the lettering was clear and unambiguous. Written in large looped letters by the coroner Dr

Mark Brighton of The Asylum, Bromley By Bow, London, were the words *Death through Insanity.*

Katie felt the blood drain away from her face. She held onto the side of the table to steady herself.

'It's true,' she whispered.

Louise looked at Katie with growing alarm.

'What's true?' she asked.

'I am going to go mad,' said Katie simply. 'I probably already am.'

'Nonsense,' Louise said firmly.

'Katie, there is no proof that Millie was mad. They used to lock single mothers away all the time. And you are as sane as I am!'

Katie looked at Louise. 'At the moment I am,' she said, 'but for how long?'

'For as long as you want to be,' replied Louise. 'Listen, we don't know what they meant by insanity. They used to make things up to suit themselves all the time especially with poor people. Millie was probably just a frightened anxious girl punished for getting pregnant.'

'I think she was a lot more than that,' Katie said.

'I think she was like me.'

XXIII

Patrick 2008

The squirrel had never intended to be there. His land was to the north, a much colder place and wetter even than Manchester. He had tumbled from an elm tree, rudely dislodged by the sudden blast of air from the 04:13 Edinburgh to Manchester mail train. It had flown by at just the wrong moment, when he had been navigating a particularly precarious branch, but the squirrel landed miraculously unharmed in an open carriage on a heap of empty mail sacks.

He scurried around the moving train desperately looking for refuge. He was frightened and wet, rain was pelting down on his head and his fur was plastered in clumps, exposing patches of pink skin. Not being a female, he was pretty big, with long black claws and in normal circumstances, a sleek white stomach which contrasted with the soft grey of his back and limbs. Today, however, as water dripped off his nose and ears his coat was anything but sleek. He shook himself and scampered up the carriage for the third time in five minutes, eventually coming to a stop when he realised that his surroundings were unlike any tree he recognised.

The ground was rumbling beneath him and the wind whipped at his face and body. He lifted his nose and smelt the air; already the familiar scent of his woodland home was growing fainter and further away. Very soon he would recognise nothing at all.

He looked around, ears pricked for the sound of danger, and spotted several large brown sackcloth bags partly hidden under a canopy of green cloth. He dived for shelter and nudged against the bags in an attempt to find warmth and protection from the continuous jarring and jolting of the train. He chewed a hole in the cloth and leapt back chattering with alarm as several hundred white and brown envelopes spilled out onto the floor of the carriage, threatening to engulf him in a sea of paper. Nudging his way through the darkness he wedged himself between two other, unopened sacks, and waited fearfully for the shuddering and rocking thing to stop. He lifted his nose, searching for the smell of a predator—the thing that was surely here to snap him up in jaws larger than any he had ever imagined. But the only scent he could find inside the open carriage was the mix of metal, the rush of cold air and the whip of falling rain.

By the time the train got to Manchester, the squirrel was sore and shaken. He had managed to stave off some of the cold by snuggling under the sacks of mail, but sackcloth was not the warmest of blankets, especially when damp. The train slowed and drew into the open mouth of Manchester Piccadilly Station, eventually stopping with a long drawn out hiss. He sat huddled in a corner, with his tail wrapped firmly and protectively around himself. His ears pricked with fear at a clanging, vibrating, shuddering sound, high pitched and echoing. Sitting bolt upright he lifted his head and sniffed, trying to sense whether the sound had an accompanying smell. It did. The squirrel's nose twitched furiously, capturing the scent that was rolling towards him in small warm waves, trying to identify what it might be. He soon recognised the scent of human. Immediately, he darted to the furthest corner of the cabin and watched as the human made its way towards the carriage where the he was hiding. The human was rather fat around its middle, with a bald head and thick rubbery lips. It was heaving the mail bags out of the carriages and hurling them onto large metal trolleys; this was the clanging sound that had caused the squirrel such alarm. He realised with a jolt that if he didn't make an escape quickly, he would be next, hurled liked a disused rag into the air then smacked against the hard metal bars of the luggage trolley.

The squirrel scurried under the mailbags and sat there, his black eyes darting about, taking in the environment and looking for a way out. He could smell that the human was coming nearer and he gathered himself for action. He squatted down onto his back legs, tensing muscles and holding his front legs steady, ready for the jump. Fear had loosened the squirrel up a bit and he knew that if he could just focus on the platform on the exact spot where he needed to land, he could get out quickly before the human noticed he was there.

With one great leap, he was over the side of the carriage, landing behind a stack of mail which was piled high on a large trolley. So far so good.

He quickly surveyed the scene. To his left the platform ran in a long straight line towards a pair of gates which led onto a wide concourse of brightly lit shop windows. He couldn't see into the shops, they were too far away, but he knew that the lights meant one thing at least—food. It had been a long time since he had eaten and he was hungry. To the right, the platform stretched out until it disappeared down into the railway track.

Suddenly a whistle blown by a red-faced human pierced the air with a high dry squeal and the platform was filled with long legged humans, running and pushing to reach the trains that stood on either side of the platform. The squirrel dived under a bench and stood stock still, desperate not to be seen, watching the creatures climb aboard and push forwards huffing and puffing to their seats. The squirrel waited, whiskers twitching, for the multitude of humans to disappear and the platform to grow silent again.

He felt his stomach rumble.

He really needed to get something to eat

From under the bench, he looked down the platform at the brightly lit shop windows and café bars. Yellow lights twinkled, beckoning. Looking from his position behind the trolley, he calculated that there were several hiding positions between the shops and his current location—a discarded trolley, a pile of luggage, a telephone box, a bench, and finally a rubbish bin. If he could jump between those bases he could reach the shopping concourse unseen. Even if he was seen, it might not be the end. It was highly probable that the humans would ignore him for he had now smelt a strong animal presence in the cavernous station. There were several families of mice nearby. He followed the familiar sweet smell until he found their little house nestled against the edge of the platform wall, positioned a safe distance from the railway track. The mice had collected pieces of rubbish—orange peel, scraps of burger buns, coke cups, large sheets of discarded newspaper and splinters of broken wood, to disguise the entrance to their house. To a human eye it would like a small pile of rubbish on the railway line, not camouflage for a mice lair. The squirrel raised his nose higher. A warm chalky fragrance mingled with the scent of urine. Ah yes; the unmistakable smell of pigeons. A group of them were staring at him from the rafters of the station ceiling.

'What you looking at, Rodent?'

He ignored them. Best thing with pigeons. They were the crudest of creatures and very stupid. They could be tricked into anything. He spun around and turned back to face the platform and the shopping concourse. His belly rumbled again. It was time to leave.

Five minutes later, the squirrel was at the doorway of Joe's Café. It appeared to be the oldest and most tatty café of all, and sat rather oddly amongst the glass and chrome décor that now dominated Manchester Piccadilly Railway Station. Unknown to the small damp squirrel who sat twitching at the door, the owners of the modern up-market retail units had tried to get rid of Joe's café, and they had the support of the station concourse owners too. They claimed it lowered the tone of the station, but Joe's stubbornly remained the most popular place to grab a cheap breakfast and was always crammed with people sitting at the blue Formica tables, spilling yolk from their fried egg sandwiches onto their copies of the Daily Mirror and supping huge mugs of over sweetened tea. Behind the counter the large stainless steel oven gave out huge guffaws of heat; the cook, a large man with a rotund belly turned pink strips of flesh over on the griddle. The bacon hissed and spat out droplets of fat which sizzled deliciously on the pan. The squirrel assimilated the greasy smell of fried breakfast but sweeter to the squirrel's nose was the aroma of freshly whipped hot chocolate. Raiding the bins of humans back home had given the squirrel a fond taste for sour milk and anything that was sugary. He glanced around. No one had spotted him, except a long skinny freckle-faced girl with short spiky yellow hair and dark eyes, sitting on her own in the corner. She seemed to be watching closely. He had better hurry up. Positioning himself, he prepared to leap up to where a collection of peanuts sat in glossy bags in a wicker basket on the counter.

'Peanuts. Sweet chocolate,' he thought. His whiskers shivered with the anticipation of the nuts between his teeth and the drops of warm chocolate running down his throat.

Working behind the counter with her back turned, was Beryl. As she busied herself with loading new stock onto the shelves, a sudden warm fizzy feeling ran down her spine and she became aware of something somewhere muttering about the delights of hot chocolate. She raised her head and looked around, but could see no one. The customers were all seated and the counter was empty. She returned to unloading the stock.

'I need to eat. Hot chocolate smells good.'

Beryl had worked at Joe's for fifteen years and in all her days she had never heard such a small, sweet and hungry voice, and it made her heart melt. She was a kind woman who loved children and would collect them like teddy bears if her husband would let her. She already had ten of her own. She thought it had to be the voice of a small boy, maybe a boy around the age of four. She lifted her head again, imagining a child with wild curly hair and bright eyes. With such a delightful image in mind she turned around to give the little lad her biggest friendliest smile. She came face to face with a wet bedraggled grey squirrel sat on her counter, its small beady eyes fixed greedily on the hot chocolate machine. The smile froze on her face, so that it didn't look like a smile at all any more, but rather as if she had eaten a clump of barbed wire that had got stuck in her gums. And then she screamed a long shuddering scream that swept past the creature's ears and flattened them against his head, causing the cook to drop the clean tray of plates and saucers he was carrying from the dishwasher. Clash! Surrounded by all this pandemonium, the squirrel decided he should leave. Grabbing a bag of nuts from the basket with both paws, he shoved it between his teeth, leapt from the counter and ran out of the door, dodging legs and feet, and skipped as fast as he could towards the station exit, leaving Beryl in a state of shock.

Outside, the sky was heavy and grey. And it was still raining. Black shiny cars stood in a queue and doors opened and slammed as passengers climbed into taxis. Engines growled, horns hooted and a paper vendor shouted, 'Manchester Evening News, First edition 30p.'

The squirrel scampered around a corner and squashed himself behind a wall. He tore off the corner of the cellophane bag with his sharp teeth, scattered the peanuts across the ground and hungrily nibbled.

He immediately became aware of the presence of another; the warm scent of bird. The squirrel looked up, then down and then behind. He could see no one. He returned to the nuts.

'Here.'

The squirrel twitched his tail nervously and jumped around to find the source of the interruption. There, sitting on a ledge was a small neatly preened robin with its wings folded, looking at the squirrel, its eyes steady and unblinking.

It was communicating with him. The squirrel stared back. The robin held the squirrel's gaze; its thoughts came in short sharp bursts at first, tumbling across the space between them. The squirrel sat still and alert.

'Why did you do that?'

'Do what?' the squirrel asked.

The robin continued to look unblinkingly at the squirrel.

'You know very well what I mean.'

The squirrel looked about and then down at the pool of peanuts at its feet. 'What take some food? I am squirrel. It is what we do.'

The robin opened its wings and flew in closer to the squirrel. It shook its head, and then bobbed its beak in towards its breast.

'You passed thoughts with the human.'

The squirrel leapt backwards in fear. 'I never did any such thing.'

'You did. I heard you.'

The squirrel shook his tail again. He could feel the fur on the back of his neck rise with indignation.

'Don't be stupid bird,' he retaliated, 'I can't do that. None of us can.'

Two other birds had arrived, flying in to sit on the wall; then another three, followed by five others. The squirrel looked about him nervously. Something did not feel right. His entire body was itching with a sense of danger. The robin fluttered its tail.

'Squirrel, we heard you.'

'I don't what you mean.' The squirrel was frightened now. 'I took food from the humans and now you are making up stories about me reaching them. Now go away and leave me alone.'

The robin chirped in anger.

'No squirrel! I don't care about you stealing their food; you steal all the food you want from this grotty, snivelling species, but for heaven's sake you don't reach them ever, and especially not via their tongue—that, as you well know, is strictly forbidden, strictly forbidden!'

The robin twitched nervously as if it expected some punishment to fall out of the sky there and then. The squirrel became increasingly perplexed.

'I didn't,' he repeated, 'I can't.'

'So you say!' communicated the robin, 'but answer me this then. How did the human understand you—how do you explain that!? You can't, can you? Of course you can't. No human can hear squirrel, which leads me to one logical conclusion; you thought in human and she heard you! Oh this is bad, oh so bad.

It shook its feathers. 'We are doomed.'

The squirrel could feel his claws tingling and the tip of his tail fizzing dramatically. He shook it angrily.

'How many more times do I have to explain, I can't...'

The robin was not listening. His head bobbed up and down furiously and his eyes darted to and fro in a wild fashion that left the squirrel feeling as frightened for the robin as he was for himself. The robin was right. It was forbidden to think in human. The robin raised its wings and fluttered its tail.

'You will have to come with us.

The squirrel felt his body tighten in fear, followed by a swell of anger in his chest. 'Oh yes, and how are you going to make that possible?'

The squirrel knew the birds had a strange gift. He had seen them often enough. They had the gift of flight; the incredible ability to be there in the trees in one moment and in the next, to be disappearing high into the clouds. The squirrel knew he would never possess this gift. He could walk the treetops but not the air. He was heavier than they were but stronger too. The bird could not *force* him to go anywhere.

The robin lifted its beak. His tone became imperious.

'You have broken a rule my friend. You will come with me to Longford Park. The Dove Queen will see you there.'

Despite the absurdity of the bird the squirrel began to feel slightly alarmed. Perhaps he had not thought in squirrel? Perhaps the fall from the tree had sent him slightly doo-lally, giving him the unusual ability to communicate directly in human?

The squirrel looked up at the robin. He knew what he had to do.

He darted forwards. Immediately the assembled birds flew up in a great cloud and descended upon him, penning him in against a bright red letter box that stood between the door to the station and the outer wall. He could not escape. All around the squirrel, birds gathered, squawking and twittering and flapping their wings. They flew in at him, darting spitefully at his eyes and causing the squirrel to spin around on his legs, using his tail as a buffer against the angry birds. The robin stood on the top of the post box, with its head held high, watching with an imperious gleam in his eye. One bird, a sparrow grabbed the squirrels back left leg. Other birds shuffled their way around him until he was surrounded in a circle of feathers and beaks. He struggled and writhed and leapt up, but was met each time by new birds that flew at him and pushed him down again with sharp beaks that dug into his head and nipped at his fur. He had almost broken free through a gap he had spotted to the right of the telephone box, when an extraordinary thing happened.

A loud humming began, followed by a rumble of thunder. The sound of an ominous storm approaching. Yet when the squirrel raised his head, he saw no darkening, but only a gap open in the greyness of the sky and a dull yellow light break through the dense cloud. All the birds fell silent. Through the split of cloud, a dark shape was gliding swiftly yet graciously towards them. As it neared the squirrel could see it wasn't really just a shape or a shadow but a creature like none he had seen before. A creature with a heavy fur coated body, densely brown wings and a long straight elegant beak, ivory coloured with a charcoal tip. Not only had the squirrel never seen a creature like it, he had never smelt anything like it either. It was an old smell, sharp, decaying, wasted, as if it had come from somewhere deep in the bowels of the earth and had lain dead for many years. Yet it was alive.

As the bird creature came in to land, it folded its wings against its body, flowed gracefully to the ground and stood beside the bewildered squirrel.

The other birds bowed their head and kept their silence.

The robin lowered its head, 'My Lord, I present to you this squirrel. We have made plans to carry him to the Council, to see the Dove Queen, on the charge of communicating with a Human.'

The creature looked deeply into the squirrel's eyes and it was then that something else extraordinary happened; the squirrel felt his back legs go weak and syrupy with his front legs soon following suit. The squirrel felt his body flop and his head begin to spin. His eyes felt heavy as if two small cold rocks had been placed upon them and in a matter of seconds he had fallen into a dark deep sleep and was completely at the mercy of the bird-like creature. The birds gathered silently now around the unconscious squirrel. The bird-creature lifted its head and cawed sharply, directing the flock silently with movements of its great wings. The birds lifted the limp body of the squirrel to place him upon the back of the creature they knew only as Lord. The creature opened his wings and made ready for flight. However they did not see that a girl was watching and waiting for the right moment to make her daring move.

XXIV

Katie had witnessed the scene in the café.

Excitedly, she pulled her chair closer to the little group of café workers surrounding Beryl who was seated with her feet up on a chair, blubbering and patting her eyes. Joan, the tea lady was comforting her.

'There, there dear,' she was saying, her arm around her shoulder, 'Calm down now.'

'But I heard it Joan, I swear I did. It was like the little thing was talking to me. It was like I could hear it saying it wanted a cup of hot chocolate as plain as the day.'

She started to cry again, big blubbering tears splashing down her apron. She patted her eyes and wiped her nose on her sleeve.

Joan looked at the cook, who raised his eyebrows in despair. Neither of them seemed to know what to do.

'It's all right love,' said Joan soothingly, 'you didn't see its mouth move now did you?'

Beryl shook her head and sniffed miserably.

'No, of course you didn't. You're just tired love, overworked maybe? I mean, you'd be in the loony bin if you heard animals talk wouldn't you?'

Beryl let out a wail and nodded her head.

'I'll ring her husband,' said Joan decisively.

Katie listened carefully. She was waiting for Laura to come and meet her from the station. It was now 4.30 p.m. and Laura was late as usual, but for once Katie didn't mind. Someone else had heard the squirrel. What was going on?

She looked across at poor Beryl. Should she confess?

'It's ok; I understand what animals think as well.'

She decided against it. Right now the lady was far too upset to talk and Katie could make things worse. She decided to go outside to see if she could find the straggly creature, the cause of all the palaver. Perhaps he knew the lady and she could ask him whether there were other people who understood him too; just maybe, Katie was not as alone as she had always imagined herself to be. Maybe it meant she was not going mad. Picking up her suitcase, she went outside to see whether the offending squirrel was still around. He was but he was not alone.

With her heart beating furiously, Katie listened to the robin scolding the squirrel and watched the swarm of birds arrive and settle around him. She watched quietly and carefully as the huge bird-like creature arrived to carry the squirrel off up into the sky. And then she did it.

She plunged recklessly into the midst of the fluttering, feathered mass. She tore the squirrel loose from the tiny cruel claws, then freeing one hand hit out right left and centre as she fought her way free. Stuffing the unconscious squirrel inside her jacket, she ran back inside the station.

XXV

Albion 23 A.D.

Lovernicus gazed around him. He was in a deep glade and trees towered above his head like benevolent giants, their thick dark trunks hairy with moss, their branches threading upwards and outwards across the sky, linking together like brothers in arms forming a latticed ceiling. Sunshine peeped through the leaves causing the light to ripple on the forest floor. All around him Lovernicus could hear birdsong; thrush, sparrow and the call of the cuckoo.

'Take care Lovernicus,' the cuckoo sang.

It was summer, the leaves on the trees were open forming a lush canopy of green, and wood poppies of orange and yellow were scattered across the forest floor like discarded beads. He listened carefully, searching for one particular sound. He found it. Satisfied, he made his way towards the gentle rush of the river.

As he crossed the forest floor, Lovernicus scanned around him for any signs of danger. The Jewel had been opened and its enemies would know, would feel its magic casting a glow over the land. They would be searching frantically for it and Lovernicus had to move quickly. He could only afford the Jewel to remain open for a short while, long enough to protect Mortunda and just long enough to speak with Sequana. Wiping his hand across his head to remove the beads of perspiration that had begun to gather on his brow, Lovernicus steadied his gaze and peered through the tapestry of branches and undergrowth, searching for Mortunda. He could sense her soul, light and ethereal wandering through the glade to meet Sequana. Following his instincts, barefoot he made his way deeper into the forest towards the river, taking care not to trip on the fallen twigs and branches that covered the forest floor. He could see Mortunda now in the distance ducking and weaving through the trees, slight and fast as a squirrel, the creature renowned for its ability to travel through the three planes of existence; the creature that was the very symbol of the Tree of

Life. Lovernicus gathered speed, ignoring the pain in his feet and made his way in the same direction as the child. All around him he was aware of the warmth of the sun and the trust of the forest. Following her form he watched Mortunda come to the river and stop. She waited. The water gushed, flowing fast at this point, brown and muscular like a dog hunting prey. Lovernicus hesitated. He was anxious not to appear too soon, respectful of the fact that Sequana had called upon Mortunda with her message and not him. He was here solely as protector and guide. He had no wish to offend Sequana or interfere with her wishes. Mortunda stood still and patient and Lovernicus again felt immense surprise and admiration at her ability to understand the ethics and rules of the inner world at such a young age. She would become a great Seronydd, perhaps even, one of the greatest. It would also be a gift to Deseus to have a peer to work alongside him in his training, a companion to break the sense of loneliness the boy felt.

A soft breeze blew in from the east and passed Lovernicus, stroking his arms and bare legs. He smiled and watched as it lifted Mortunda's hair and caused her to spin around to greet it. As Mortunda did so, she found facing her, a young woman, with long brown hair and eyes the colour of cornflowers. Lovernicus witnessed the Goddess reach out her hand and stroke Mortunda's face, gently and lovingly. Mortunda's mouth broke into a wide smile.

Lovernicus waited in the shadows of a large oak tree. He heard Sequana speak, her voice young and melodic, filling the forest with song.

'Mortunda, I welcome you. There is much I have to say.'

Mortunda, looking into the eyes of the Goddess, was spellbound by her beauty; it was if the entire forest hummed with the scent of water lily and lilac.

'So why have you come to the dream forest to meet me child?' the Goddess asked Mortunda, 'can you remember why I summoned you?'

'I heard you in my dream,' said Mortunda. 'You said something about the tribes in the South of Albion but I did not fully understand what you meant.'

The young Goddess smiled, 'Yes you remember well. I am glad you called upon the Request. That was clever of you.'

Sequana smiled at Mortunda then looked directly towards the oak where Lovernicus stood waiting.

'I think we should invite Lovernicus to hear my message Mortunda.'

Mortunda looked astonished. 'You mean Lovernicus is here? But how?'

Sequana touched Mortunda's arm lightly.

'I will let Lovernicus explain. He and I have spoken on many occasions and it is best that you hear why from him.'

Stepping out of the shade, Lovernicus made his way across the clearing to where they stood.

'Forgive me Mortunda,' he began, 'I accompanied you because I fear we do not have long before certain enemies, dangerous enemies, attempt to stop your meeting with Sequana.'

Mortunda frowned. 'What enemies? You mean Rome?'

'Not just Rome. But I will explain later. I came with you today because you are young and I promised your father I would protect you.'

Sequana nodded, 'Lovernicus will protect you Mortunda and you are to trust him at all times, but Lovernicus, you are right about our enemy. We haven't long. The Jewel is open and he and his Travellers are not far away.'

Mortunda looked bewildered, 'What Jewel?'

Sequana placed her hands gently on Mortunda's shoulders.

'That is not your concern. One day you will know more. But for now, are you ready to hear my message?'

Mortunda swallowed. She nodded.

Sequana smiled again and her eyes shone with an inner radiance that filled Mortunda's soul with peace,

'Come let us sit down,' she said. Once all three were seated Sequana began.

'Mortunda I am here to tell you that one day you will be Queen of the Brigante and beyond. But before that time there is much that needs to happen. This island of Albion faces great danger, the greatest danger in all of her history. The tribes of Albion are playing into the hands of those that come to conquer her.'

Mortunda interrupted, 'You mean the Romans; the Romans are coming?'

Sequana nodded.

'In many ways they are already here. They may not have successfully invaded the shores yet, but they will one day very soon. Their presence is visible already through trade and I fear the influence Rome has over the minds of certain tribal leaders.'

'The tribes from the south,' Lovernicus murmured, 'our elders warn them daily of Rome but I fear we are losing the battle.'

Sequana turned to Lovernicus. Her voice was hard and cold. A shiver ran through the forest, 'You may well lose the battle Lovernicus. Some of your elders are not all they seem. Some use their abilities to acquire wealth and influence and forget their true path.'

Her eyes held his.

'Yes I know,' he said.

Sequana continued. 'The very future of the Seronydd lies in the battle ahead. If the Seronydd lose their true focus, then they will lose their way, and all of Albion will be lost forever. Lovernicus, the future of the Jewel is tied into Rome and the path the Seronydd take.'

The Goddess turned to Mortunda, 'As for you child, you must tell your father to go south, but I warn you, do not expect him to listen to you. If he were a wise man he would forego any future wars with his neighbours and ask them to follow him south. He would call upon all the tribes of Albion to unite and face Rome together. But I fear men of the tribes of Albion are not ready for such a message. They prefer to fight with each other.'

Sequana's eyes saddened.

'It will fall to you Mortunda. You must tell Brennus the real enemy is Rome, not the Parisi, not the Atrebate, nor any of the neighbouring tribes. This is the message you must deliver. Tell Brennus to form a council with Lovernicus at its head and for all tribes to send delegates to this council. The task for the council is unification of Albion. The tribes must find a common purpose through the wisdom of the Seronydd and the strength of humanity. Albion must be united before the Romans arrive and time is running out.'

Mortunda felt herself dizzy with apprehension. She looked at Lovernicus. 'My father will not listen to such advice,' she said plaintively, 'He will grow angry and tell me not to interfere with matters I do not understand.'

Sequana placed her hand on Mortunda's head and Mortunda felt her apprehension fall away from her shoulders like a heavy cloak. 'You are right Mortunda, your father will not listen, but you must deliver the message anyway.' Sequana glanced at Lovernicus, 'for there are others in the room that need to hear it. Lovernicus, there is more at stake than even you realise.'

Lovernicus frowned, disturbed by what Sequana had said.

Mortunda stood up. 'Is that all?' she asked Sequana.

The Goddess smiled, 'Almost,' she replied, 'except what is to become of you in the immediate future.'

Mortunda waited her heart pounding. This is what she had been waiting for. Her destiny. What was to become of her?

'Mortunda, you are to go with Lovernicus to Mona. Train to be a Seronydd and then, when you have passed the age of eighteen summers, you will return to the Brigante and in your heart you will know what it is to be done.'

Mortunda spoke quietly. 'But what will be in my heart? How will I know what needs to be done?'

Sequana answered as quietly. 'Mortunda, remember your mother's words. Look within and find the heart of the matter. Let nothing lead you astray. You will know what is to be done when you return and you must make sure you do it. Be true to the knowledge your heart holds.'

Mortunda smiled. Joy surged warmly through her. Training to be a Seronydd would not please her father but it was the right thing for her; she had always known it, just as her mother had known it too. Surely even her father would have to listen now she had been through the Request and returned with a clear answer. Her thoughts were interrupted by Lovernicus who suddenly shot to his feet looking startled.

'What was that?' he hissed.

Sequana froze. 'They are here Lovernicus,' she whispered. 'They have found us. You must return with the child immediately and close the Jewel.'

XXVI

Sequana faded into the trees and Lovernicus and Mortunda were left alone in the forest. Lovernicus watched carefully. Large shadows crossed the forest floor and smaller ones darted behind the trunks of the trees. It had grown dark. Mortunda came closer to him and instinctively took his hand.

'I am frightened,' she whispered. Lovernicus squeezed her hand to reassure her and put his fingers to his lips, 'Sssh,' he whispered, 'I need to concentrate. Now stay close to me.'

Mortunda fell into silence and followed Lovernicus, weaving in and out of the trees back towards the open ground where they had arrived. The forest was old and thickly populated with trees that stood close together. Where once they had appeared to be friends, protectors almost, now Mortunda and Lovernicus were aware of an insidious feeling of menace creeping towards them from the low, crowding branches. They glared down at the pair with sinister intent. Hidden eyes seemed to follow their every move. Mortunda felt the skin on her back prick with fear. The shadows were not far behind; Mortunda could sense them stretching, darkening, moving towards them, growing larger. She turned briefly and saw dark folds unwinding like skeins of fine charcoal cloth, covering the forest, shrouding the green in cold grey. Soon they too would be covered; snared, snatched away, their life drained out of them. She had never felt so afraid. Lovernicus was moving faster now and Mortunda was afraid he would forget she was there; forget that she was only a child whose legs were shorter and slower. She tried to call out to him, to ask him to slow down but the words got caught in her throat and would not come out. Her foot got snared in a patch of bramble and suddenly she was on the ground, the wind knocked out of her lungs and her hand twisted beneath her body. She cried out in pain and Lovernicus turned to help her up. He caught sight of the shadow that was sweeping down towards Mortunda, its face grey and twisted in a look of pure hatred for the child lying injured on the ground. Lovernicus picked Mortunda up and pulled her quickly towards the open glade. The shadow swept across the empty patch where Mortunda had lain, its fingers emerging empty, without its prey, feeding only on the remains of her body heat, the faint, sweet smell of human flesh. It cried out in anger at having missed the child and writhed with frustration as Lovernicus opened his arms and began the recitation, his ululations of praise and request filling the air. Above a crow shrieked and a crack of thunder tore the sky. Grabbing Mortunda by the hand, Lovernicus pulled her into the swathe of red light that shot up from the ground and bathed them in its hue. The light flew high into the sky, above the tops of the trees, soaring above the hills and covered the land with a soft red glow. Within moments both Mortunda and Lovernicus were back in the circle in the house of Brennus, and the dream forest melted behind them into thin air.

XXVII

The circle of watchers waited while Mortunda and Lovernicus came round from their long sleep. Mortunda had called out several times in her dream journey and Brennus had fought hard not to rush into the circle to comfort his daughter in her distress. At one point Mortunda had cried out as if she were in great pain, and he imagined her eyes had shot open to reveal her terror. Brennus had feared for her sanity, for her life and berated himself for allowing her to enter such a dangerous inner journey. The Flame was for experienced journeymen and even though Mortunda was being accompanied by Lovernicus, Brennus had been afraid his daughter may not return. He waited anxiously; fear prowling in his chest like a chained bear, until Mortunda gradually sat up and rubbed her eyes. Lovernicus too, awoke and stretched his limbs. But, his face was etched with tiredness and something else. Brennus detected a look of uncertainty in Lovernicus. It was something he had never seen before in the Seronydd elder. It unsettled him.

'The Request was successful Brennus,' Lovernicus declared falteringly. Yet he did not smile. Still his eyes carried a look of worry. He continued speaking to the circle, 'Everyone present may open their eyes. The message has been delivered and Brennus, your daughter will pass it to you shortly. But first we will need food and ale.'

Brennus tossed aside his concerns. He crossed the circle and threw his arms around his daughter.

'Thank the spirits you are safe,' he whispered and kissed the top of her head. Tears fell freely from his eyes. The party broke hands and soon everyone, including Mortunda was feasting ravenously upon freshly cooked meat and supping ale sweetened with honey.

Once they were refreshed and Mortunda had left the room to wash her face, Lovernicus called Brennus to his side.

'I will allow Mortunda to tell you what she saw and heard Brennus, but if she is unsure of any part of the message, would you permit me to assist her?'

Brennus nodded sagely,

'Of course' he replied, 'shall we begin now?'

The circle reassembled. Outside the light shifted in the sky. Dark rain clouds chased across the moon and covered her with trails of black mist. The wind blew in and the fires began to die down. The merriment of the camp tuned down towards sleepiness and people began to turn into their beds. They would hear any announcements in the morning.

Inside the house of Brennus, the circle heard the story of Mortunda's journey to meet the Goddess Sequana. She told the story well, stumbling only over the part where Sequana talked of the need for a council of men and Seronydd to unify Albion. Lovernicus stepped in as he had promised.

'The Goddess spoke of the need for men and Seronydd to work together to unify Albion,' he explained.

'She was adamant that Brennus was fit for this task,' he added, looking intently at him.

Mortunda looked at her father, her eyes pleading.

'What do you say Father?' she asked.

'Will you go to the other tribes and unite them? Will you help Lovernicus form a council?'

Brennus shook his head.

'I fear it is impossible. If I go out to my people tomorrow at first light and explain that from now on, the warriors of the Brigante will lay down their arms and fight no longer to protect our land from those tribes that would dare to steal it from us, I will be King for no longer than a day. Also there is no guarantee that other tribes would listen. I would be vulnerable to attack and the sovereignty of the Brigante could become compromised.'

Torrance nodded his head.

'This is true, but what is also true is that the Romans are a bigger enemy than the Parisi or the Atrebates or any other tribe that lives on this island.'

Brennus sighed. 'Yes to a point I agree,' he said, 'But we can not forget that there are scavengers here who would steal our land and starve our people.'

He turned to Mortunda. 'Daughter, are you sure you understood the method by which Sequana wants me to unite Albion? Perhaps she meant I should unite by my sword. Conquer the lands to the south and bring them under the rule of the Brigante. Maybe a strong Brigante tribe is Albion's only hope?'

Mortunda shook her head. 'No Father, this is not the message at all!' she said despairingly. 'Sequana spoke of peaceful means, a council of warriors and Seronydd from all tribes, led by Lovernicus, a way in which Albion can work as one.'

Brennus looked at Lovernicus. 'Surely my daughter got this wrong, Lovernicus? Such a message would sign my death warrant. These can not be the words passed on to us by the Gods?'

Lovernicus looked at Mortunda. *She warned you he would not be able to hear the message Mortunda.*

'The Goddess spoke of the need for Albion to unite, King Brennus,' said Lovernicus. 'How men go about such matters is probably best left for men to decide. Sequana comes to us from the Spirit world. She is not a warrior.'

Lovernicus lowered his head. It was the only explanation Brennus would understand and he hoped Mortunda would grow to forgive him. Mortunda's face was grey. Dismay haunted her eyes.

'You have much to learn Mortunda,' Lovernicus said with his mind. 'Patience is the first lesson.'

'At last!' shouted Torrance, 'Now I think we are getting somewhere! The Request was a success and your wonderful daughter has brought us a plan from the Gods themselves! Come King Brennus, let us bring out the map of this Island of Albion, let us make plans to build upon this tribe of yours so we can be strong to fight the Romans. Yesterday it was the Parisi, tomorrow the Atrebate. But we fight with only one purpose in mind and the tribes we take will learn this quickly—we fight only to defeat our most dangerous enemy; the Roman Empire and the greed she stands for! Come Brennus, let us plan! You have my service in full!'

There were cries of agreement from around the circle and Brennus felt cheered by the sudden decision thrust upon him. He lifted his cup and raised it to the ceiling,

'To a stronger Brigante, to a stronger Albion,' he toasted.

Others lifted their cups to his, and cheers broke out around the room. Lovernicus noted that Sego was smiling, although he had not gone so far as to raise his cup.

The next four hours were spent poring over the map of Albion and planning the invasion routes into neighbouring tribal lands. Mortunda felt sick and betrayed by Lovernicus. She had heard his silent messages to her but she could not understand why Lovernicus had not pressed the true meaning harder. He could have made Brennus understand if he had really wanted to. He was the leader of the Seronydd after all! If anyone could make her father see the reality of the true situation, Lovernicus could. She felt lost now, unsure what to do and deeply afraid that she had sent her father on a false mission, possibly a mission that would lead to his death. Her father was about to embark on what he thought of as a request from the Gods, when in fact it was not. It was the opposite. He assumed he had the protection of the Gods when in fact he did not have. He was acting exactly in the way the Goddess had feared. She had to do something quickly to stop him. There had to be a way to buy some more time. Of course! The solution came to her in a breath. The second part of her encounter with Sequana; the matter of her leaving the Brigante. A King's daughter's leaving ceremony would take days of preparation and force her father into a cooling off period. If she could only buy some more time, she may be able to convince him that war was not the way forward.

'Father,' she called out, 'You can not prepare for battle just yet. There is something else you should know.'

Brennus looked up, 'And what is that?'

Mortunda took a deep breath.

'You have to make ready my leaving journey. Sequana has ordained that I leave with Lovernicus to train as a Seronydd, and that it should be as soon as possible.'

XXVIII

Katie, Manchester 2008

Katie stood inside the station panting and feeling a little shaky.
'What now?' she asked herself.

She looked around trying to figure where to place the rescued squirrel and was about to head over to the Virgin ticket office to put him behind the bright yellow sofa, when a familiar voice called:

'Katie!'

She turned to see Laura waving irritably at her. Arms folded impatiently, she came striding across the concourse.

'Katie, where on earth have you been? How many times do I have to tell you to wait where I ask you to wait? Seriously Katie, you can be the most selfish person sometimes! Anything could have happened to you and then how would that have made me look?'

Katie scrambled around for an excuse.

'Sorry. I wasn't feeling too well so I went outside for some fresh air, and I was just making my way back to the café.'

Laura tutted and felt Katie's head. Ever since Katie's fever at the time of the fortress, Laura had become obsessed with checking her temperature.

'Yes, just as I thought, you have a temperature again. You're probably tired. Exeter is far too far for you to travel by yourself! I told your father that! Of course, he never listens.'

Her face darkened as she mentioned Katie's Dad.

'Come on let's get a taxi home.'

They made their way to the taxi rank. Laura talked quickly and incessantly about their new house which was apparently in a wonderful leafy suburb south of the city with a back garden that overlooked a large park, whilst Katie worried all the time that the squirrel would wake up. How would she explain to Laura why she was carrying an unconscious squirrel under her jacket?

'You're very quiet Katie,' Laura said. She stopped suddenly and pulled her mobile phone from her bag. Belligerently she began pumping in Katie's Dad's number. Katie's heart sank. She sensed a row brewing.

'Jim is that you? Good. Yes she is here with me. No, she is not ok!'

Katie could hear the faint indignation of her father's reply.

'What? No Jim it was too far and your daughter is unwell because of it. You should have driven her back as I asked you to. Well she has a temperature now and of course I will have to deal with that, won't I, because you are not here. Well she won't be travelling to see you again until you can be bothered to come and fetch her yourself. Goodbye!'

She switched the telephone off and looked at Katie.

'Your father has no idea. Men are stupid selfish creatures.'

The pair stood in silence in the taxi rank until an empty cab drew up beside them. Laura climbed in first, grabbed Katie's luggage out of her hand and arranged it against the back of the driver's seat. She sat next to Katie and felt her head once more.

'Katie, when we get to the house, you are to go straight to your new room and have a lie down. I will make us some very late lunch and bring you a cup of tea.'

Laura felt her daughter's forehead yet again and tutted.

The taxi drew up in a tree lined street of semi-detached houses. Number 27 was theirs and for one minute Katie forgot the events at the station, the squirrel asleep inside her jacket and her parents' incessant fighting, and eyed with pleased surprise the freshly painted windows, and the neat brick path leading to the front door. The house looked welcoming and pretty with its green front door and ivy growing over the brick arch porch. A brass plaque *Ivy House* glinted above the arch. With apprehension mother and daughter opened the front door. Stepping inside the airy hallway, Katie could smell the fresh paint and turned to smile appreciatively at Laura.

'The house looks good.'

Laura nodded. 'I know,' she said, 'Now go up to your room and unpack and I'll bring you a cup of tea.'

Katie had no trouble finding her room. Laura had organised all her books on shelves, her collection of soft toys was lined up on her bed waiting for her and there were even her old posters on the wall. It had been painted in a cool pale blue and the floorboards had been fashionably stripped and varnished and over laid with a large cream rug. The room was large and beautiful but a small pang in her chest reminded her that she wished her Dad were with them. She sat on the bed and wondered how and when she would ever stop wishing that. Was it possible, she asked herself, ever to get used to having the person you loved more than anything else in the world, living 300 miles away from you? A slight movement in her jacket interrupted her thoughts and reminded her of the passenger she had brought home from the railway station. Peering anxiously inside her jacket, she saw that the squirrel had merely turned over in its sleep.

He was snoring. Gently, Katie undid the buttons of her jacket and lifted the sweaty sleeping squirrel out onto the bed. She rummaged around in her cupboard and retrieved a shoe box containing her new trainers, which she removed and placed under her bed. She placed the squirrel inside the shoe box, tucked the white layers of tissue paper that had protected her precious trainers over its legs and under its neck, and then pushed it under her bed with the trainers. She sat there for a while taking in her new surroundings before realising that Laura had probably forgotten the cup of tea. She got up, shut her bedroom door, and made her way downstairs to join her in the kitchen.

XXIX

Laura had forgotten the tea. When Katie got to the kitchen she found her holding a text book on interior design in one hand and stirring something with the other. To Katie's surprise Laura had prepared a meal for them both; croissants, scrambled egg, soya sausages and grilled tomatoes. She immediately noticed something different about Laura. Her shoulders were less hunched and her lips were not pinched together in the cross, pursed way Katie had grown accustomed to. Despite the row with Dad on the phone, Laura appeared more relaxed. She almost seemed happy.

Katie sniffed hungrily, and attempting to quieten her tummy rumbles, took a look around the kitchen.

Laura had obviously been very busy during Katie's stay with her Dad; paintbrushes were standing upright in a jar of white spirit by the sink, and the kitchen walls gleamed with new paint.

'I like the colour,' Katie said conversationally whilst picking up a croissant and putting it to her mouth.

As she hoped, Laura smiled.

'It's called terracotta. I thought I'd go for the Mexican look, you know add some blue accessories, maybe paint the back door blue and then lead into the garden with a terracotta and blue glass tiled patio with lots of flower baskets. The idea is to bring the garden into the kitchen.'

Laura picked up a new book she had bought recently, *Interior Design and Garden Rooms*.

'Here, I was inspired by this writer. Read it Katie you may learn something.'

Katie reluctantly leafed her way through the book.

The pages were heavy with photographs and line drawings of light angles and room rearrangements. Try as hard as she could Katie could not get excited by authentic Victorian fireplaces, the Art and Craft Movement or choices between Indian Silks and Tweed. She stared at the pages, willing them to make sense.

'So how was it with your Dad?' said Laura suddenly, spooning scrambled eggs onto two plates.

'Fine,' replied Katie.

'So what did you do?' Laura continued.

'Nothing much, we went swimming, and bowling and ate lots of ice-cream.'

There was silence for a while. Then the inevitable question came from Laura.

'So what is she like then?'

She was referring to Knickers.

Katie shrugged.

'She's all right I suppose.'

'Just all right?'

'Well, you know, she is a bit over the top, maybe. She went out of her way to be nice to me. She talks a lot and she has smelly breath.'

Laura nodded.

'Is she pretty?'

'Not as pretty as you.'

Laura scowled.

'She has to be prettier than me at least!'

Katie did not say anything. She hoped the questions would stop.

'So what does she look like?' Laura persisted, 'I mean, I know she's younger than me, trust your father to follow the stereotype wherever he goes. But she must have something else I don't have; apart from the inconvenience of having a child of course, but what is that something else that she has that I am so clearly lacking? Maybe she's a better cook!'

Laura ended with a hollow laugh and shoved a piece of croissant into her mouth chewing angrily. Any signs of relaxation were disappearing quickly. Katie bit upon her bottom lip to prevent herself from crying. It worked well. The pain distracted her. Laura wanted to know why her Dad had left them and yet the truth was quite obvious. Laura had named it herself only moments before her outburst. She was sat there in front of the reason and the reason's name was Katie—'The inconvenience of having a child.' It had nothing to do with Knickers being prettier or cleverer than Laura. The truth was that Knickers was quite vile! She talked a lot and talked very quickly too, so that sometimes Katie's head had gone dizzy trying to listen to her. And she was shorter than Laura, and not nearly as clever but she did have pretty green eyes, which only made Katie hate her even more. She settled for a different version, one that was easier to say and one that would allow Laura to feel happier.

'She has short red frizzy hair and ok-ish green eyes, but she talks far too much. Dad likes her because she plays the piano and she thinks his job is way more important than hers. She tells him how wonderful he is all the time.'

'Ah ha,' said Laura, 'I just knew it! Of course, Katie you have hit the nail on the head. All that male chauvinist ever wanted was for some woman to worship at his feet and sacrifice her life for his. Well do you know what? She is welcome to him!'

Laura triumphantly smeared butter into her croissant and grinned.

'Anyway, I have a big surprise for you. We have someone coming over. I have invited him for tea tonight. I think he quite likes me.'

Katie put on her bright voice, 'Who is he then?'

'Well,' replied Laura smugly, 'that is the surprise! All I am prepared to say for now is that he's a very interesting man. Much more interesting than your father ever was with all that boring sales talk of his! He is very nice, and he is not married.'

Katie's heart sank. Great, she thought, just what I need, another parental romance in my life, but she gave Laura another bright smile.

'Wonderful,' she said, not meaning it one little bit.

XXX

After lunch Laura insisted they should explore the park at the back of the house. A walk would be good for them she declared. It would allow her to show Katie their new surroundings before she started her new job the next day. Before they left, Katie popped upstairs to her room, on the pretence that she just had to put on her new trainers. Ducking her head under the bed, she saw that the squirrel was still snoring, and dreaming too, for its eyes were darting to and fro under closed eyelids. Tip-toeing over to the wardrobe, she foraged inside for her jacket, retrieved her new trainers from under the bed, then left the room, shutting the door quietly behind her.

Laura and Katie went out of the back door, down the long thin garden and out of the back gate into Longford Park.

Longford Park was not as big as East Dulwich Park; there was no duck pond, boats or café where you could stop to get buy a drink and cream scone. But it was pretty enough. Large horse chestnut trees outlined the pathways and just beyond the under five toddler playground was a mini zoo containing goats, rabbits, hens, ducks, geese, and exotic birds; blue breasted budgerigars, cockatoos, parrots and dainty yellow canaries. Katie and Laura plodded around the animal pens, Katie listening to Laura's plans for reforming the house and her ambitions to please her new boss and be made regional manager within the year. It was not until they reached the chicken pen that Katie felt that something was watching her again. She turned her head to see who or what was there, when a twittering coming from the tree above made her look up. There, on a branch of an old elm tree sat the robin, and beside him sat several sparrows and thrushes, all fixing Katie with their glittering, reptilian eyes. They must have followed her from the railway station. She looked around to see if she could see the strange looking bird-creature, but it was nowhere to be seen. She turned away quickly, her heart pounding. 'Think,' she muttered to herself, but try as hard as she could she could not decide what to do. She knew that if she was to start communicating with the birds, Laura would become angry and it would spoil any chance Katie ever had of making a new beginning in Manchester. She desperately wanted to stay on the right side of Laura. She found she was regretting saving the squirrel and hiding it in her room; she should have just walked away and pretended she had not seen or heard a thing. Katie swallowed her anxiety and moved quickly out of the robin's view, moving tentatively closer to Laura. The robin wasn't scary as such, but the glare he was giving her reminded her of the bird-like creature. Her instincts told her it would not be long before he joined the birds. She did not relish being hypnotised!

Katie and Laura moved across the enclosure. Immediately the birds rose in a rustling, flapping cloud and settled on the tree nearest the pair. Lizard-like, their small heads thrust forward, they stared unblinkingly. Katie shivered.

'Are you chilly again?' Laura enquired.

'A little, would you mind if we went back? I feel rather tired.'

'This morning has obviously worn you out!' Laura said.

More than you know, thought Katie.

Crossing the park to her house, Katie peered anxiously over her shoulder to see what the birds were doing. It was as she thought. They were following her and they had grown in number. Now there were around a hundred birds flying in groups from tree to tree, tracking Katie and Laura back to the house. The trees alongside the path to the house were filling up with birds of every feather. The branches swayed under the weight of preening magpies, thrushes, swallows, sparrows, doves. They clucked and twittered and cooed to each other, and their voices entwined one with the other, so that Katie had difficulty understanding what they were saying. She moved her head slightly to one side in an attempt to catch the meaning, but there were too many different bird languages all being spoken at once. It sounded like a garbled mess of tweets and chirping, interspersed with the crude caws of the crows that had now joined the branches of the trees.

Laura looked up as they entered the back gate.

'My! Look at those birds. They must have sensed the storm coming.'

Glancing up at the sky, Katie noticed the clouds had thickened and darkened. The cold smell of impending rain caught in her nostrils. The two rushed through the gate to the back door, reaching it just as the first soft blobs of rain fell from the sky.

Once inside, Laura sent Katie upstairs, instructing her to change into pyjama's and get into bed. Katie did not argue. She had a squirrel to inspect and questions to ask. This time, amazingly, Laura kept her word and as soon as Laura had brought her a cup of tea and a digestive biscuit, drawn the curtains and left the room, Katie reached under the bed, dragged the box out and plonked it onto the duvet. Lifting the lid she peered inside. The squirrel was still snoring, its small body rising and falling in short sharp breaths. Katie shook it gently. The squirrel twitched and jumped but remained firmly asleep. Katie shook it harder and hissed, 'Wake up!'

One eyelid flickered. Katie reached for the teaspoon that lay in her saucer and drew a small drop of tea. She dribbled it onto the squirrel's mouth. A small black tongue stirred and then popped out to lick the drops. One eye sprung open, followed by the other.

The squirrel stared at the girl and then with a flash, leapt out of the box and scampered onto the top of the wardrobe where it eyed her suspiciously.

Katie eyed it back. She needed to persuade it to leave as quickly as possible before Laura noticed it was there. She closed her eyes and concentrated on the space at the back of her head until the fizzing began in her arms and legs and warmth rushed through her body. She opened her eyes and could instantly sense the squirrel's fear and knew that it was male.

'It's OK,' Katie hissed. 'I rescued you. My name is Katie. I think we may have a problem. Would you mind coming down from the top of the wardrobe so we can talk?'

The squirrel did not come down. He looked as if intended to stay put. He sat upright on his back legs, balancing on his tail, and looking at Katie with unblinking black eyes. His nose twitched ceaselessly and in a flash of inspiration Katie grabbed a digestive biscuit and waved it at him. It worked. The squirrel began to move down the wardrobe door. Katie took a step forward. It was too soon! In a flash the squirrel had leapt to the top of the wardrobe once more. Katie sighed. She would have to engage deeply with the creature. She took a deep breath and within seconds the fizzy feeling started again in her stomach, and she could feel the anxiety of the creature in her room. She closed her eyes and began to focus on his feelings. Very soon she could hear the squirrel's thoughts; his fear that Katie was out to trap him, his confusion on being understood by a human and his conviction that the birds would be back for him at any moment. There was no way the squirrel was going to be caught holding a conversation with a human. His eyes darted about the room searching for the wretched birds, and then back again to look at the face of the skinny girl with short dirty blonde hair and a nose turned up at the end smothered with freckles.

'My name is Katie and I rescued you from those birds,' said Katie. 'The strange looking bird hypnotised you and put you into a deep sleep. You have to know as well, that the birds are waiting outside in the park. They followed us here.'

Suddenly Katie felt a strange sense of relief wash over her. She realised it had been more of a strain on her not to talk to the creature and that despite the fact it probably meant she was mad, it felt good to be talking to an animal again. She was glad she had listened to the squirrels in her old park. Communicating with the squirrel was more difficult than it was with Lottie; she had to focus very hard. After a while though she found she could read its thoughts and the chunters and clicks the squirrel made at the back of its throat began to make more sense to her. She looked up at the squirrel.

'By the way, you don't have to worry. I am talking to you in your language. I've always been able to speak to animals. I speak Dog beautifully and Sparrow, although I prefer Dove. I don't like Pigeon, mainly because it is so harsh and crude.'

'Don't talk to me about pigeons!' The squirrel immediately twitched his tail nervously. Now he'd done it.

Katie continued, feeling his anxiety. 'Oh, I hate them too, real scroungers the lot of them, always after your lunch, or pestering you for something. Squirrel, do you mind if I call you Patrick? I can sense you are a male squirrel and it feels easier for me as a human if I can give you a name?'

The squirrel did not reply.

Katie continued. 'Do you understand what is going on? I mean in the café I heard you and of course I understood you. I've been speaking Squirrel since I was five years old. When the waitress understood you, at first I thought she was afflicted like me, but now I am not so sure. I mean if she can hear Squirrel or understand it at least, why did she get so upset in front of all those people? It just doesn't make sense. I never let anyone know I can do Animal Talking if I can help it.'

Patrick just stared at her, his black eyes never leaving her face.

'Patrick, please believe me I am on your side.'

'They think I spoke in human tongue.'

Patrick hopped down from the wardrobe and scurried about looking for crumbs. The long sleep had left him feeling hungry, and hunger was, when all was said and done, far more urgent than fear. 'I can't reach the humans...only squirrels and ISP.'

'ISP?'

'Inter-species or ISP is how we reach other animals outside the squirrels. I have no idea why you can understand me or why I can understand you, but there you go, what do I know after all?!'

'Oh. How clever. I have never heard of that one before.' A thought sprung into Katie's head. 'Patrick, where you come from, are there others like me who can speak to your kind?'

Patrick stood up on his back legs, his black eyes darting around the room spying out more crumbs. Humans always left crumbs of food.

'No,' he said uninterestedly, 'can't say I've ever met any and I can't say I know anybody who has. You're the first.'

'Oh,' she said, disappointed.

She sat down on her bed. Cupping her chin in her hands, she thought deeply. There was a puzzle to be solved here. The birds and the bird-like creature believed Patrick had broken a taboo by thinking human. But he hadn't because he couldn't. Katie had heard him think Squirrel but the waitress had understood him also. Perhaps the waitress had always had the ability to Animal Talk but just never knew it until today? She fiddled with her hair thinking hard all the time and then chewed her thumb nail. As she did so she caught sight of her birthmark lying like a single railway track on her hand. It winked at her, reminding her of Nana's story. Perhaps Nana's story was connected in some odd way although Katie did not know how. Then she remembered the diary and a darker thought entered her head. No, it was far more likely that she was mad like Nana, thinking she could hear squirrels speak and other such nonsense. The resolution she had made in the basement of the Sanctuary came back to her and the relief she had felt in talking Squirrel evaporated; she had stop tuning in to Animal Talk. The sooner she got rid of the squirrel the better. Surely, all that was needed was for Katie to go outside and explain to the birds that Patrick had done no wrong—he had not broken any law. Then she would walk away and ignore any future sensations she had around animals and her ability to understand them. She would cure herself of this strange affliction, and get on with her new life as Laura's normal daughter, forget the squirrel and the strange birds and focus on school and making friends. She was about to explain this idea to Patrick, when an almighty thud against the window caused both of them to jump. Pressed against the window, shaking its head from the impact of body meeting glass, was a large grey pigeon. It shook its feathers, settled itself on the window sill and began to peck against the glass with its beak.

XXXI

Albion 23 A.D.

Brennus had begged Mortunda not to leave. It was the custom that daughters or sons left their tribes to train as a Seronydd at thirteen, but Mortunda was on the cusp of her twelfth year the day she set off for Mona with Lovernicus, Deseus and Sego.

The morning of her departure arrived on a cloudless pale sky awash with streaks of gold; the spring following the long hard winter of war was unusually warm. Purple crocus prodded their heads up through the earth and the crops growing in the fields around the oppida below were flourishing well already. Many of Brennus' people had returned to the lower lands and taken up their old familiar lives, relieved to resume their farming and their crafting, pleased to be back in their own houses, feeding their chickens and chastising their children. Brennus and his chief warriors remained on the fort with Sego to draw out the peace treaty with the Parisi. It had been a difficult time. Many Parisi had been killed in the battle and their heads were staked around the fort on long poles, their empty eyes looking across the hills of Brigante as tragic reminders of what happened if one dared to enter battle with the Brigante tribe. The hostages the vanquished King had sent across, some twenty young men and a few women were sullen and angry. Brennus had made the vow that his people would not attempt to take any more land, and the Seronydd elders had taken this promise to the Gods. Suspicion and deep mistrust glared in the eyes of the Parisi. Brennus felt the weight of Sequana's message heavy in his heart; sometimes he wished he did not know the message of the Gods. They asked him to pay a heavy price. If Brennus could not gain an alliance with the Parisi against Rome, then he knew his vow would be broken. The Brigante would be forced to invade again, this time not to take the narrow stretches of fertile land to feed their growing tribe but to conquer the entire territory and place Brennus on the throne. The hatred in the hostage's eyes told him in no uncertain terms that the Parisi King would not fight with him against Rome or anyone else; the Parisi would prefer to slay Brennus in his own bed! The shadow of the next war was already looming before him even as they signed the peace treaty.

Then of course, there was spring. Brennus greeted the coming of spring with mixed feelings; on one hand he was pleased to feel the warmth of the goddess on his back but on the other, it reminded him of Leticia. Leticia had loved spring; she had always rejoiced in the time for new beginnings and new life. Spring reminded Brennus that Leticia's life was no longer on the Middle Plane with him, but in the Lower Plane of ancestral souls and he ached to speak with her. His dreaming skills were weak so he had no access to her, no way of reaching out to her and talking with her. He was a man of the land and, although he was proud of his own warrior prowess, since Leticia had left him he longed to hear her voice and know what she was thinking. Brennus had consulted Sego of course, asked him to journey to the Lower Plane to seek Leticia's guidance on matters he felt unsure of, but he felt embarrassed to ask too many times; he did not want to appear desperate. Sego was unable to reach Leticia anyway. Despite several journeys, Sego had come back from his trance with nothing; it was almost as if Leticia had as much time for Sego in death as she had had in life. The only message Brennus received from the Lower Plane was silence. He sighed. His one link to Leticia was leaving him today; Mortunda his beloved daughter was about to travel to Mona and train as a Seronydd Seer. From today onwards, his only bond to his wife would be gone.

Brennus crossed the enclosure to the house. Mortunda was inside. He stood at the doorway watching her in the same way she had watched him on the night she made the Request. She looked so small, so fragile and yet so determined. He watched her busily loading her furs into her pack, sorting through her stones and then folding her tunics into a short neat pile, reading to pick up and pack alongside the furs. She stood up suddenly to stretch and gave a gasp of surprise.

'Father,' she said and ran towards him.

Brennus pinched her cheek.

'I have something for you,' he said. He took her by the hand and led her outside.

'Here,' he said simply.

Tethered to the trunk of an oak tree was a beautiful brown mare. Mortunda's eyes widened.

'She is your favourite,' she said shaking her head, 'I cannot take her!'

Brennus smiled,

'Oh yes you can,' he said, 'I want you to have her. She was also your mother's favourite horse and a part of me knows that through her, your mother will be with you at all times to keep a watchful eye over you.'

Mortunda buried her head against his broad chest.

'Thank you Father,' she said, her tears choking her throat. 'Mother is always with me. I dream of her all the time.'

Brennus stroked her hair, 'You are truly blessed then,' he said quietly.

'Are we almost ready?' a voice said behind them.

Mortunda lifted her head and looked up at her father.

Brennus nodded. Mortunda turned to Lovernicus,

'Almost,' she said, wiping her hand across her runny nose.

'First she has to say goodbye to Aed,' Brennus said, looking at Mortunda with one eyebrow raised.

Mortunda nodded and pulled herself away from her the warmth of her father's arms and ran across the grass to find her brother. 'You will find him by the chariot yard,' Brennus called after her. Mortunda raised her hand to show that she had heard. Lovernicus and Brennus watched her disappear across the enclosure towards the perimeter of the fort.

Brennus looked at Lovernicus.

'Walk with me to the ale house?' he asked.

The ale house was across the way from Brennus' residence in the part of the settlement reserved especially for festivities, dancing and rejoicing. Today the house smelt sweet; there had been fresh ale brewed recently and the barley used to make the ale was still warm and pulpy inside the oak barrels. The ale house itself was a rectangular house built of mud and stone with one chimney and a roof that had been assembled quickly, after the last one had burnt down due to an over excited display of drunken torch dancing. Brennus smiled wryly to himself as he remembered the incident. The culprit, a respected warrior with dubious dancing skills, had, with great cheers and encouragement from the crowd, balanced a lit torch on the end of his nose and leapt up too high. He had caught a piece of grass hanging from the ceiling and within moments the entire roof was covered in hungry leaping flames. Several barrels of ale were wasted putting the fire out but luckily no one was hurt. The dancer was not a popular man after that incident. Luckily he was able to make amends. In peace time when his warrior skills were not needed, he was a good house builder and he and his brother got to work the next day building a new roof and part of the walls. By the end of the fourth day, the tribe had their ale house back and all was forgiven.

Today several full oak barrels were lined up against the inner wall, waiting to be taken down to the oppida. The ale house was quiet at this time in the morning, only the birds rummaging in the rough thatch above disturbed the serenity of the place. Brennus filled two goblets with the warm brown frothy ale and handed one to Lovernicus.

'May Belisama bless us,' said Brennus raising his goblet to Lovernicus.

Lovernicus took the ale from Brennus, 'Why Belisama?' he asked curiously.

Brennus laughed,

'Mortunda likes Belisama,' he said. 'She collects her stones. She often says she would like some of Belisama's power for herself.'

'Does she indeed?' said Lovernicus. 'I wonder what your daughter would do with such power,' he added thoughtfully.

Brennus looked down at his goblet.

'I suppose that is partly what you will teach her in Mona?' Brennus said, 'How to use her connection with the spirits.'

'Ah,' Lovernicus said, 'I think your daughter already knows how to connect with the spirits Brennus. It is her connection with the Gods that we must channel. That is far more powerful, and requires far greater skill.'

Brennus nodded.

'She is talented I think. Her mother always said so. I was blind to it for a long time.'

Lovernicus gulped some ale and leaned over to refill his goblet. 'Yes she is' he said. 'In Mona, Brennus, we will teach Mortunda how to fully use all of her talents. We will teach her how to journey to the Upper Plane to converse with the Gods. And as you said, we will teach her how to use her connection to the spirits.'

Lovernicus took a gulp of his ale and continued.

'Mortunda can already call upon the wisdom of the spirits that reside with us on the Middle Plane—I could sense that the first moment I saw her; the spirits were all around her. It is a remarkable feat for one so young. Her connection with the Gods needs to be refined. Once we have accomplished that we can then teach her to use that connection to heal. There are many broken bones and bruised souls out there waiting to be mended. The training is hard but Mortunda is gifted; the most gifted I have seen in a long time. She will learn quickly.'

Brennus was quiet.

'It is odd that Sego always advised me that Mortunda was not to be chosen as a Seronydd pupil,' he said after a moment. 'I was, of course, always relieved to hear his advice for selfish reasons perhaps; I did not want Mortunda to leave us. Yet I can't help wondering why Sego did not see things the way you have?'

Lovernicus said nothing to this, but his face darkened at the mention of Sego's name. Brennus refilled his goblet, splashing some of the honeyed liquor on his hand. He licked it off, and drank from his cup, letting out a small belch when he had finished.

'Tell me Brennus, what do you think of your son?' Lovernicus asked.

'Aed? Why he is a good lad, proud and trustworthy.'

Brennus frowned and looked at the ground.

'He is not a natural King I fear. But Aed will be a fine diplomat, in many ways he is already. He has a silver tongue, people love and trust him and he is fair minded. Yet he lacks a killer instinct. He would not fare well on the battlefield and I fear he sees only the good in people. I am not convinced he would see betrayal until it was right upon him with a sword at his throat.'

Brennus glanced up at Lovernicus. 'Why do you ask?'

Lovernicus shrugged. 'I wondered perhaps, what will become of Aed now that Mortunda is to train with our order?'

Brennus gave a short laugh.

'I am not sure yet. I trust we will be appointing a new Seronydd elder soon and will request that he or she call upon the Gods for advice on the matter. Perhaps with more practise Aed will make a warrior, and I can certainly prepare him for the throne. The young woman he has chosen as a wife could, I suspect, make a good Queen. There is a strength about her, I can read it in her eyes. She would wear power well I think.'

The two men stood silently for a while.

'I always wanted Mortunda to be Queen,' Brennus said forlornly as if it were a secret confession.

Lovernicus nodded, 'Yes I know,' he said, adding, 'And you know the Seronydd ruling on such matters Brennus?'

Brennus nodded. 'I do,' he said, 'A Seronydd cannot become a king or queen. Once a child has embarked on the Seronydd path there is no turning back.'

Lovernicus looked Brennus in the eye. 'There is more,' he said, 'to do so is punishable by death.'

Brennus looked startled. 'I thought the Seronydd were forbidden to kill their own.'

Lovernicus placed his goblet on the ground.

'We are,' he replied. 'It is against the Seronydd Code to harm or kill another Seronydd, unless the Seronydd has betrayed their oath and placed the order at risk. When Mortunda reaches Mona she will be sworn in as a trainee Seronydd. Part of the oath a Seronydd takes is to promise that they will never use the knowledge for their own personal ends. To lead a tribe as a ruler would compromise that Code. Mortunda must also swear to never divulge the Seronydd knowledge with anyone outside of our order. This would compromise the very existence of the Seronydd.'

Brennus frowned, 'But Mortunda is a child,' he said. 'If she were to promise not to share what she learns then surely there is always time for her to change her mind if she were to decide the life is not for her?'

'No. You forget Brennus; it is the Gods who have chosen her, not the other way around. The line of connection between Mortunda and the Gods is a strong one. She cannot break this, it is impossible. It is stronger than the cord that binds a baby to its mother's womb, and just as vital to life. Mortunda has to become a Seronydd in the same way that she had to leave her mother's womb. It is inevitable.'

Brennus was silent.

Lovernicus placed his hand on the other man's shoulder.

'It's not all doom and gloom,' he laughed. 'Seronydd use the knowledge they receive to heal, and to teach the people how to understand the Gods. We do not keep the knowledge to ourselves—we use it to keep the connection between the planes open, to make sure we are all connected to the wisdom around us, both on this Middle Plane that we share with the spirits, and those planes that we journey to, in order to mend fragmented souls or seek guidance from our ancestors. We use the knowledge to interpret dreams. We play an important role for humanity. Without the Seronydd the world would stumble in darkness. You should be proud of your daughter.'

Brennus gave a half smile. 'She is stubborn, you know that don't you? You will have your work cut out for you.'

'Yes I have noticed,' Lovernicus said.

The two men were silent for a moment.

'One thing that does concern me,' Brennus said, 'is that Mortunda believes that Sequana told her that she will be Queen one day. I am afraid that she does not understand the full consequences of leaving here today. I think she believes she can return to take the throne and remain a Seronydd.'

He looked at Lovernicus anxiously, 'If this is not possible, then why did the Goddess lie to her?'

'The Goddess did not lie Brennus! Sometimes the true meaning of the Goddess takes time to unfold. The Goddess spoke of Mortunda being Queen of Brigante and beyond. It is my belief she did not mean in this plane, but another. Perhaps your daughter's destiny is to change the very course of Albion. We shall have to wait and see. But, Brennus please understand that the Seronydd order could never allow Mortunda to sit on the throne of Brigante. To do so would be to renege on her oath.'

Brennus nodded.

'You will tell her this is not possible? I do not want my daughter falling foul of any oath, Lovernicus. Seronydd or no Seronydd, I would have to kill anyone who as much as laid a finger on Mortunda.'

'That will not be necessary Brennus,' said Lovernicus. 'I will explain all to Mortunda, and that is a promise.'

Mortunda had felt a stab of guilt at the mention of Aed. Ever since his open declaration of courtship with Sirona, she had avoided him. Her jealousy had felt too overpowering to manage; like a growth gnawing at her stomach, eating her up. A terrible sickness seemed to rise in her, when she thought about them. Every time she had gone to find her brother, to talk with him or spend time with him Sirona was there, smiling smugly, her arms wrapped around her brother's waist, holding him possessively, interrupting Mortunda's conversation with constant pecks on Aed's lips. It made Mortunda feel invisible. She had tried greeting the pair of them as one person, to appear friendly and light hearted but her voice always gave her away; it came out thick with resentment; hoarse and unsteady and so she had avoided the canoodling pair as much as she could, choosing instead to spend time with her father and Giles.

However, Brennus was right. There was no way she could leave the tribe without saying goodbye. With a heavy heart she searched around the fort looking for her brother, hoping she would find him alone. She eventually found Aed leaning against the granary, chewing thoughtfully on a stalk of grass. She was glad to find him alone. Sirona was no where to be seen. He looked up as she approached and she was shocked to see tears in his usual cheerful green eyes.

'Aed?' she said, 'Are you crying?'

With a sudden movement he swept her off her feet in a bear-hug. 'Make sure you look after yourself,' he said, his voice muffled. 'I am going to miss you.'

Mortunda hugged him back, her eyes clouded with tears. 'I am going to miss you too Aed.'

Aed wiped his nose on his sleeve and looked at his sister. 'I guess Mother was right about you all along?' he said. 'She always knew you were destined to be a Seronydd.'

Mortunda smiled. 'Yes. But now the time has come, I am not sure I want to go. I feel scared Aed. What if I am making a mistake?'

'It's not a mistake Mortunda. It is what you have to do.'

Mortunda sniffed.

'I think that is right. But it means leaving everyone I love and I could be gone for a long time. When I come back everything here will have changed.'

She felt a wave of sadness rush over her and again a jolt of realisation that she really was going to leave her family behind and not know how they were, if they were well or sick or if they were safe. She felt dizzy and held onto Aed tightly. Aed kissed the top of her head.

'Things always change Mortunda, and change hurts sometimes.'

Mortunda sighed.

'I know,' she replied and then added sheepishly, 'Like Sirona. One day she's just a girl who I find slightly annoying and the next she's the person I hate more than anyone else in the camp. I feel very jealous of Sirona, Aed. I was so used to having you to myself.'

Aed held his sister away from him and looked into her eyes.

'I did realise,' he admitted, 'but you forget that Sirona is to be my wife, whereas you and I, we are joined by blood and blood is the strongest bond. You will always and forever be my sister.'

Mortunda laughed and hugged her brother tightly.

'I will be back Aed, I promise. The Goddess told me in my dream journey. I will return to Brigante the summer I turn eighteen. And you must promise never to forget me!'

Aed smiled, then joked, 'Forget you, never. Er, what's your name again?' Mortunda poked him in the ribs and then threw her arms around his waist and hugged him so tightly she thought her back would break.

XXXII

As soon as they left the settlement, passing through the outer wall of the fort and into the rugged countryside surrounding the Brigante homeland, Mortunda took off the crown her father had tenderly placed on her head before she left, and removed her Brigante cloak. From now on she would have to dress as a Seronydd in order to ensure safe passage through the territories of Albion. If other tribes recognised her as the daughter of King Brennus, her life would be in danger. She could be kidnapped. Be held for ransom in exchange for land and cattle; at worst she could be murdered. Although it would take days to pass through the entire Brigante land and into other tribal territory, Mortunda wished to prepare herself as soon as she could for the transformation from princess to trainee elder. She packed her crown into her saddlebag and donned the dark grey hooded cloak of the Seronydd. The material, of tough wool, felt heavy and alien. The hood chafed her skin. She pushed it away from her cheek, where it prickled, and resisted the urge to scratch her shoulders. Sego was watching her. He had noted her discomfort and obviously found it amusing. A flicker of contempt showed in his eyes. Blushing with a mixture of embarrassment and irritation, Mortunda pulled the hood around her face, determined to allow the material to chafe as much as possible so she could accustom herself to the harsh clothing of the order and show everyone, particularly Sego that she was prepared to do whatever it took in order to be a successful Seronydd. She kicked her horse and coaxed her forward leaving Sego riding behind her.

They travelled for five days before arriving at the outer reaches of the Brigante lands. They had met with nothing but kindness and hospitality on the way and had left each of the small settlements well rested, and with full stomachs. The battles with the neighbouring Parisi had been fought mainly in the north and the settlements in the south had not been unduly affected; the food stocks were high and the people were in good spirits. On the sixth day they reached the border with the Coritani. Mortunda felt nerves stir her belly. It was the first time she had travelled beyond the borders of her people's land and everything here felt different; the air smelt saltier, the sky held more clouds, which appeared to lie lower to the land; the landscape was flatter and even the trees seemed unfamiliar. She looked around seeking somewhere to hide in case of an ambush. In Brigante land the hill forts were plentiful, safe havens where the whole tribe could seek refuge in times of battle but in this land of wide open spaces she was not sure where they would hide should they be attacked. She felt uneasy and exposed; as if her skin had been turned inside out. She glanced at Lovernicus; the old man was her only hope. If any of her father's enemies guessed she was not Seronydd she was certain he would not be able to protect her. Deseus noticed her whitened face and clenched knuckles and he rode in closer to her.

'Don't worry' he said, a smile playing in his eyes. 'You don't look like a princess anymore. You have become almost as scruffy as me!' He shot out a bare foot, muddied and darkened from walking without shoes and grinned.

Mortunda gave a tight half smile. 'I suppose so,' she said ruefully, 'I hope I look the part.'

'Well you do, it's true,' he said, leaning towards her, 'Pooh, you even smell like a Seronydd!'

Mortunda laughed despite her fear. 'Are you trying to tell me that the Seronydd do not wash,' she said screwing up her nose.

'Of course we wash,' he said pretending to be insulted. 'I'd be quite happy not to ever, but Lovernicus makes sure I don't get too stinky.' He nodded his head at the old man, 'He's quite an old fusspot actually, it's only when we are travelling that he lets me get away with not bathing.'

The pair rode on in silence for a bit. 'How old are you Deseus?' Mortunda asked shyly.

Deseus smiled, 'I am almost fourteen summers old,' he replied proudly, 'soon I'll be old enough to be enlisted into a tribe of my own.' Mortunda looked across at the boy on her left. He had a lovely smile that showed a set of even white teeth; dark eyes and dirty blonde hair that insisted on falling forward into his eyes. He had a smattering of freckles on his broad nose.

'How long have you been training to be a Seronydd?' she said.

'Since I was eight,' Deseus said.

'Eight!' replied Mortunda. 'That is young isn't it? You must be very gifted.'

Deseus let out a snort of derision. 'Not at all!' he said. 'I am no where near as gifted as you are.'

His face grew sad, 'I came to train with the Seronydd because Lovernicus knew my mother. My father died when I was small and my mother was unwell. Lovernicus felt I could be moulded to the Seronydd ways. So when I was eight years old, my mother packed me a saddlebag and allowed Lovernicus to take me to Mona to train with the elders.'

Mortunda frowned, 'Was there no one else in your tribe that could take care of you?' she asked, thinking of her own people. In the Brigante it was common practise for children to live with different family members—aunts, uncles and foster parents—adults who would love the children like their own and be their guides through life. In times of war, children were often left without a mother or father, sometimes both, and so would enter the care of other adults. In the Brigante, the care of the children was seen as a responsibility that sat with the entire tribe. She could not imagine any child being sent away because there was no one to care for them.

Deseus shook his head. 'No. Apparently Lovernicus insisted I went to Mona to train. He said he could see something special in me, although I sometimes think I am a bit of a disappointment on that front.'

Deseus lowered his voice, 'I am not the best student,' he whispered.

Mortunda nodded. She wanted to ask what Lovernicus had seen in Deseus to make him want the boy to be a Seronydd, what calling the spirits had made upon the boy, but at that moment, Lovernicus turned his horse around and galloped back towards them.

'We need to rest,' he said. 'The horses are tired and we should all eat soon, and for the spirits' sakes boy, you need to find a river and have a bath. You are beginning to smell!'

The party stopped to rest in a field that bordered a forest. Mortunda could hear the running water of a river near by and longed to dip her sweaty body into the water and wash away the traces of dirt that had collected under the rough cloth of her Seronydd cloak. She tied her horse to a tree and came to sit down. Lovernicus came and sat beside her. 'You look deep in thought Mortunda,' he said.

Mortunda pulled a face, 'There is one thing you will learn quickly about me Lovernicus, and that is I am always deep in thought. My brother Aed used to tease me for it!'

Lovernicus smiled, 'A good trait for a Seronydd,' he replied. 'Now tell me what is on your mind?'

Mortunda drew breath. 'I am puzzling over how happy the people were in the south of the Brigante. They seemed more at ease with themselves than my people in the north. I mean they are all part of my father's Kingdom but they are also...' she struggled to find the right word, finally plumping for something that wasn't quite right but as near as she could possibly find, '...different.'

Lovernicus thought for a moment.

'I think,' he said, 'that your people in the north have endured great loss. War comes with a price Mortunda. Men may boast about the glory of the sword but when it comes to the fields of battle and the likelihood they will feel the blade cut through their flesh to bone, the glory suddenly fades. If men were honest they would talk of fear and terror, not glory.'

Mortunda thought for a while. 'I suppose it is not easy to forget what you see in battle is it?' She was thinking of Giles. His smile had faded since his son died; the light had gone from his eyes and for days after he had hardly spoken. He had walked around the settlement and his eyes had seemed somehow dead, expressionless and empty.

'It is impossible to erase, Mortunda,' Lovernicus continued. 'War, once waged, leaves behind it deep wounds that never quite heal; that stain the rivers, the trees, the sky with blood. War spreads through and saturates everything. The memories of seeing people die in pain, of the looks on the faces of those you cut down stay with you. War is passed on Mortunda. A father's pain will be passed to his children and that pain in turn goes down the line. Pain can so easily be transformed to anger and anger to more war. It falls to us, the Seronydd, to help men avoid war. Too many times we fail.' He looked away saddened.

Mortunda was quiet for a moment. 'My father wished for me to be a warrior. It never felt right.' She thought of Aed, and shivered, 'I hope my brother stays safe. Somehow I feel he should be a travelling poet and storyteller rather than warrior. He is too gentle to fight.'

'Maybe, but he is still young and there is time for him to learn, and learn he will, for your father is a persistent man. The Brigante has big plans

I suspect. He will want Aed to involve himself in these. They have taken half of the Parisi lands and even now your father is looking to the land we have just travelled through, the land of the Coritani. Torrance will, I fear, persuade him that further conquest is necessary.'

'Why did you not tell him the true words of the Goddess?' Mortunda asked shyly.

'Ah,' said Lovernicus, 'I have been waiting for that question.'

He took a deep breath.

'He could not hear it Mortunda. And sometimes we have to allow men to make their own mistakes.

Mortunda looked horrified. 'But he will die!' she gasped. 'How can you allow him to follow a path that is so clearly the opposite of what was advised knowing that it could mean the death if him and maybe everyone in the tribe?'

Lovernicus smiled. 'Ah Mortunda,' he said affectionately, 'you misunderstand the nature of the Seronydd. We are not here to order men around and neither can we control their actions. Men have to make their own destinies. You have to understand that we all find our path towards the Gods in the end. The stars shape us, they tell us of our strengths, and our capabilities, but all they can offer us are our choices. The Seronydd can only serve in the same way. We are of the stars Mortunda. Now come, we must eat and then move on. We have a long way to travel before night falls.'

Lovernicus stood up and brushed himself down. He patted Mortunda on the head and walked away. Mortunda looked across to the horizon. The land had grown flatter and the sun had grown red and was resting on a straight line of fields. She had never seen land so flat and empty. The vast expanse of green and yellow stretched before her and threatened to swallow her up. She had lived in the hills and had grown accustomed to their undulations; the way they marked the land and gave it character and height. In the north, the land could be named by the hills it sat beneath. This place seemed like a soulless wasteland that appeared to stretch on and on forever. Mortunda suddenly wanted to flee. The flesh on her arms prickled with uncertainty.

They rode on until the moon tipped over the edge of the sky, and then stopped to camp on the edge of thick forest land. As the night drew in Sego set about lighting a fire. Mortunda gratefully warmed herself by it. The night promised to be a cold one and she could already feel the chill in her hands and feet.

They unpacked the saddlebags and laid out their rugs of fur and skin. Mortunda took out a crumpled dress and rolled it into a pillow for her head. She unravelled a second fur and laid it on the one already on the ground. It would suffice easily as a blanket and should ward off the cold. She hoped that she would sleep well. She watched Sego unpack the provisions kindly given to them by the last settlement they stayed in and lay them out before the group. He broke off pieces of bread and uncorked the carafe of ale. He passed the bread around the group and took deep swigs of the sweetened ale, finally stopping to belch loudly. He wiped the top of the carafe and passed it to Lovernicus who drank equally deeply upon the liquid before passing it on to Deseus and then Mortunda. The group ate hungrily upon the bread, chunks of pork and crisp apples. When they were full they repacked the remaining provisions into the saddlebags.

Sego went off to the trees and found more fallen branches and twigs to fuel the fire and soon the party were being warmed by tall blazing flames. Gradually their eyes grew heavy. Feeling tired from the journey and relaxed by the heavy food and ale, as the moon sailed to centre stage in the night sky, all four fell into a deep sleep.

XXXIII

Lovernicus awoke just as dawn was breaking. He listened carefully to the bird song emanating from the trees and caught word of some disturbance going on in the forest. 'What is it?' he asked.

The birds replied, 'We are not sure Lovernicus, but we are afraid.'

Lovernicus looked at Mortunda, Sego and Deseus; all three were still sleeping. He heard the bird song again,

'Lovernicus it is worse than we feared.'

Steadying his nerves, Lovernicus crossed the field to the outskirts of the trees and slowly entered the forest. The bird chatter grew louder,

'Be careful Lovernicus, be careful.'

Lovernicus kept his hand on his sword and deftly picked his way across the bracken and fallen leaves, taking great care not to make a sound. A badger bravely scurried past him, and Lovernicus immediately tuned into the creature's fear. There was something alien in the forest, something that should not be present in the Middle Plane. Something dark and sinister had crossed over. He caught the scent immediately, a pungent sickly sweet smell that filled his nostrils and coated the back of his throat. A sense of foreboding crept over him. He scanned the forest and amongst the lower branches saw shadows dart under trees and disappear into the thicker parts of the forest; goblins were present in the woods, agents of Travellers turned bad, probably Travellers working for the God that could not be trusted. A sound made his ears tingle. An owl hooted, once then twice and then again. Lovernicus focused his mind into the tone of the hoots. 'What can you tell me?' he asked with his mind.

The owl answered, 'Something strange is here. I have seen it. Dark shadows crossed the forest and a tall gangly creature the size of a young tree, with arms like branches and legs that could run like wind. It smelt bad.'

Lovernicus felt his heart contract wildly.

The Chief Traveller, the one that served the enemy of the Jewel had crossed into the Middle Plane and had taken a physical form. This was unknown! Such a law had never been broken. Lovernicus felt panic fill his lungs. Things were a lot worse than he had feared. If the God had granted his Chief Traveller a physical body on the Middle Plane, then it meant they were here in the woods right now. They had been followed and Lovernicus knew why. He turned and quickly made his way back to the others, running across the field to where his horse was tethered to a tree. He checked his baggage and felt for the Jewel wrapped in its cloths. He found it. It remained cold and silent, undisturbed by those who sought it. They had to get out of there as fast as possible and return the Jewel to Mona.

Quickly he woke the others; 'We should move on,' he said. 'The Cornvoii are aware we are here.'

Sego blinked his eyes open, sat up and looked at Lovernicus. 'We are travelling Seronydd,' he said, confused. 'There is nothing unusual about our presence. The Cornvoii meet Seronydd often in these parts.'

Lovernicus dismissed Sego's words with an impatient shake of his hand. 'These are strange times Sego,' said Lovernicus shortly, 'I would rather be gone by the time they arrive and I would rather you not question my authority.' Anger flashed in the old man's eyes. 'Now do as I say.'

Sego lowered his eyes and tightened his jaw.

'I apologise Lovernicus,' Sego said, 'of course we shall leave immediately.'

Lovernicus began gathering the bedding and commanding the party to pack up and mount their horses. Deseus rubbed his eyes and yawned. He looked across at Mortunda, 'What's going on?' he mouthed silently.

Mortunda shrugged.

Lovernicus clapped his hands loudly, 'Deseus you stupid boy, will you get up and get moving!'

Deseus, shocked by Lovernicus' uncharacteristic outburst of impatience, hurriedly stood up, brushed himself down and gathered up his belongings. Within a short space of time, the party had mounted their horses and were galloping across the fields.

Lovernicus thought quickly. He had underestimated their persistence. More importantly he had failed to understand the dangers of bringing the Jewel with him to Brigante. How stupid he had been! Yet he reasoned silently, he had had no choice but to bring it with him. For many moons now he had known it was no longer safe in Mona without his being there. Daily he had grown aware that the Jewel was in danger of being found, and the Jewel had known it too. Several times, it had burned brightly and thrown its rays of red light across the temple with no calling needed from Lovernicus. It was trying to tell him something. Strangely on the day they left for the tribal lands of the north, Lovernicus also knew he would need the Jewel with him for some other purpose than merely keeping it safe. He had not known what that purpose was until Mortunda made the Request. It appeared that in some way that Lovernicus did not yet understand, the fate of Mortunda, Albion and the Jewel were all connected. The Jewel had saved both him and Mortunda from annihilation inside the Dream Forest, yet being open had allowed its enemies to enter Mortunda's vision. This had never happened before. Only the God or Goddess requesting the hearing could enter the vision, but in Mortunda's case an enemy had broken through and now these same enemies were present in the Middle Plane. The enemies of the Jewel were growing in strength. The power of the Seronydd was waning on so many fronts; increasingly many of the southern tribes looked towards Rome as the bearer of peace and bringer of prosperity—if Rome were to conquer the tribes of Albion, what would happen to the Seronydd then; what would they do with the Jewel? They would not understand its power; they would not be able to protect it! It would be handed to the enemy. Already, Lovernicus could feel the clammy skin of a goblin hand upon his back and the poisonous breath of a Traveller blowing down his neck. Their presence was physical even from this distance. He pressed his leg against the bag containing the Jewel and begged the spirits that had protected it for so long, to help them return it safely to Mona, unseen by its enemies. If he could get to Mona they could formulate a plan but they had to be quick. Time had grown thinner in these last few days and darker forces had grown stronger. He thought of the Upper Plane, the land of the Gods and knew instinctively that a great war was brewing there, a war that would determine the fate of humanity for many ages to come. If the Gods of the Jewel lost...

Lovernicus shivered; he could not bear to think of the terrible consequences. The Gwr Doeth of the Seronydd, as appointed Keeper of the Jewel, had kept the channel between the Gods and men open through the ages, but something had weakened them, and strengthened the one God that would destroy them all. Lovernicus pushed his horse to gallop faster and the others followed, breathless and alarmed by the old man's obvious and uncharacteristic panic.

XXXIV

They galloped through the fields, avoiding forest land and sticking to the wide open meadows. Eventually the horses tired and slowed to a trot. Lovernicus pulled his horse back so he was riding beside his companions. They rode side by side for a short time in silence.

Eventually Lovernicus spoke. 'I think we will touch on the edge of the Cornvoii's main settlement and cross the river there. There is someone I know who will lend us his *curragh*. We can also rest a while there. I believe we should travel across the mountains to Mona,' he said.

Sego looked thoughtful. 'I thought you were afraid of meeting the Cornvoii. Crossing the land to the river will deliver us straight to them.'

'Only a few Cornvoii are enemies, Sego,' said Lovernicus shortly. 'Mainly they remain friends of the Seronydd. They have not sold out to Rome just yet. No, let us have hope. If we focus on tracking the river we will pass by the Cornvoii and eventually cross to the lands of the Ordovician. From there we can travel home to Mona.'

Mortunda glanced at Sego watching his reaction to Lovernicus' words. It was obvious that Sego felt irritated by the old man, and embarrassed at having been spoken to so sharply. She saw that Sego dropped behind her and Deseus so that he was riding at the very back of the party. She could feel his eyes boring into the back of her. Once again she felt his contempt for her. She glanced backwards and as she suspected, Sego was glaring at both her and Deseus as if their very forms irritated him. Physically he could crush them all in his bear like hands, but Mortunda guessed that would be too messy and far beneath him. No, she could imagine Sego destroying them in far cleverer, more subtle ways. She pressed her knees in against her horse's flanks and coaxed him to speed up so she was riding closer to Lovernicus, away from Sego. Once again she questioned how it was that he had come to train as a Seronydd elder. She decided she would ask Deseus the next time they stopped. She would also ask the boy why he had been chosen as well. It had begun to appear to Mortunda that the choosing of Seronydd was not as straightforward as she had always been led to believe.

Deseus certainly did not give the impression of ever feeling that he had been hand-picked by the spirits and Sego looked as if he would be happier on the battlefield.

Sego trailed behind Lovernicus and the two youngsters, watching them and thinking. He watched Deseus riding happily next to his beloved master Lovernicus and new friend Mortunda, and remembered back to when he first came from his land, Catuvellauni, to Mona to train as a Seronydd. Sego had shared the same enthusiasm and excitement as the two young people he now watched. Yet his excitement came from a different source. He came to Mona to escape his past, to have a chance to acquire self respect, not because of some deep wish to become a spiritual elder. He smiled to himself as he looked upon Deseus's thin undeveloped frame. He had looked so different from the skinny boy upfront; Sego had been huge even as a child. His large arms, strong legs and barrel of a chest had marked him out as a fighter immediately.

'Sego, our warrior,' his father had called him right from being a baby barely out of his mothers womb,

'Sego will fight for the Catuvellauni until every last drop of our enemies' blood has been spilt.' When Sego was merely five summers old, his father had paraded around the settlement with Sego on his shoulders boasting how his son would one day fight alongside the King of the Catuvellauni and single-handedly take the lands of their enemies. Most people smiled and ignored Sego's father; the man was a powerful warrior, but away from the battlefield he was a simple man with limited farming skills. When times were peaceful amongst the Catuvellauni, Sego's father could be found drinking ale and brawling with his friends. It was well known that the father would hit the mother. Sego recalled his mother's bruised eyes and once a broken hand when she had tried to defend herself against her husband's drunken advances. People gossiped about how the son would no doubt follow in his father's ways, for the young Sego did not exhibit any traits to suggest otherwise. Sego, however, was afraid of his father and had no wish to be like him. In many ways he despised him.

All that changed the day he saw him prepare for battle.

The battleground transformed the rough bad tempered man Sego knew as his father. His father's beard had been tied in preparation for battle and his face painted in bright blue woad, and a dye made from red berries and mud. On his head his mother had placed a richly decorated silver helmet with concentric swirls and the mark of the Catuvellauni, a gold embossed *curragh*. His body was left naked and painted the same blue woad his mother had used for his face. Sego watched as his father lifted his arms whilst his mother tenderly decorated his father's skin with the dye, moving over the arms, to his fingers, then down to his chest and stomach, legs and feet. His father had become an animal; muscle and skin glistened through the blue and white teeth shone out of a blue painted face. He looked both terrifying and beautiful. The scene left an indelible impression upon Sego's mind. For the first time ever, he longed to be like his father. Before him stood a Catuvellauni warrior, someone his mother could be proud of. From that day onward Sego swallowed his dislike for his father and began to believe that the contempt people clearly felt for him in peacetime was unearned and unfair. He began to allow his father to teach him sword skills and to perfect the chant of a warrior as he entered battle. He watched his father carefully; whereas once he thought of his father's brawling as crude and showy, he soon learned there was skill to the way he tackled and threw his opponents upon the floor, standing on their neck until they desperately surrendered. Sego learned all he could and soon he too could fight almost as well. He relished the praise his father heaped upon him.

Unlike his father however, Sego never neglected farming and nor did he ever strike a woman. On some level he understood the pain his father inflicted on his mother and their household by not attending to the land. The family needed to eat, and Sego's mother valued the respect of the small settlement they lived on and wished for her family to play an equal role in the community. As well as tending the land and feeding the pigs, she was a valued midwife and delivered many of the babies born there. This brought in food and clothing. Sego played a large share in helping his mother tend the land, and when his farming work was done, and if his father was sober enough, he practised his battle skills with him and perfected the art of charioteering and sword play. Then war broke and it was time for Sego to fight.

He relished the rush and fear he felt in his belly the first time he went into battle alongside his Catuvellauni people. He remembered the time in great detail. The sky had been a deep blue and the fields were full. It had been a good summer for his settlement and food was plentiful, but the

Catuvellauni had been plagued by raiders from neighbouring Atrebate, intent on stealing food and cattle. Then the Atrebate king declared a large settlement on the southern border to be Atrebate land and moved his warriors in, not merely to steal food but to slaughter men asleep in their beds, and to seize their families and belongings. He had offered the remaining women and children as ransom for the land, confident that Cunobelin, King of the Catuvellauni would be far too busy securing the rich lands he had stolen that same summer from the Trinovante, to worry about a small handful of farmers. Verica, the King of Atrebate, was young and arrogant. He had a sister, a beautiful woman with hair the colour of sun-kissed wheat. Maybe he had felt his sister's beauty would captivate Cunobelin—some had suggested Verica hoped Cunobelin would woo his sister, bring her into the Catuvellauni camp, and make her his wife. Through his sister, Verica could wage control over the actions of the Catuvellauni. He could not have been more wrong.

Cunobelin waged a bloody battle against him and the Atrebate were badly beaten. The battle was hard and exhausting. Sego came home from battle, returning to the hill fort where Cunobelin held court, too rigid with shock to speak. He had seen many men and women slaughtered; their deaths had been agonising. Yet the worst for Sego was witnessing the cutting off of the heads.

He had seen decapitated heads before, of course, as a young child watching the warriors bringing them back to the settlement, holding them up proudly, for all to see, held by their hair, the skin of the neck still pink, streaked with traces of blood and ragged, eyes still open. Then they had seemed somehow not to be real. Sego had never associated the dead heads with once alive people like him, or his mother or father. They were just enemy 'heads.' Yet to be there at the point of the slaying had left Sego reeling with nausea and fear. He watched his father wielding his sword, crashing down on the enemy, and gasped as he heard the sick thud of the head hitting the ground followed shortly by the still twitching body. He knew of course that the soul of a person lived in the head and wondered whether he would see it rise and leave, but he could not. There was nothing there. Just a body, its legs and arms thrashing about and a head, its hair still warm, the lips still pink and the eyes open and staring wildly; then the silence that followed and the greying of the skin. Life had simply gone. Sego was only sixteen summers old and he did kill that day; fear for his life and a fierce protectiveness for his father and their way of life carried him through the battle; anger rushed through his blood, powering his muscles, his limbs and allowing him to kill. He plunged his sword deep into many sweating, labouring breasts, cut Atrebate men and women from their horses, but he could not sever their heads. Every time he raised his sword to do so, his arm trembled and his stomach grew sick. He left the slain to die slowly on the ground, intact. Sego went home with the victorious Catuvellauni a changed boy, but not as the hero his father had hoped for. His father rode in silence beside him and Sego could feel his disappointment seeping through him like persistent rain. His son had killed but had nothing to show for it; no trophies to bring home. However, what was worse was the fact that he had left those he had killed with their souls still in the living realm. This would bring bad omens to the Catuvellauni; the souls of the dead would walk the Middle Plane and haunt them forever. Sego had brought shame and ill fortune upon the tribe.

When they reached the hill fort, his father abandoned him, turned his back on his son and walked away. Sego was left miserable and angry at himself for being such a coward. It was while he was in the camp that Sego first caught sight of King Cunobelin. He was a young king then; a tall man with dark hair and wild beard, and he spoke with a fluidity and passion Sego had never heard before. His voice thundered across the heads of the gathered warriors as he thanked them for their courage and promised more killing, on which the fighters still stained with blood and sweat from the battle just gone, roared in joy.

Sego joined in the feasting that night but with a heavy heart. His father had still not spoken to him and he felt a longing for his mother's comforting arms and loving voice. He would not see her for another few days yet. He saw his father becoming progressively looser on sweet ale; he was now doing a carousel with a plump, equally drunken, woman that Sego did not recognise. There was no hope of dragging him away from the merriment of victory; his wife would just have to wait for word that her husband and son were still alive. Sego sat in the midst of the celebration, surrounded by laughter and drunken brawling, a pretend smile on his face whilst inside his heart bled. He could not understand why he had been unable to bring home the heads of those he killed. He felt the heat of self loathing flush through him. He would have been lifted high upon the shoulders of his father and his neighbours if he had just been able to do what all warriors must do; remove the head of those they kill; already several had been staked above the settlement gate, their empty eyes staring out at the lush green living fields of Catuvellauni. Only Sego's trophies were missing. Again a wave of anger swept over him; he should be here as a warrior amongst warriors, glorying in the showers of praise, bathing in the waters of his fathers love and admiration; dancing with girls and laughing with his friends. Instead he was alone, shunned and ignored.

'You seem preoccupied,' a voice had said. Turning around Sego saw a young man in Seronydd clothing, looking at him quizzically. Sego shrugged, 'Maybe I am,' he replied, wishing the man would go away and leave him to sink even deeper into his own misery.

'Here,' said the man, and handed him a cup of ale. 'Drink this, you'll feel better.'

Sego took the cup and swigged hard. Immediately he felt the effects of the alcohol softening his muscles and sedating his angry thoughts. 'Thanks,' he muttered.

The young man smiled. 'So Chief Cunobelin is happy,' continued the young man, obviously determined to squeeze a conversation out of the grumpy sullen youth sat beside him, 'The Atrebate are thwarted for another day and Cunobelin can sleep peacefully in his bed.'

Sego looked sharply at the young man. There was something inherently disrespectful about the way he spoke of Cunobelin. This in itself did not worry Sego unduly; the Catuvellauni people had long held a tradition of not placing their elected kings on too high a pedestal; it was healthy to mock rulers when necessary, but nevertheless the remark did intrigue him. This Seronydd elder, though young, had arrogance quite unseen before by Sego. The Seronydd had in fact, always appeared in Sego's eyes as pious and without humour; quick to tell tribesmen and women to respect their rulers but happier to shirk from battle. This one appeared, unnaturally, to enjoy poking fun at the tribe's elected King. He felt curious and pressed the young Seronydd elder.

'I hardly think we fought a battle just so that *King* Cunobelin can sleep well at night,' he said. 'I thought we fought for our land.'

The Seronydd laughed; 'That is one interpretation I suppose,' he said, taking another long drink from the cup. Sego sat up tall and looked at him with incredulity.

'What are you suggesting? You are saying worrying things Seronydd; we are in a time of war. I hardly think it is your place to cast doubt on King Cunobelin's motives!'

The Seronydd laughed at Sego, and made as if to push him playfully on the shoulder. Instinctively Sego's fist came up and punched his hand out of the way.

'Ow!' howled the Seronydd. 'You are far too quick with your anger. You should have fought today and used up your anger on the battlefield!'

Sego glared at him. His interest was rapidly turning to intense dislike for the Seronydd, who was clearly a fool. He also did not need reminding of the battle. As if he could forget. Another wave of pain ran through him.

'Go away and leave me to my thoughts,' he snapped.

He turned his back on the young Seronydd and stared moodily into the distance. He turned the Seronydd's words over and over in his head and thought on how little he, Sego, really understood the world of men. His father had cast him aside, he had proven to be a useless warrior and now someone, a Seronydd no other, was mooting the possibility that it had all been for nothing. He kicked at the grass.

'I'm sorry,' said the Seronydd. 'I was jesting with you and perhaps looking for some light relief amongst all this frantic joviality. I did not mean to offend you. You looked troubled.'

Sego ignored him.

'My name is Alvaris by the way. What is your name?'

Sego turned back to face Alvaris. The Seronydd elder was probably only a few summers older than Sego, a faint beard shadowed his chin and his eyes were the keenest grey. He smiled showing straight teeth and a dimple formed in his cheeks. Sego nodded in greeting. Perhaps he had been too harsh. Maybe he could spend some time with Alvaris, although the Seronydd were not his usual choice of company, it had to be better than sitting alone stewing in his own despair. He glanced over at his father a few steps away, lying now on the grass cavorting in a highly familiar way with the woman he had been dancing with earlier.

'Sego,' he said and outstretched his hand in a reluctant, half hearted greeting.

As the evening wore on, the two young men drank a lot more ale. Sego found himself pouring his heart out to the fledgling Seronydd; Alvaris had only joined the Seronydd the summer before and remarkably, he hadn't lost his sense of humour. He also proved himself to be a keen listener as Sego told him of his father's disappointment and disgust for Sego's cowardice. He explained how his stomach churned and how his arm had been paralysed when he had tried to bring his sword down upon his slain enemy's head.

Alvaris supped his ale. 'Hmm,' he remarked, 'maybe it is not cowardice but knowledge you displayed Sego.'

Sego shot him a contemptuous look,

'Knowledge, huh. You Seronydd are full of knowledge but you rely on the warriors to protect you. Knowledge doesn't keep our enemies away, only the sword.'

'Ah,' replied Alvaris, drunkenly holding up his finger as a point of emphasis, 'that is a common myth but unfounded in reality. The Seronydd can fight when they have to. No, Sego, my point is this—' He paused to let out an almighty belch and Sego could not help but grin.

'That is a good point,' he smirked, 'Even if it was a bit smelly.'

Alvaris beamed, 'That is nothing. You should hear me fart,' he said and lifted his rear off the grass and let rip a shot of gas. The pair rolled about laughing helplessly holding their sides and wiping the tears away from their eyes. Eventually they regained their composure and Alvaris continued.

'What I am trying to say dear friend,' he said, 'is that maybe you understood what the average warrior sometimes fails to comprehend. The fact is this; the soul resides in the head and to release it is an act of wonder. Maybe, just maybe, you knew what you were doing and could not bring yourself to do it lightly.'

Sego snorted. 'I know where the soul resides,' he shouted, 'Everyone knows that. Tell me something I don't know!'

'Ok,' said Alvaris, 'well tomorrow morning when all the warriors are nursing their sore heads and queasy stomachs, the Seronydd will clear this mess up.'

Sego looked around at the empty barrels of ale lying on their sides but Alvaris shook his head.

'I don't mean that mess,' he said, 'I mean the mess out there!' He pointed to the horizon, in the direction of the battlefield. He took a swig of ale. 'Tomorrow we will take our journeying tools and appease the spirits. We will release any souls that are still trapped in broken bodies and attend the funeral rites of the dead. The Seronydd will return harmony to the pain and upset that war brings to this land. Cunobelin may have won new lands but it will be the Seronydd that will restore the spirit.'

Alvaris leaned in to face Sego so closely that their noses were almost touching, his tongue made loose by the ale.

'If you want real power and glory my friend, then train to be a Seronydd. Follow in my footsteps. It is we who hold the real power.'

Sego looked at Alvaris dubiously. 'What power?' he slurred.

'I can see you doubt me my friend. If you need evidence, then take a look at your King. Who has his ear right now? Is it a warrior or is it a Seronydd?'

Sego looked across at Cunobelin. The King was standing on higher ground above the revellers, listening intently to a tall, slim, red-haired Seronydd elder, nodding gravely at his words. Sego stared, trying to focus on the Seronydd elder. He had never seen him before.

Alvaris grinned. 'That is Borvo, my cousin,' he said proudly.

'He has just been appointed to your tribe as chief elder. He will have the ear of your King for many moons to come. Some say that one day soon, he will be the Gwr Doeth of all the Seronyddion.'

Sego frowned, 'Haven't the Seronydd just appointed their lead elder?' he asked.

Alvaris snorted. 'Yes!' he replied. 'They have! Lovernicus an elder from one of the northern tribes has just been appointed, but...,' and Alvaris leaned in yet closer to Sego and lowered his voice so he was barely audible, 'not all of us agree with the decision to appoint Lovernicus. He is of the old school. Some of us say that he is out of touch with the needs of the tribes. Lovernicus is a bit, how shall we say, serious, a little bit removed from the needs of men.' Alvaris tapped his nose and grinned drunkenly at his new friend.

Sego shrugged. He was not that interested in the machinations of Seronydd politics, but he repeated Alvaris words in his head, 'If you want real power and glory my friend, then train to be a Seronydd.'

He looked at Cunobelin again. His head was bent inwards to the elder Borvo, his arms clasped behind his back and a deep frown creased his forehead. Alvaris was right. It was not a warrior who had won the attentions of the King, but a Seronydd. Sego knew then with a clarity he had never experienced before that he would be far wiser to train his mind than his body. He turned to Alvaris.

'But how can anyone like me ever hope to train as a Seronydd?'

Alvaris raised his eyebrows and then smiled. 'Leave it to me,' he said. 'I will nominate you through my cousin and your King will be delighted. It is known to our order that Cunobelin is never happier than when his children are appointed as Seronydd.'

Sego leaned up on his elbow and looked Alvaris in the eye.

'You would do that for me?' he asked with incredulity. 'But why?'

Alvaris hiccoughed. 'Let's just say that you can never have too many friends in this world Sego,' he replied. Again, he lowered his voice to barely a whisper. 'All I ask of you, in return, is that you do not forget me or my cousin. We certainly will not forget you.'

Sego nodded gratefully. He had his way out, a path to restoring some glory and pride for himself. The next day, he declared his wish to train with the Seronydd. He was accepted a few days later. He never spoke to his father again.

XXXV

These memories drifted through Sego's mind as he rode behind the rest of the party. He had not thought of home for a long time and felt a pang of sadness. He remembered his mother; the way her hair had fallen across her eyes, the fine lines around her mouth, the unevenness of her teeth. He wondered whether she was still alive and whether she had questioned his father about her son's sudden decision to go to Mona. She may have demanded to know why her husband had come home from battle without their son; maybe his father had told her that Sego had been killed and for years she had mourned the loss of a son. Inwardly Sego shrugged; he would never know and he could not allow his feelings of regret and loss to cloud their plans. Not when they were so close to realising them. Borvo had been very specific about this. Nothing must stand in their way.

At midday the party stopped by the river. The place where they would cross by *curragh* was further south but the horses needed to drink and rest. Their flanks glistened with beads of opaque sweat and one of the mares had a loose shoe. Mortunda was grateful for the break. The muscles in her legs and back ached from the hard riding of the last few days and she had not slept properly since leaving her fathers main settlement. She needed a reprieve from the relentless physical activity and longed to be able to lie down and close her eyes, falling into a deep undisturbed slumber. She thought of her warm bed back at home and the sadness at leaving her family and friends welled up into her chest and pricked at her eyes. Making her way to the river, Mortunda knelt on the bank and gazed at her reflection in the water. She saw tired dark rings under her eyes and a small pinched face now streaked with tears. Taking a deep breath she reminded herself that this was her destiny and her choice. She had to be brave; it was what Brennus would expect of his daughter. She cupped her hands and scooped up the clear river water, splashing it over her face. The water was icy sharp and took her breath away.

'I expect it is hard for someone like you to tolerate such privations. Cold water is not what a Princess is used to,' said a voice behind her.

Mortunda looked up. Sego towered above her his sword drawn. She glanced nervously at the sword and then back to Sego. His eyes were hard and unsmiling. 'No one to heat your water for you or ensure your sleep remains uninterrupted. I should imagine also that you are not used to sleeping with the stars for company Princess.'

Mortunda could feel her heart beating hard in her chest.

'I am very used to the cold of the river Sego,' she replied hesitantly. 'My brother and I have swum many times in the river close to my father's settlement and we have slept outside on many occasions. I am well accustomed to the company of stars.'

Mortunda watched his eyes narrow at her response. His dark eyebrows knitted together in his frown and his sharp thin lips turned down. Sego did not like her, and although Mortunda was used to other children displaying caution and suspicion around her, she was accustomed to having the admiration and respect of adults. She could not fathom why Sego disliked her so and why his dislike was so strong that it clearly bordered on hatred. She looked around to see where Lovernicus was, hoping he would appear from behind a tree or bush and rescue her from the cold man looming above her. Sego continued to stare at her.

'People say you have powers Mortunda,' he said, his lip curling in a sneer. 'Well let us see how you progress now you are in the company of others like yourself. Do not expect to be treated with undue kindness child. The way of the Seronydd is a hard one. It will be interesting watching how you fare away from your father.'

He turned on his heel and walked away, his large feet crunching on the ground, ducking his huge head under the trees and making his way back to the horses. Mortunda could feel her heart thundering against her ribs. She quickly splashed more water onto her face to wash away the gloom she felt descending on her. It had been a mistake to come here. She should have stayed with her father and taken the throne as he wanted. At least she was not hated there; back home she had a life and a family. Now she had no one.

'Do not heed him Mortunda,' she heard someone say.

She turned around quickly to see Deseus standing behind her.

'Deseus,' Mortunda stammered, 'How long have you been standing there?'

Deseus looked down at his feet.

'Quite a while,' he admitted. 'I followed you to offer you some food and water. I thought you looked hungry and tired. I remembered how I felt when I first left home to join the Seronydd. It seemed the journey would never end! So I thought I would just see how you are.'

He blushed and briefly looked away.

Mortunda smiled and felt comforted by these early signs of friendship and welcome being offered to her.

'Thank you Deseus,' she said, 'I need a friend right now. Deseus why does Sego hate me so much? I do not know how I have offended him so.' Her eyes stung.

Deseus seated himself beside Mortunda.

'He is jealous of you,' he said matter-of-factly. 'He can tell you are going to be a much better Seronydd than he is and he doesn't like it.'

He leaned in closer towards her and said hesitantly, 'Actually he is not a very good Seronydd. I heard Lovernicus call him slow once. He said Sego was slow to learn and arrogant. The worst two qualities a Seronydd can have—stupidity and a big head.'

Deseus glanced quickly about him to make sure they could not be heard. He patted Mortunda's shoulder.

'I wouldn't worry about him Mortunda. He is all bark and no bite. He only joined the Seronydd order because he could not be a warrior.'

Mortunda gasped. 'I thought you had to be special to train with the Seronydd,' she said.

'Well, in some ways that is true,' Deseus replied. 'In order to be a Seronydd you have to have something the Order needs and you have to be willing and able to learn the craft. However Lovernicus is fearful, as we all are, that the tribes are losing respect for the Seronydd and turning towards Rome. Sego was picked because he had strong links with the Catuvellauni. Cunobelin, their Chief, hates Rome and has been aware for many years of the designs Rome has on Albion. The Catuvellauni are always delighted when one of their sons or daughters is picked to train with the Seronydd. It makes them like us more and trust us more. Lovernicus accepted Borvo's nomination of Sego for political reasons. Everyone knows Sego is really a second rate elder, but he is useful to the Seronydd.'

'Who is Borvo?'

Deseus spat on the ground. 'He is one of the Seronydd elders from the south. Lovernicus does not seem to care for him much.'

'Why does he not like him?'

'It is known that Borvo would like to lead the Seronydd. Lovernicus says Borvo would do anything to replace him. There is much tension between Borvo and Lovernicus.'

'Can Borvo replace Lovernicus?'

'No. Well not unless Lovernicus dies before he appoints a new leader. The Gwr Doeth announces his chosen heir. Then the elders of Mona will journey to the Upper Plane for three nights and three days. They consult with the Gods. It is the Gods who then approve or disapprove of the Gwr Doeth's chosen heir. But for as long as the Seronydd have existed the Gods have never disagreed.'

Mortunda looked thoughtful for a moment. 'So who will Lovernicus choose?'

Deseus threw a stone across the water, watching it skip and skitter on the smooth surface of the river.

'I have no idea,' he replied.

Mortunda shook her head.

'What is it?' Deseus asked.

'I am sorry. Sometimes I do not follow the world of adults very well. They confuse me!'

Deseus laughed.

'I know, they confuse me too. But Mortunda, one thing you will learn quickly in your training is that to be a good Seronydd, you have to understand the grown up world of politics—it doesn't always make sense. I guess it will one day!'

Mortunda smiled. She liked Deseus, with his crop of floppy blonde hair, keen dark eyes and wide grin. His front tooth was chipped slightly giving him an almost cheeky look when he smiled. As they stood to return to the horses Mortunda turned to him.

'What made them choose you Deseus?'

The boy laughed.

'Well,' he replied. 'It was not for the same reasons they chose you that's for sure! I am no great scholar nor do I have a natural pathway to the Spirit world like you. I have to work hard to understand the rituals and teachings. I try my best all the time—well for most of it anyway.'

He grimaced, 'Lovernicus has not let me journey to the Upper Plane yet. He says I will scare the Gods with my stupidity! He is still trying to teach me how to journey to the Lower Plane, but I keep messing that one up too! And the hardest of all is the study of the stars. There are so many of them!'

Mortunda frowned, 'So why were you chosen? Not for political reasons surely?'

Deseus laughed.

'No, it wasn't that! Lovernicus knew my mother although she would never tell me how. When I was born he came to see her. Apparently he took one look at my hands and saw this.'

Deseus turned his left hand over so Mortunda could see his palm. There on his left hand was a wiggly silver line that ran from the base of his thumb to the top of his wrist. Mortunda ran her finger over it, feeling the raised skin, following the line down from the top to where it finished on the boys wrist. As she did so she felt a shudder run through her back and her blood turn cold. A strange sense of foreboding fell upon her shoulders and the sky turned momentarily darker. Within a fraction of a second it had passed, but Mortunda was left with a sense of uneasiness.

'Did you feel anything?' she asked Deseus quickly.

Deseus shook his head and gazed indifferently at the birthmark.

'It's just a mark and to this day I still have no idea why Lovernicus got so excited about it. However he has promised to tell me the day I turn eighteen summers. In the meantime he says I have to work hard at being a good Seronydd elder and that is precisely what I intend to do.'

He looked at Mortunda. 'It will be all right you know,' he said reassuringly, 'you are going to love Mona. The settlement is great and the Seronydd elders will look after you.'

Mortunda smiled, 'Thank the Gods for that!' she said. She paused, wondering whether to ask Deseus the question that had burned in her mind like a persistent flame ever since her meeting with Sequana.

'Deseus,' she said tentatively, 'what is the Jewel?'

Deseus screwed up his nose and shrugged, 'The Jewel?' he said, 'I have never heard of it. Why?'

Mortunda shook her head.

'I'm not sure,' she said. 'The Goddess mentioned it to Lovernicus in the dream forest. She said Rome would want it and that the enemies of the Jewel were getting closer. Lovernicus seemed to think it was very important. I think it may have been that which saved us from the

Travellers. They got into the dream forest with us. At one point I was sure we were going to die.'

Deseus raised his eyebrows mockingly. 'Lovernicus knows how to deal with Travellers! They would not frighten him. But I have no idea what the Jewel is. But there are lots of things I do not understand about the ways of the Seronydd. I am still learning.'

Mortunda nodded.

'There was something else,' she said shyly. 'In my vision of Sequana, she very clearly told me that one day I would be Queen of the Brigante and that I should tell my father to build unity with the tribes in order to fight Rome. But when I relayed this to my father, Lovernicus did not support me. He walked away. It was as if he did not want my father to hear the words spoken by the Goddess.'

Deseus laughed.

'Mortunda,' he said, his voice firm and gently mocking, 'Lovernicus is the leader of all Seronyddion. He talks to the Gods all the time. He is the cleverest Seronydd that has ever lived. Believe me he knows what he is doing. If he did that, there would have been good reason for it. You just have to trust him. Like this Jewel thing you mentioned. All will become clear when he thinks the time is right.'

Mortunda smiled, relief washing over her.

'Fine,' she said.

Deseus grinned impishly. 'Race you to the horses?'

Mortunda laughed, 'OK, if you like your behind being whipped,' she said.

In one short moment, the two of them forgot the surly Sego, the long journey in front of them, tales of strange Jewels and meeting with Gods. They scrambled to their feet and, whooping with laughter, chased one another across the meadow back to where the horses were tethered.

XXXVI

Katie 2008

Katie grabbed one of the books off the shelf and threw it against the window.

'Shoo!' she shouted at the dishevelled looking pigeon pecking against the window. 'Go away!'

The pigeon fixed her with a contemptuous stare and continued pecking hard at the shiny glass. Outside amongst the sound of falling rain and pigeon pecking, a strong wind picked up. It blew across the roof tops, gusted across the empty streets towards a house marked with a brass plaque that read *Ivy House*. It reached the front door, effortlessly whooshing through the key hole, howling its way around the house, temporarily dimming the lights as it went, sending an icy blast under Katie's door. A swishing noise came from the direction of the window and now flying towards her window ledge were thirty or forty birds, cascading in a flush of different colours and types, landing on the ledge and pecking in unison against the glass, sending shivers down the window pane and down Katie's back. The squirrel Katie had named Patrick dived under the bed, but Katie felt angry. How dare they do this! Remembering suddenly that she was large and they quite small, she went to the window and shouted at them through the glass.

'Go away now! Or I'll fetch next door's cat.'

The noise stopped and along the ledge, pushing others out of his way, shuffled a small red breasted robin. Immediately Katie felt her arms and legs begin to fizz. Within moments she had tuned into the bird.

It had come for the squirrel.

'Patrick, we need to talk with you. And bring the human too,' it puffed, watching Patrick under the bed, ignoring Katie altogether.

Katie began to speak to the robin, 'You talk to me not him. He's done nothing wrong. I can talk your language you know, so maybe your quarrel is with me or the waitress, but not Patrick. He can't speak a word of human!'

To Katie's surprise, the robin bobbed his head as if in agreement.

'Madam, we know. I owe you an apology. I have been made aware of our error, but we urge you, beg you, to come with us. We have an emergency of the utmost terribleness and the Lord Bird requires your assistance.'

'I am not going anywhere near that creature!' Patrick piped up from under the bed.

Katie turned to the robin. 'You heard him! We are not going anywhere with you, *especially* if that bird-like creature you call Lord is nearby!'

'Madam you have nothing to fear. Our Lord has no wish to harm you or the squirrel; I am afraid you do not understand the seriousness of our troubles.'

Katie turned to glance at Patrick quivering under the bed and then back to the small red breasted bird on her window ledge. There was a forlorn look in his eye, which was quite different from the pomposity he had shown at the railway station. His feathers were bathed in sweat and his eyes were glazed as if all the effort of finding them had exhausted him to absolute weariness and despair. Indeed, now she looked closer, all the birds gathered outside had a weary, almost frightened look about them, all except the pigeon; he seemed to be enjoying himself. The rest peered in at Katie, shuffling their feet anxiously on the ledge, eyes darting to and from Katie to Patrick to the robin.

She turned to Patrick.

'Perhaps we ought to speak with them?'

'Are you mad?!'

'Probably, but I think it's only polite, and I honestly think they have no wish to hurt us.'

Patrick snorted, 'It's all right for you, its not you they want to carry away. Well if you want to speak with them, go ahead, but only once I've made my escape.'

'Will you speak with me alone?' Katie asked. The robin twitched and jumped about on the ledge. 'I am afraid you don't understand!' he said, 'We need you to come immediately, oh my word we do. Have you not heard? The world as we know it is being turned upside down and we need you two to help us.'

The robin pressed his face up against the window. 'Animals and people are in mortal danger...we need you to help us on a mission.'

'It's a trick!' yelled Patrick from his hiding place.

Katie felt intrigued by the robin's words, but she needed Patrick to be on side and guessed he was not to be rushed into anything dodgy or dangerous. She looked at the robin and made her eyes as narrow and as suspicious looking as she possibly could.

'How do we know we can trust you?'

The robin bobbed his head up and down,

'That's a fair question. Allow me to consult with my flock.'

Patrick poked his head out from under the bed and bared his teeth at Katie, 'What are you doing?'

Katie waved her hand for him to be quiet, 'Nothing, I'm just curious to know what this mission business is all about.'

'The only mission they have for me is to drop me from the sky! Just tell them to go away,' he said.

However Katie was adamant. 'Wait. Let's see what they have to say.'

A minute later the robin, having finished his consultation, turned back to Katie.

'I will suggest to the King and Queen that they come here to your home wherein you shall be duly informed of our calamities. I will also respectfully request that the Lord does not attend this meeting but remains at the palace until further notice.'

'Forever, you mean!' Patrick shouted from his under the bed cave.

'That Lord of yours sent me into a trance. I've got the most mammoth headache. He's evil!'

The robin bowed again, this time ignoring Patrick and focusing instead on Katie, 'I can assure madam that his Lordship placed the squirrel under a spell only to restrain him from struggling to escape whilst on the flight home. We wouldn't have wanted him hurt in any way, and falling from the sky in mid flight would have most surely killed him. We only wished to try him in our courts for the treacherous act of speaking in human tongue. However our investigations have taught us that the squirrel is indeed innocent of such a crime and that there are more dangerous plans afoot than we could possibly have known.' The robin shuddered.

'May I suggest that unless you hear otherwise, you can expect their majesties the King and Queen at around midnight? We will come to your window and pray you will let us into your chamber. The Queen has a delicate beak which is sensitive to the wet and cold, and midnight will most definitely be both wet and cold.'

Katie looked over to Patrick. She believed the robin to be genuine but could not agree without Patrick's consent. Patrick however had by now seemed to have accepted he was beaten and given up on listening. He had found Katie's discarded digestive biscuit and was busily munching. Katie shook her head with disbelief. The attention span of a squirrel was very short, she concluded, even when the future of the world was being discussed. She understood then that squirrels minds are a lot like their movements; scurrying, nimble, but equally quick to move onto the next thing, and food always seemed to come first.

'You eat too much sugar,' Katie shot at him. 'Muffins and biscuits are not good for you. Your teeth will march out of your mouth in disgust!'

Patrick shot her a scowl and dived under the bed with the biscuit firmly clasped in his jaws. He was taking no chances. It was his biscuit now and he was sharing it with no one.

XXXVII

When Patrick had been carefully deposited back into his shoe box, Katie went downstairs to take tea with Laura. She exaggerated her yawns, and made an excuse of wanting a hot bath and an early night. Laura however had other plans. She had invited the mystery guest to tea, and had promised him that he would meet Katie. At 8 p.m. the door bell rang, and Katie watched her mother take a deep breath, check her hair in the mirror and then open the door.

'David! How lovely to see you.'

Laura proffered her right cheek for a light kiss.

'Laura,' returned the man at the door.

Katie stood rooted to the spot. She recognised the voice immediately. Dr. Bennett. Her mother had invited Dr Bennett to tea! To Katie's disgust Bennett handed Laura some flowers, a bottle of wine and planted a second soggy kiss on her mother's cheek. Katie followed them both into the kitchen and politely offered to find a vase to house the stupid flowers. She noted with some pleasure that Dr Bennett had brought Laura lilies. They happened to be her mother's least favourite flowers. They made her sneeze. Dad would have known what to bring, even on his first date. He would have thought of a way to find out what Laura liked and what she didn't—no lilies from him! She gave the Doctor a polite smile and held out her hand, 'Hello Dr Bennett.'

'Good to meet you again Katie. And do call me David.' He held out his hand and limply shook Katie's. His hand was wet with nerves the way it had been in the hospital the first time she had met him. He rubbed his head and stood awkwardly on one leg.

'How was Exeter? My aunt lives there you know,' he said.

His voice sounded thinner and reedier than Katie had remembered; she wondered what on earth her mother could like about this man. He was so skinny and insubstantial. And, yet, tonight his eyes were steadier and fixed upon Katie. For a passing moment she sensed him searching her eyes as if he was looking for something hidden there. It made her feel uncomfortable and she quickly turned to offer Laura some assistance with taking plates to the table.

During tea, Katie tried to work out what else it was she didn't like about Dr Bennett. He had terrible table manners. He ate his food quickly, taking small fast bites one after another. He talked at the same time too so Katie could see the spinach rubbing against his teeth and pasta shells masticating in his salvia. It put her off her own tea so much that eventually she gave up eating and placed her fork down beside her. She sipped a little of the wine—a special treat her mother said to celebrate the move to Manchester. So far, Katie could see no cause for celebration. If it meant having to listen to Dr Bennett for more than one evening, Katie thought she would go mad with frustration. His conversation was mainly about his patients, the hospital, the extensions being made to the building and his new post at Manchester University Medical School. He was just plain boring! Laura sat mute, nodding interestedly in all of the appropriate places. But there was definitely something else about him that Katie could not fathom; something that was different. As he talked, he shot glances across the table at Katie; the same small searching glances he had passed when he first arrived. Katie could sense Laura too passing glances at Dr Bennett, as if the two of them had something they were hiding from her but were preparing to share with her as soon as they judged the timing to be right. For one terrible moment she imagined her mother announcing that she and Dr Bennett were to be married. She felt both sets of eyes upon her. Here it came. The point of the evening was about to be announced. Laura spoke first,

'Katie, as David is a doctor of the mind, and as he is here, having tea with us, I wondered if it would help if you told him a little bit about your...' Laura broke off, too embarrassed to say the words.

Katie glared at Laura. She felt her cheeks grow warm. Laura was going to betray her to the goblin. She looked at Dr Bennett.

'There is nothing wrong,' she said quickly. 'Would you like some apple pie? Laura made it especially.'

Dr Bennett spluttered slightly on his glass of wine.

'I would love some thank you.' He glanced again at Laura.

'Katie, I think it is time we discussed this 'problem' of yours,' said Laura firmly. She looked quickly at Dr Bennett, 'before it becomes...unmanageable.'

Katie shook her head. 'There is nothing wrong.'

She got up and went into the kitchen. From the dining room she could hear Laura and Dr. Bennett talking in hushed whispers. She felt anxious. She leaned her head against the fridge. The clock ticked above her; it was now 9.30 p.m. In two and a half hours she was due to meet with the birds. Who was she kidding; rescuing squirrels, conversing with robins, scolding tatty pigeons? Of course there had to be something wrong. Yet she also knew it was real. It felt real. It had to be real. And there was no chance on earth that she would ever share any of this with Dr Bennett. She busied herself with collecting the pudding plates and slicing the apple pie, desperately trying to think about how she could change the subject with her mother and Dr Bennett, when a voice behind her made her jump and drop the knife. It clattered to the floor. She bent to pick it up.

'Katie, your mother is worried about you.'

Dr Bennett was leaning against the door frame watching her. He had his wine glass in his hand and was sipping at it, confidently.

'Where's Laura?'

'She has popped upstairs to powder her nose.'

Laura never powdered her nose. Katie focused on the apple pie. Something felt wrong. Dr Bennett strode across the kitchen and took the knife out of Katie's hand. Katie stared at him.

'We wouldn't want you to do anything silly would we Katie?'

'What do you mean?'

'Well sometimes, people who see things and hear things that are not really there can become frightened and hurt themselves. Or others around them.' He was looking deeply into Katie's eyes now. There was something about him that was different. He smelt strange, musty and slightly decaying, as if his clothes had been left too long to dry. His voice too was older; it had a rasp to it.

Katie felt her throat grow dry. 'I do not know what you are talking about.'

'Your mother fears you are becoming ill Katie.'

'There is nothing wrong with me,' Katie repeated, more loudly than she intended to. She could hear the panic in her voice.

Dr Bennett looked down and seemed to be studying his hands.

'Sometimes people do not realise that they are unwell. The things they see or hear seem so real, so authentic, so true to life, that really it is not their fault that they believe them to be true. If I saw or heard the things some of my patients do, I too would believe they were real.' Dr Bennett stepped closer to Katie and took her hand. 'But that doesn't mean that they are,' he whispered gently.

'I don't see stuff,' Katie stammered. Her head was reeling a little. So Laura had betrayed her to the Goblin. She wished Dad was here now. He would punch Dr Bennett right between the eyes!

'I am not mad Dr Bennett,' said Katie. 'I just feel prefer animals to people. Is that such a terrible thing?'

She shook her hand loose from the doctor's and proceeded to set the three pudding plates in a straight line. She noticed she was shaking. If she could just focus on looking normal maybe Dr Bennett would leave her alone. But Dr Bennett was not so easily derailed. He leaned against the counter, watching her dole out three slices of apple pie.

'Tell me about the fortress.'

Katie flinched. How did he know about the fortress?

'What fortress?'

'The fortress you saw in the garden. Can you describe it to me?'

Katie looked towards the kitchen door. Never in her entire life had she hoped for her mother to appear as much as she did now.

'I do not know what you are talking about.'

'So are you saying your mother made the story up Katie?'

Katie looked at the Doctor. His eyes had become harder and they glinted like steel. It was as if all Dr Bennett's timidity had left him completely. He seemed like a different man; his stature appeared larger, his shoulders were bigger, his legs longer. His form wavered before her eyes. She rubbed her eyes.

'My mother knows about the fortress?'

The room was dancing now before her. The walls shimmered as if they were made of water. What was happening to her?

'Yes she does. You became delirious Katie. You spoke of a fortress wall in your sleep. You worried your mother so much that she rang the hospital and asked to speak to me?'

'There was no fortress,' Katie murmured. 'I just came down with a fever and like you said, I became delirious.'

'That is not how your mother saw it. She said the fever came on after you were found wandering in your neighbour's garden. Your mother said you were terrified when she found you.'

Katie looked around the room frantically searching for an escape. The dark had drawn in and through the kitchen window she could see a fog had gathered over the trees and was floating down towards the lawn. The park would be washed in dense white vapour and the meeting with the Birds seemed a much less attractive proposition than it had seemed several hours ago. Doctor Bennett had her captive in the kitchen and she could see no way of him letting her go. Where was Laura?

'Where is my mother?' Her senses were going completely. Her legs felt as if they made of jelly and she held onto the worktop to keep herself from falling down.

'I told you Katie, she is powdering her nose.'

Katie forced herself to look directly into Dr Bennett's eyes. There was something familiar about them. She felt herself go dizzy. She looked away to prevent herself from being swallowed up by his gaze.

'Laura does not *powder* her nose.'

Her voice sounded as if it was detached from her, floating in from miles away. She tried to move her legs. If she could just get out of the kitchen she would be fine.

'Tell me about the coin?' said Dr Bennett.

'What coin?'

'Your mother said when you were feverish you kept on repeating what sounded like Roman numerals. I understand they were inscribed on a coin that you found inside the wall. I thought I could help enlighten you of its meaning.'

'But you just said it wasn't real!'

Her thoughts were racing now. How did her mother know about the coin? It had only been there for a few moments before it disappeared in her hand. Not that remembering it was a problem. She could recall every last detail.

'But Katie, it was real to you. Maybe telling me about the coin will throw some light on what is happening to you.'

'How do you mean?'

Dr Bennett put his glass upon the counter. It clanged against the surface.

'Because Katie, everything you see or hear when you are having one of your delusions, is really just a part of you. The fortress wall, the coin, the things you hear, are split off parts of yourself. If we can understand why you split these bits off from yourself we might be able to help you.'

'Liked you helped my Nana you mean!'

There she had said it. Dr Bennett frowned.

'Katie your Nana was very ill.'

'So you say. She looked fine when we left her!'

'Ah,' said Dr Bennett, 'you think I killed your grandmother.'

'Well did you?' Katie could feel her eyes burning with anger.

Dr Bennett smiled softly. 'Now that is classic paranoia. No Katie I did not kill your grandmother. But I do want to know about the coin.'

'I wrote some of the inscription down.'

Katie turned as did Dr Bennett.

Laura stood swaying by the kitchen door. 'Sorry,' she slurred. 'I think I drank more wine than I intended to. I feel rather drunk. How embarrassing!'

Katie felt a wave of relief. She moved away from the counter and stood beside Laura. She glared at Dr Bennett.

'I have it here.' Laura waved a piece of paper at them.

She pushed Katie gently back into the dining room and placed a pencil and paper under her nose.

'Just draw the coin for Dr Bennett Katie,' she said.

Katie knew she had no choice. If she could pass this off as a dream it might be all right; hadn't her mother told Bennett she had been feverish? She would let him analyse her and tell her about her 'cut off' bits of herself, she would promise to stop doing whatever Laura had told him she did and everything would be ok. She picked up the pencil, turned over the paper and began to draw. She could recall every detail perfectly; the worn edges and slightly raised centre, the red gold coloured bronze that had developed green patches with age; the face of the woman looking haughty, beautiful and proud in the centre, and even the inscription written around its circumference.

She wrote carefully.

MORTVNDA

And then beneath the inscription she wrote the date, pausing to recall the exact positioning of the letters.

DCCXCVII A.U.C

Bennett was watching Katie's every stroke. As she wrote the letters he stepped closer to her so that by the time she had finished he was leaning over her shoulder. He had turned a deathly white.

'This isn't possible.'

He sat down and put his head in his hands.

'What is it?' asked Laura, worry etched in her voice. 'What isn't possible?'

Bennett pulled the piece of paper towards him and ran his fingers over the woman's face, tracing the letters and shaking his head.

'How have they done this?' he murmured.

'Done what? David what are you talking about?'

Bennett ignored Laura. 'Katie, where did you find such a coin? Tell me now, I need to know?'

'David, I already told you. Katie was calling out these letters and numbers in her sleep—when she was ill!' Laura sounded perplexed. 'Now what does it mean? What is wrong with my daughter?'

'This coin,' began Bennett, his voice steady and quiet, 'is from the reign of Queen Mortunda and there is no evidence this person existed; only myth; no coin or other artefact has ever been found to corroborate her existence. Not that this matters—we often learn more from mythology than physical finds.' He took a deep breath. 'Mortunda is an archetype—a legend. She represents all that is rebellious in women; all that is unsavoury.'

'Well maybe it is mere coincidence then,' said Laura sounding relieved. 'Probably just something Katie read about somewhere and it came out in her dreams.'

'I doubt it. Mortunda is not known to many. Her name was wiped out. It had to be that way.'

'Who was she?' Katie remembered the words whispering to her from the fortress, '*She knows you are coming…*'

Dr Bennett laughed a short cold peeling laugh that chilled Katie's heart. 'Mortunda—feared Queen of the Brigante tribe. She made a pact with the Romans that eventually led her people to death. This coin is dated 44 A.D., only one year after the Roman Emperor Claudius invaded Britain. Now I am asking you one more time Katie, how did you find this coin? How do you know of Mortunda?'

Katie instinctively covered the birthmark on her hand. 'I just dreamt it,' she lied.

'David what does all this mean? You are scaring me.'

Bennett turned to Laura. He gave her a fixed stare.

'I am afraid it means Katie is more unwell than either you or I had ever imagined. She is showing classic signs of early onset of schizophrenia; the calling to mind and regurgitation of primitive archetypes is a common starting place for this illness. Her clear identification with the Mortunda figure is a definite sign of paranoid delusion, as are her beliefs that I killed her grandmother. It means I have no other choice.'

Laura had almost stopped breathing.

'What is your choice?'

'I think Katie should be admitted to my care for immediate psychiatric assessment.'

XXXVIII

Dr Bennett left the house. He instructed Laura to pack some clothes for Katie, saying he would expect her at the hospital in the morning.

Laura appeared dazed. She attempted to tidy away the dinner things but her arms and legs did not seem to want to work; she stumbled into the kitchen clutching her head.

'That wine was stronger than I realised,' she mumbled.

Laura glanced at the bottle. It did not look like strong wine—the label said 10% alcohol.

'Must be because I am not used to it,' Laura said.

Or he has drugged you thought Katie. But she did not dare say this. Instead she sat down and glumly picked at the label.

'What will he do to me?' she asked.

'Nothing,' replied Laura, 'because you're not going.'

Katie looked up, shocked but pleased.

'I'm not?' she asked.

Laura sniffed. 'No. I would rather us deal with this ourselves. Besides, I don't trust him.'

'You don't?' said Katie.

'No, I don't. What was it he said...something about that ancient woman being the archetype of all that is rebellious and unsavoury about women? I didn't like that. Made me wonder what century David Bennett lives in.'

'So I can stay here?'

'Yes Katie you can stay here. But don't think this nonsense of yours can go on forever. It has got to stop you understand? We will talk tomorrow. Right now I have to go to bed. My head is thumping. Lock up for me and don't forget to turn off all the lights.'

Feeling very shaken, Katie went upstairs to find Patrick. She discovered him fast asleep, snoring gently in his shoe box, nestled under the trainer wrappings. 'Not sleeping again,' she said, shaking the box firmly. He awoke with a start, 'I thought you were not coming,' he said crossly.

'I nearly didn't make it,' retorted Katie. 'Patrick, my Nana's psychiatrist turned up. The thing is he was horrid. He grabbed my arm and wouldn't let me go. He threatened to take me into hospital, probably pump me full of horrid drugs and lock me away in a cell. I think he drugged Laura too—she was acting all strange. And he kept staring at me and asking me all sorts of questions when I was dishing up the pudding!'

'I don't suppose you brought any pudding up with you have you?' asked Patrick. His belly was popping again.

'No! Is that all you think about?' snapped Katie.

'Sorry! It's my nature. I am a squirrel you know. I'm supposed to eat every time I wake up.'

Katie sighed heavily, 'Well, right now there are more important things to think about, like why we are being summoned to this meeting and what do they want us to do?'

'It's your fault we are having a meeting in the first place,' snapped Patrick. 'I would have stayed hidden under the bed until they'd gone away, but you had to be all polite and listen to them and invite them back!'

'Maybe I should have left you to be kidnapped then. If it wasn't for me you'd be dead right now, accused of a crime you didn't commit!'

There was really nothing Patrick could say to that, so he decided to close his mouth and stay quiet. They sat for a few minutes in silence, both glum and fed up, until a sudden thud against the window made them leap off the bed and shout out together, 'What's that?!'

Carefully and with a nervous hand Katie drew back the curtain. Sat on the window sill looking very perturbed and sweaty was the robin.

'Open your window!' he chirped.

'Her Majesty will be here shortly and she will not be of glad mind if she is left sitting in the damp.'

Katie undid the latch and secured the window as wide open as she could. Robin flew in gratefully and landed on the bedside table. He shook his feathers and rubbed his beak into his glistening coat.

'That was a long flight,' he groaned. 'I had to come the long way around because of the fog. Phew I'm hot!'

'Before we begin Robin,' Katie said, ignoring his plaintive moans of having wind in his wings, 'we need some ground rules about Patrick's safety. I have here a very nasty spray.' She brought out a can of air freshener she had stolen from Laura's room earlier and waved it under the robin's beak. She continued, 'This line to the left side of the bed is strictly our territory. You and your clan are not allowed to cross over. If you do, I will spray this in your eyes and you will be blinded, and don't think I won't spray your precious King and Queen, because I will! The right side of the bed belongs to you and the others, and we promise not to cross over to your side.'

'She's a suspicious creature isn't she?' Robin said to Patrick, but Patrick only glared at the robin. He still had not forgiven him for the way he had been treated outside the station. 'Ok then,' said Robin gloomily. 'Have it your way. We have Miss suspicious and Mr grumpy to deal with tonight. I'll make sure to warn their majesties the King and Queen.'

Nothing happened for a while. As the clock hands edged towards midnight, the wind outside grew stronger and Katie's curtains began to flap, softly at first then moving to a wild crescendo of slapping. Katie hugged herself to keep warm. She longed to close the window and feared the wind flapping against the curtains would awaken Laura. Just as both hands came to rest on twelve, a flurry of beating wings announced the arrival of the royal party. Katie and Patrick saw a column of birds, of all colours, shapes and sizes, stretching as far as the end of the street and flying in an arrow straight formation through Katie's window. They gathered on her bookshelf, on top of her television, her wardrobe, and when those spaces were taken, they perched in long lines along her wall. All eyes were fixed on Katie and Patrick, until a shrill song broke out from one of the sparrows. The rest of the birds bobbed their heads in excitement as through the window flew two silky grey collared doves. They settled gracefully onto Katie's bed, and waited for the head bobbing and chattering to cease. The Robin stepped forward.

'Your Majesties,' Robin turned to Katie and Patrick, 'I present these two servants to your Majesty. Please bow before His Majesty the King of Longford Park and Her Majesty the Queen of Longford Park.'

'It's all right Robin, there is no need for bowing. We are in greater need of our two friends than they are of us, I'm afraid.'

The darker of the two doves spoke, her voice calm and melodic, 'You must be Katie and you, my grey friend have to be Patrick. You have caused quite a stir my dear.'

'I've done nothing wrong!' exclaimed Patrick, moving closer to Katie and holding onto her ankle. Katie bent down and scooped him up into her arms. Katie spoke, 'It's true. Patrick may be a pain in the neck your Majesty, but he isn't lying. I was there. He spoke in his own tongue—'

'What do you mean, I'm a pain in the neck?' interjected Patrick forgetting his trepidation for one moment.

'Ssshhh,' Katie hissed.

Patrick gave a sulky look, but had to admit to himself he felt much safer now that Katie was holding on to him, and pleased she had defended him.

The Queen moved closer to the forlorn looking pair.

'Rest,' she said gently, 'We bear Patrick no malice. We know he did no harm. We know now he spoke in animal tongue. As Robin has explained to you both, we need you to help us.'

She cooed and nestled briefly against the King.

'What we are about to tell you must travel no further than this room. Katie, Patrick; you must prepare yourselves for a long and arduous journey, a journey to lands you never knew existed, and a journey to lands our wings cannot take us to. It will be a dangerous journey, but a necessary one.'

Katie listened hard to what the Dove Queen was saying. She reminded her of Nana telling one of her stories and Katie felt immediately trusting of the grey bird with her deep black eyes and ivory coloured beak. It was the King who spoke next in a voice that sounded like feet crunching on gravel. 'This thing we need you to do for us will determine what happens to us all. There is darkness all about us, Katie. Utter chaos will follow if the thing we need you to protect is taken.'

Katie looked at her birthmark and rubbed it gently.

'The Jewel,' she said quietly.

There was a rush of excitement in the room before the Queen said softly, 'You know of the Keepers' Jewel?'

Katie nodded. 'My Nana told me the story. I did not believe her. I must admit I thought she was making things up. She did that sometimes; it was, well we thought it was all part of her illness.'

'You speak of your Nana in the past tense,' said the King gently.

Katie felt the tears well behind her eyes. 'She died a couple of weeks back,' she said. 'It was a heart attack that killed her. It was very sudden.'

She recalled her Nana's face and tired brown eyes and felt warm tears splash onto her cheeks. She hastily brushed them away.

The Queen looked at Katie gently and then at the King. 'It may have been the Travellers who killed your Nana,' the King said softly; 'It would not be the first time a Traveller from the dark side of the Upper Plane killed a human being.'

Katie stared at the King. 'What do you mean?' she stammered.

The Queen opened her grey wings and flew in closer to stand beside Katie. 'Travellers were good once,' she whispered. 'They used to carry messages from the Gods in the Upper Plane down to humans who live in the Middle Plane. They helped humans listen to the wisdom in their hearts. But then the Jewel was lost, stolen from the world of humans and thus the ability that humans had to understand the deeper meaning of the Gods was lost forever. Some of the Travellers turned bad. They continued to whisper things to humans as they always had done, but they chose only bad things, and angry things. They find joy in frightening your kind knowing that the humans of today's world have lost the knowledge of their inner wisdom.'

Katie shook her head in disbelief. 'But why would they do that?' she said. 'If they were good before and used to help humans understand the wisdom of the Gods, why would they suddenly turn bad?'

The King came to stand beside the Queen. 'Once the Jewel was lost, the Travellers had nothing to do. They began working for the jealous God. They began destroying all the belief the humans ever had in knowledge and wisdom. They created madness in its place. Only a few remained true to the ways of the Jewel and the Gods who created it. But sadly they are outnumbered. Katie, what did your Nana tell you of the Jewel?'

Katie thought hard not knowing how much she should say. There had been far too many strange and terrible things happening to her recently, not least the incident with Dr. Bennett tonight. She cleared her throat, trusting her instincts to share some of what she had heard, but not all of it.

'I know it has magical properties,' she said weakly, 'and my Nana believed it had been lost. She tells me it once sat on a tower. That is all I know.'

She held back on the notion that she was a Keeper. Somehow she feared Doctor Bennett may be hiding and listening to her conversation. The King nodded.

'Katie, there is a lot more for you to know but it is not I who needs to tell you. The knowledge of the Jewel has always remained with the animal world. It is the human world that has forgotten its existence. We need to introduce you to someone who can explain better than I can the terrible predicament we find ourselves in. He is from another place but he has been watching you and waiting for the right time. Will you allow us to bring him here?'

Katie pushed her hair behind her ears and looked at Patrick.

'It is rather odd I know,' she said thinking aloud, 'but odd is fast becoming the normal nature of events in my life.' She looked at the King.

'All right,' she said, 'I don't mind who you bring or from where, as long as you can promise me that it will not wake my mother up.'

XXXIX

Albion 43 A.D.

Somewhere on a mountain, an elderly man picked up his staff and struggled to his feet. He was immediately helped by a younger man, who watched his master with a mixture of deep anxiety and hope. Lovernicus had felt the calling of the Dove Queen and had been preparing for the journey all day with incantations and spells. Signalling to his companion Deseus for his goat skin coat, he stood now and looked across the mountains to the west.

'Have you prepared sufficiently Lovernicus?' asked Deseus.

Lovernicus smiled at the young man standing bedside him. 'I have,' he replied, and clasped his companions shoulder.

'Nerthus, spirit of the Earth, will keep me safe. Together we have focused intently on the incantation of Safe Passage. I do not want to be scorched by the flames.'

He looked deeply into Deseus's eyes. 'Have you prepared for our return journey? You know what to do?'

'I do,' replied Deseus, 'The remedies are waiting and the incantation tools are complete and in place. Your journey home with our new companions will be safe. We will be waiting for you on Mona at the designated place.'

Lovernicus nodded in approval, 'You have done well Deseus. We are in good hands. The tides have turned in our favour again, I can feel it. Now I must prepare to go.'

He took up his staff, and turned to Deseus and held him tightly against him, 'Remember Deseus do not follow me. Watch from here and you shall be safe, but do not follow me into the Grove for there the light will blind you. I shall see you soon my good friend.'

Deseus wiped the tears from his eyes, 'Good speed my Mentor,' he called as Lovernicus made his way to the bottom of the ridge and into the clasp of tall trees.

Deseus was left alone on the mountain. He wondered whether he would see Lovernicus again, but then scolded himself for even doubting it. No one had ever used the Incantation of Safe Passage before. The knowledge of Safe Passage lay only in imaginations and the oral tradition of the Seronydd, passed down from leading elder to successor elder over the passage of time. Seronydd apprentices heard of the knowledge only as they prepared for their final initiation and understood that the secret of its power had never been tested as far as anyone could remember. It had never been called upon, for its secret had never been needed. How different it was now in these dark times. No one was more qualified to call upon it than Lovernicus, leader of the Seronydd, powerful seer and Keeper of the Jewel. Deseus doubted there was anyone with a brave enough heart to endure such a journey, except for Lovernicus. He had made it clear to all that he, Deseus, was not fit to follow in Lovernicus' footsteps. He ran his fingers over the mark on his hand. The sadness returned and threatened to engulf him, but he pushed it away; pushed all thoughts of Mortunda from his mind. If only his heart was as willing to banish her.

A sudden change in the hue of the sky from blue to violet interrupted Deseus' thoughts. He looked over to the grove as a sudden blast of light emanated from the woods and lit up the valley. Shielding his eyes with his hand he squinted at the crowding mass of trees marking the entrance to the wood. A tall white shield of light had risen from the ground and stood high above and amongst the trees. It looked as if it would be solid to touch and within its white glow, Deseus could see the Guardians of the Journey, the keepers of Safe Passage. Balthus half man, half goat, his long face brown from his life in the forest, his beard black and silky like the goat hair on his hind legs, writhed within the shield representing the wisdom of all animal knowledge; their dance and their language of woods and mountains. Then there was Ereton, Queen of the wood elves. Ereton was fair and beautiful. Her sharp features danced in joy within the shield and she held out her hand to Lovernicus who took it gently and for a while they spun around and around together singing chants and sharing news of the Upper World. Lastly, Deseus could see Icena, Queen of the first tribe of Men and Women. Icena was strong and dark and dressed in a pig skin tunic. Her muscular arms carried scars from many battles and her face wore the blue daubing of a warrior Queen. They entwined themselves around each other, and held Lovernicus in their arms, smiling into his face. Lovernicus was smiling in return and his face wore a look of peace and serenity that Deseus had not seen him wear for many months. The Incantation had worked. Lovernicus would be safe. He watched as the shield shimmered in the weak sunlight, throwing its glow across the entire mountainside, lighting up the dark purple crevices and giving life to the plants that slept within the rocks. The figures within the shield had mingled until Deseus could not make out Lovernicus from the Guardians. They were bestowing their power upon him, allowing their forms to become absorbed into his. They would regain their own shapes only when he returned.

Gradually the shield shimmered in and out of view, growing weaker with each appearance, until finally it was absorbed into the trees that it had surrounded, gradually becoming part of the landscape. Now an endless display of white flowers covered the branches of the trees and formed a white canopy of blossom that smelt like the taste of freshly collected honey, spreading down the trunks of the trees, carpeting the forest floor, bringing the forest out of winter and temporarily into spring. The forest had given its permission to Nerthus, to allow her to awaken the glade from sleep to ensure Lovernicus' Safe Passage. It was now up to Deseus to ensure that Lovernicus and the new companions could be brought home again. He made his way down the mountain and set out on the journey to Mona, aware of the enormity of the task that lay before him.

XL

Lovernicus travelled across many seas and over many lands before he finally broke through into Katie's bedroom. He arrived swathed within a bubble of white light and to Katie it looked as if he and the bubble materialised through the bedroom wall gradually, piece by piece. It reminded her of a nature programme she had seen where a zebra had given birth. First the bubble of water emerged, followed by long gangly legs and arms, then the plop of a body hitting the ground. Katie wondered how the wall did not splinter into shards of plaster, bringing Laura running from her bedroom to see what all the commotion was, but there was no noise, only the creaking of Patrick's breathing as he huddled under Katie's tee-shirt for comfort.

Within five minutes the man inside the bubble was in the room. He had his eyes closed and his knees bent under him. It did not look as if the journey had been comfortable. The man inside the bubble murmured, 'Sail on, sail away, let light break into day.'

The bubble folded in on itself, peeling away layers of light one upon another until the man stood tall, stretched and waved his hand at the white transparent folded membrane that had been the bubble, and now sat folded like a newly washed bath towel on Katie's floor; it disappeared soundlessly. The old man pulled his goatskin coat around him. The journey had not been a warm one and despite the central heating being on full blast, Katie could tell the man felt cold. He shivered and then looked over at her, his eyes the brightest blue she had ever seen.

'You are larger than I expected,' he said, his voice flat and certain. 'But then again you live in more prosperous times. I take it you do not have any difficulty growing grain and harvesting the fields?'

Katie stared at him and felt Patrick clamber deeper beneath her tee shirt, his sharp claws scratching her skin.

'How many summers have you lived?' the man asked her, his deep blue eyes never leaving hers.

'I beg your pardon?' said Katie.

'Your age?' the old man clarified. 'Tell me your age child.'

'Oh I see,' said Katie, understanding finally dawning on her.

'I am thirteen years of age.'

'Ah,' he replied, 'And, are you betrothed?'

'Certainly not!' she said. 'I am still at school!'

'Ah,' the man said again, 'I see. Well things are certainly different here. But that's good. That's good.' He nodded to himself. 'It means less people will miss you.'

He stared at her for a bit longer and Katie grew uncomfortable under his gaze. It was as if he could see right into her very being and knew all her deepest fears and secrets. Then, without warning he quickly withdrew his gaze and turned to face the Dove Queen perched on Katie's bed. He bowed deeply to her.

'Thank you your ladyship for your clear calling.'

'Thank you, Lovernicus, for heeding our call. We are deeply indebted to your bravery.'

Turning to the stunned child and the glaring squirrel, the man called Lovernicus nodded.

'Greetings Katie, and greetings to you too…Squirrel, companion of the World Tree.'

Katie managed a small nod, but Patrick, his courage dismembered by the old man's booming voice, fled from under Katie's tee-shirt and dived under the bed. Another human wanting him to talk was just too much for one day. Lovernicus poked his head under the bed after him and called to him gently,

'It is fine Squirrel of the Grey Coat. You have nothing to fear. I come as a friend.'

Patrick gradually opened one eye and looked up at the tall old human with his white grey hair and bearded chin. Cautiously he poked his black nose from under the bed and met the face of the old man.

'What do you want old human?' asked Patrick.

'I would like the opportunity to talk with you and Katie. And I bring you a gift. I have here in my bag, some hazelnuts, picked fresh this morning. If you come and talk with me, you can have my entire hoard.'

Patrick shifted along the floor. First his nose, then his paws and then his entire body eased out from under the bed. He sat up.

'Really,' he asked Lovernicus. 'Have you really got fresh hazelnuts?'

Lovernicus smiled. 'I have.'

Katie tutted impatiently; did the creature think of anything else but food?

The old man untied the string at the top of his pig skin pouch and tipped out eight large green nuts. Patrick's eyes popped with excitement.

'Have you never seen hazelnuts before then?' asked Katie, failing to hide the sarcasm in her voice.

'Not like these!' replied Patrick 'In the woodland back home, you get the odd measly looking specimen, but nothing as beautiful as these!'

He greedily picked one up and placed it to his jaw, splintering the shell with his teeth. He was about to dive under the bed again to start nibbling on the succulent flesh, but Lovernicus, the old man, was far too quick for him. With a flash the he had swept Patrick up into his arms and placed him swiftly upon the bed.

'Katie, would you take a seat please.'

Katie sat down next to Patrick automatically following the command in the old man's voice. His voice seemed to have different layers to it. On the bottom layer she could hear a rich deep tone that pulsated in her ears when he spoke but over the top of that layer was a calming melodic tone like water running over stones in a brook. Katie felt captivated by his voice, like she could just sit and listen to him speak for hours and not notice the passing of time.

'I think you will need an explanation on the meaning of my presence here today and indeed who I am,' Lovernicus began. He put his hands behind his back and began walking around the room in a circle.

Katie looked the old man up and down. She had certainly never seen anyone like him. He wore a tunic of animal skin that stretched down to his knees, revealing long gangly legs that were cut and scratched. He had some form of wrappings on his bony feet. They were definitely animal skin of some sort because Katie could see tiny hairs populating the material. Lovernicus had long hair, steel grey in colour and matted together into tight dreadlocks and his chin was unshaven, sporting a short, curly, tangled beard. Despite his ragged appearance, his face was like his multi-layered voice, steady, calm and kind.

'I expect you to be alarmed by these evening events. You will, no doubt have many questions and I am willing to answer them all. But first let me introduce myself. I am Lovernicus, and I am the leading elder, the Gwr Doeth, of the Seronydd Order.'

'What is the Seronydd order?' Katie asked, her forehead creasing into a puzzled frown.

'Ah,' said Lovernicus, 'Of course. We are extinct by your time.'

He looked sad when he said this and stopped his pacing, looking around the room to take in the surroundings that were familiar to Katie but seemingly foreign to him.

'Yes, the Seronydd order does not exist in your time of 2008,' he repeated as if trying to make the reality of it stick in his own mind.

'You might find this hard to believe Katie, but a very long time ago we were the heart of this land. The Seronydd were once the guides and wisdom keepers for all the tribes of Albion.'

The old man's eyes grew misty. 'Of course, everything changes. Sometimes I fear change does not bring progress.'

He fell into a long silence, until Katie blurted out, 'I am afraid that I do not know what you are talking about. What do you mean by your time, and where is Albion?'

The question brought the old man out of his daze and he smiled.

'They are good questions Katie and the answers are strange but they are true nevertheless. Allow me to explain.'

Katie stroked Patrick's ear—the squirrel had climbed upon her lap and had fallen asleep. Lovernicus' eyes scanned Katie's room.

'Have you a map of this place in which you live?' he asked.

Katie frowned, 'Do you mean a street map of Manchester or a map of England?' she asked. 'It's just that we have not lived here very long. In fact I only arrived today.'

She felt her heart pull as she said this, remembering her promise to herself that in Manchester she would become a normal girl for her mother's sake. Well so far she had failed miserably. She gathered herself together and stood up, carefully placing Patrick on the pillow.

'I have a map of England somewhere,' she said. Sorting through her various books and comics which were filed neatly upon her shelves, Katie hunted for her *Atlas of the British Isles*. She found it stacked tightly against an old *Bunty* album of 2001.

'Here,' she said, pulling it out.

She took it over to the bed and opened it to the first page which showed an overall map of the British Isles. Lovernicus studied it closely, running his fingers across the land and sighing deeply.

'It has altered somewhat,' he said.

'How do you mean, altered?' Katie asked.

Lovernicus glanced up at the freckled child. 'See here?' He pointed to a tiny island remotely detached by a thin strip of water just off of Wales. Katie nodded. She recognised it immediately.

'Anglesey,' she said. 'We have been camping there before.'

She recalled it raining persistently for the entire week; huge sheets of water falling continuously from a dark sky that never cleared and long days hunting in vain, with her parents, for a cinema or bowling alley—anything to escape the wet and cold. Anglesey had seemed a dark and mysterious place to Katie, full of ancient ruins and angry marsh lands that whispered to you to go home. She had been relieved when they left.

'This place you call Anglesey, is what we know in my time as Mona,' said Lovernicus. 'It is the land of the Seronydd and the home of our temple. Now I can see there is hardly any water between us and the mainland. In Albion's time the water was broader and deeper. We were more protected.'

'Protected from whom?' persisted Katie, 'And where is Albion?'

Lovernicus looked at the Dove King and Queen and then back to Katie.

'Albion is here Katie. It is the old name for your country, our country.'

The old man took a deep breath and exhaled gently. 'I am from the past Katie, from a long, long time ago; the time when the land of Albion was the home to many Celtic tribes.'

Katie swallowed, her head reeling. She asked, 'How far from the past?'

The old man took a deep breath as if he was going to answer her. Instead he returned to the map. Katie stared at him and Lovernicus ignored her obvious frustration, his eyes shifting away from hers and back to the map before him.

'See this?' he said, pointing to the part of the map that marked the county of Yorkshire. He ran his lined hand across Yorkshire down to the tip of Manchester.

Katie nodded. 'That's where my Nana died,' she said pointing to York.

'How did your Nana die?' he asked her quickly.

'They said it was a heart attack,' replied Katie, and then she added, fearing that Lovernicus would not know what a heart attack was, 'It's when the heart stops working and so the person dies.'

Lovernicus nodded. 'Quite possibly your Nana was taken by spirits that crossed over from the Upper Plane into the Middle Plane,' he said matter-of-factly. 'We call them Travellers.'

'The Birds have said the same,' Katie said.

'Are you all really telling me that my Nana was killed by spirits?'

'Oh yes, it is more than likely. Now this land I have shown you, this is the heart of the Brigante tribe. The peoples of my time are a tribal people united in spirit by the Seronydd order but divided from each other by war, fear, greed and uncertainty. In the time I come from, the water helped a little, to protect us from the enemies that plagued Albion.'

Katie looked confused. 'What enemies are you speaking of?'

Lovernicus ran his hand through his tangled hair and sat beside her.

'There have been many enemies of Albion,' he said. 'Some have grown from the land itself, for the tribes are constantly at war with one another. But at this present time in our history we face both an enemy from outside and an enemy within. You asked me what time I am from?'

He did not wait for confirmation from Katie but hurtled ahead with the explanation.

'I am from the time you would know as 43 A.D. Even now as we speak, the Romans are due to invade Albion. They have planned it for many moons and many of the tribes of Albion have failed to understand their true motives and have seen Rome as a friend, a protector from other tribes. However, when the Romans arrive, they will come for our gold and silver, they will take our land and worst of all, they will destroy our ways forever.'

The old man stared into space again and his eyes clouded with tears.

'Of course the Romans come,' Katie said quietly, 'Everyone knows that. You are not suggesting that I can help to stop the Romans are you? That's impossible! It's already happened. You can't play with time, or turn it back, undo things that have already happened, can you?'

Lovernicus hesitated and twirled his beard in his fingers.

'No you can't, well not completely,' he said slowly. 'The Romans will arrive. I fear we are too late to stop that. But there is something you can do to help us, to help all of us. There is a Queen, Katie, a dangerous Queen. Her name is Mortunda, Queen of the Brigante tribe.'

Lovernicus pointed to Yorkshire on Katie's atlas.

'Queen Mortunda has discovered the secret of the ancient Jewel, the Keeper's Jewel and she knows that it is protected by our order on the Island of Mona. She will do all she can to steal it from us, and she will use the Romans to help her. This is why I have come here today Katie. We need you to help us stop Mortunda. If you do not, I fear the Jewel and all it teaches will be lost to us forever. If it becomes lost to us, it becomes lost to humanity.'

'You are the Keeper who has struggled to pass on the Jewel?' she said quietly, remembering what Nana had said about the Jewel being lost in time.

'I am,' he said. 'And I need you to travel with me Katie, back to my time. You are our last hope.'

Katie swallowed. 'And then what?' she asked, although she had already guessed what the answer would be.

Lovernicus did not answer at first.

He struggled to find the words. Eventually he explained, 'Once you have the Jewel, you will bring it back to your time, where it rightly belongs,' he replied simply.

Katie looked at the floor. 'Why me?' she whispered.

Lovernicus leaned over and gently took her left hand, turning it over so her palm was exposed.

'Because you are a Keeper of the Jewel.' He smiled. 'It belongs with you; it belongs now in your time. We have had our time of the Jewel and now it is right that it leaves us. Humanity depends on you child. The question is this; are you strong enough to undertake such a journey?'

Katie did not reply.

Lovernicus squeezed her hand. 'You have the marking of the Keeper Katie. The first mark made on the Builder's hand when he wrenched it from the Tower to safety from the wrath of the jealous spirit. Your family are the natural line of Keepers and it is to you we must return the Jewel. I have cut through layers of time to take you to it.'

Katie sat in a stunned silence, her head reeling.

'May I see your hand?' she asked suddenly. Lovernicus held out his left hand to Katie who took it within her own and turned it gently over so she could look at his palm. There, barely visible amongst the many lines of age on the old man's hand, just below the thumb, was a white raised squiggle.

'Our enemies grow stronger. We are running out of time,' Lovernicus said gently and slowly, his hand holding Katie's tightly.

Katie thought about her strange evening and remembered the coin and the Fortress and the strangeness of Dr Bennett. She cleared her throat.

'I think this Queen Mortunda person may already know about me,' she confessed. 'A man was here this evening. Dr Bennett. He was my Nana's psychiatrist. But he seemed different tonight. His eyes were cold, hard and he smelt odd. It was if it wasn't really Dr Bennett at all. I told him about a coin that I found.'

Katie told Lovernicus about the fort that had appeared in her garden in East Dulwich, where she had found the coin and the voices she had heard warning her. She described the inscription, Dr Bennett's behaviour, Laura's reaction and how she had appeared to be drunk.

As she told Lovernicus the whole story, the thought suddenly dawned on her, 'It was almost as if I was being hypnotised by Dr Bennett in the same way the birdlike creature hypnotised Patrick!'

There was a twittering of bird chatter and Lovernicus glanced at the Dove King and Queen.

'Where is the Lord of the Birds?' he asked.

The Dove King bobbed. 'The squirrel asked for him not to be present Lovernicus, and so we honoured that request. Surely you do not suspect that the Lord of the Birds is working for the enemy?'

Lovernicus held up his hand.

'We can not be sure of it in these strange times,' he said. 'Maybe he is not all we believed him to be.'

The Dove Queen spoke up, 'But the Lord is a trusted Traveller Lovernicus. He is one that you appointed yourself; surely you are not accusing him of going over to the side of the Jealous God, of taking human form, after all these centuries of serving the Jewel and what it stands for?'

The birds in the room were now becoming noisier and more flustered. The Dove King cooed loudly and immediately they fell into an obedient silence.

Lovernicus stood up.

'I am not sure of anything any more,' he said. 'My trust has been betrayed before; in ways that have wounded me so deeply I thought I would never recover. But nevertheless, this is not our concern. Right now what matters most, what our very lives depend on, is taking Katie back to Albion to retrieve the Jewel. Only then will it be safe.'

He turned to Katie, 'This man of whom you speak, the one you called Bennett, did he see the mark on your hand?'

Katie looked quickly down at her birthmark.

'I am not sure,' she said.

Lovernicus sighed. 'If he is one of Mortunda's spies, if indeed he is a Traveller working for the Jealous God, the Wretched Spirit, and if indeed he had seen the mark, we have very little time.'

Katie stared in disbelief. 'You mean he will be back to kill me?'

Lovernicus nodded. 'I am afraid so. They want to possess the Jewel Katie and one sure way of controlling the Jewel is to destroy the line of Keepers. They have destroyed many before you and unless we return to Albion tonight, they will be back to destroy you.'

Katie felt sick, 'So what do you want me to do?' she asked weakly.

Lovernicus looked at Katie and around the room at the waiting birds.

'My friends I am afraid we must act fast. Darkness is falling upon us and we must return to Albion and the Jewel immediately.'

Turning to Katie Lovernicus said, 'Will you help us by coming to Albion to retrieve the Jewel, and will you bring your little friend to help us on this quest?'

Katie looked at Patrick who was snoring gently on the pillow.

She stood up and took a deep breath.

'Yes Lovernicus, we will both come to Albion.'

To be continued...

About Kings Hart Books

Kings Hart Books is a small, independent publisher, based in Oxfordshire, England.

Our other fiction titles:

The Invisible Worm by Eileen O'Conor
ISBN 978-1-906154-00-4
The Reso by Ambrose Conway
ISBN 978-1-906154-01-1
Meeting Coty by Ruth Estevez
ISBN 978-1906154-03-5
Apartment C by Ruth Learner
ISBN 978-1-906-154-06-6
The Price by Tony Macnabb
ISBN 978-1-906-154-08-0
St Anthony's Fire by Rod Sproson
ISBN 978-1-906-154-10-3
Nyabinghi by Shamarley Fontaine
ISBN 978-1-906-154-09-7
Beyond the Reso by Ambrose Conway
ISBN 978-1-906-154-12-7

Coming Soon:

Leaving Coty by Ruth Estevez
ISBN 978-1-906-154-04-2

Please visit our website at **www.kingshart.co.uk** for extracts and further information.

Available to order at all bookshops or through online retailers worldwide.

Lightning Source UK Ltd.
Milton Keynes UK
23 September 2009

144081UK00001B/8/P

9 781906 154141